Sara Banerji's first book was longlisted for the Man Booker, and her last published novel won an Arts Council of England Award.

Sara and her husband now live in Oxford, where she teaches writing for Oxford University's Department for Further Education. They have three daughters and five grandchildren.

THE WAITING TIME

Julia has given up on love in her middle age, but is searching for a vanished brother and a lost identity. In doing so, she collides with Kitty, a woman of a different age, lifestyle and aspirations. The proof of Julia's identity lies somewhere under Kitty's home. This literal digging up of the past changes life for both of them, though what they find is very different to their expectations. Ahead are surprises, conflict, terror, disappointment, love — and unexpected happiness.

SARA BANERJI

THE WAITING TIME

Complete and Unabridged

ULVERSCROFT
Leicester

First published in Great Britain in 2005 by
Transita
Oxford

First Large Print Edition
published 2007
by arrangement with
Transita
Oxford

British Library CIP Data

Banerji, Sara, 1932 –
    The waiting time.—Large print ed.—
    Ulverscroft large print series: fiction
    1. Middle aged women—Psychology—Fiction
    2. Missing persons—Investigation—Fiction
    3. Large type books
    I. Title
    823.9'14 [F]

    ISBN 978–1–84617–818–4

ULV 28·6·07

Published by
F. A. Thorpe (Publishing)
Anstey, Leicestershire

Set by Words & Graphics Ltd.
Anstey, Leicestershire
Printed and bound in Great Britain by
T. J. International Ltd., Padstow, Cornwall

This book is printed on acid-free paper

DEDICATION

I would like to dedicate The Waiting Time to Marina Oliver without whose work and inspiration the book would have lacked shape, order, title and perhaps even existence.

I would also like to thank The Authors' Foundation for giving me much-appreciated help when I greatly needed it.

1

Jem has started forgetting our mother so I am going to write down everything I can remember about her and about our home, then I will read it to Jem to remind him.

I will start with the evening my mother buried our precious things. She wrapped them in pieces of yellow cloth cut from an old souwester and put them in a metal box. Carrying it, me and Jem following her, she went into the garden. I felt awed, my skin tingling with the thrill of what I recognised as a holy moment.

It was dark. There was no moon. My mother talked in whispers, as though there might be Germans listening.

'We are like smugglers,' I said softly and shivered with excitement.

'I want to be a pirate, not a smuggler,' shouted Jem, brave because of the tight grip he had on his mother's hand.

'Hush,' said my mother.

That was a year ago when I was seven and I have grown up a lot since that evening. I realise now that my mother must have put on the whole show partly for our fun. She was always thinking up adventures for us. I don't think she really believed Britain was just about to be invaded. Perhaps she partly did, but also she pretended because it gave our night-time adventure more reality.

The three of us dug the hole for the box.

'It has to be deep,' my mother said. 'And we have to remember the spot so we can find all our precious things after the war is over. Six paces from the pear tree and seven from the house.' I think that is what she said. I must remember, because at my first chance I must go back and dig up that box again.

Next day my father came home on leave. Jem, my mother and I rushed out to meet him as he came up the path. He wore his officer's uniform, with shining brass buttons and carried a polished swagger stick that he tossed from hand to hand, his blue eyes crinkled with smiling and happiness.

Jem and I clung to his legs all the way up to the front door and even through the hall while my mother, a drying-up cloth in her hand, watched half laughing and half crying. Later she had told me her eyes had not been full of tears because she was sad but because she was so happy to have our father back.

'How long are you home for, Charlie?' she asked.

'Weekend leave,' said my father, hanging his hat up on the coat hook and starting to look more like his usual self. 'Then I'm being sent abroad.'

'Where?' asked my mother, clinging to his arm.

'Military secret,' he said. He grabbed up Jem and me in a single hug and kissing us both at once, added, 'They haven't told even me.'

'How shall I write to you?' begged my mother and now her eyes started to become full of the other sort of tears.

'Come on, silly girl,' scoffed my father putting us down and grabbing her instead. 'Here am I, back for five minutes and you're already crying about me going.' He kissed her on the end of her nose and said, 'We've got the whole weekend ahead of us and the first thing I'm going to do is to mow the lawn. It looks dreadful.'

'Sorry, Charlie,' whispered my mother.

'So you should be,' laughed my father.

It was not till later, after the lawn was mowed, when we were just about to sit down to tea, when he saw that the silver candlesticks were missing.

'Have we been robbed?' he asked in a horrified voice, and became even more horrified when my mother told him she had buried all our valuable things in the garden.

'Whatever could you have been thinking of,

you silly girl?' he raged at my mother. 'All our silver out there in the wet? And the share certificates. And the children's birth certificates? The deeds to the house?'

My mother said in a tiny voice, 'I packed them carefully, Charlie. I was trying to keep everything safe till you got back. In case we got invaded.'

'Silly Dorry,' said my father, putting his arms round her. 'What made you think that might happen?'

'They were talking about it in the village,' said my mother contritely. 'That it looked as though Hitler might be invading Britain at any moment and because we're so near the sea, I just thought . . . '

'Silly, silly girl,' said my father. 'We'll dig it up at once.'

'Have your tea first, darling,' my mother said. 'I've cooked you your favourite lardy cake.'

Every time I get a chance and remember something I am going to write it down like this. (Julia Pritchett's diary, 1947)

★　★　★

Julia Pritchett closes the grubby exercise book and puts it back into the briefcase among all the others. She had never thought, when she had written her diaries, that one day she would be searching among them for clues to where her mother had buried that box.

The trouble is that she cannot remember the name of the village in which her family lived, she does not even know which town is near. She knows it is not far from the sea, the house was near a corner shop, that a shallow river runs at the bottom of the garden, that in the garden there is, there was then at least, a pear tree. That the house is gone. She knows her family's name is Pritchett, yet has so far managed to find no record of it.

She sits on the edge of her bed in the seedy London hotel room and feels washed with sadness because that day of long ago has gone so utterly. She looks round the shabby little room, with its cheap furniture, the best place she dared afford and compares it to the lovely home of her childhood. She has been to England several times before, hunting for her missing childhood, searching fruitlessly among birth certificates, church registers, marriage licences and each time has been so overwhelmed with depression that she is glad to go back to Canada, where at least there is nothing to remind her of the things she has lost.

Julia carries her diaries everywhere she

goes in England, hoping that somewhere, somehow, she will come across a clue leading her to the place of her childhood. Sometimes at night in lonely hotel rooms she riffles through one, letting it fall open anywhere, in the hope that fate will let drop before her eyes the very lines she needs. Often she has been ablaze with hope, thought she was there, felt certain this was the place but every time her search had ended with disappointment. It always turned out to be the wrong village, the wrong family, the wrong convent, the wrong little adopted boy. For years she would try to forget the whole thing, get on with her life, concentrate on her career, on making a go of it in her adoptive country. But then the longing and the guilt would rise in her again. Again she would gather up whatever she could save, make yet another trip to Britain and resume her probably hopeless search.

Some of the pages had been ripped away. Even now, after all these years, the voice of the Boys' Sister would sometimes ring in her ears. 'You were very kindly treated when you came to us. These things you have written here are wicked lies and you are an ungrateful child.' She had ripped Julia's laboriously written pages apart and punished Julia for her falsehoods, though Julia had been trying her very hardest to write the perfect truth, a truth that would sustain her and her brother for the rest of their lives.

*   *   *

A fine drizzle crinkles the surface of the slow-flowing river, plonks damp spots on the battered bits of tin and cardboard sprouting from a rubbish tip in the middle of the waste land, settled in shining wobbles over the 'For Sale' sign on the cottage front.

A grey cottage on a grey day. It stands awkwardly on the unkempt land, not a riverside cottage, not Kitty's idea of a cottage at all. To her these were thatched affairs, honeysuckle round the door, more often seen embroidered on tea cosies than in actuality. This one has a garden bordered by a drooping fence of rusty barbed wire and rotting plank fencing which goes down to the water's edge and takes up about a third of the land. The rest of the land has been returned to a sordid wilderness. Brambles sprawl over rank trees. The ground is tangled with elder, dock and nettles. Ash saplings and buddleia rampage. Rubbish protrudes from every bush and grass hump. In this dank place man's dirty hand is pressing hard on nature's careless one.

Kitty surveys the area mournfully, considers silently how unattractive the countryside is compared with the parks of London, orderly with flower borders, clean and careful.

Matt, however, gazes around him as though looking upon Paradise. His face, thinks Kitty, radiates when he smiles. Little laughter lines crease his mouth. Tim, who is Matt's best friend and has a veterinary surgery in the village, has found this cottage. He laughs happily. 'I knew you'd like it, Matt. I knew it would be the perfect place for you.'

'This is the place I have been looking for,' Matt says. 'I want the rest of the land as well, and I shall make an offer for that too when I can get the money together. All this will be ours one day, Kits.' He waves an imperious hand, gesturing like an emperor.

A bird, perched silent in a gnarled old tree, stretches its wings and starts to sing as though contradicting him. 'Not yours, mine.'

'A thrush,' breathes Matt, peering up among the twisted branches. 'You don't see them so often nowadays.'

Tim says, 'It's a bargain, folks. Snap it up or someone else will.'

Kitty sighs, conflicted. 'It looks spooky.'

'I'll protect you from the ghosts, Kits,' laughs Matt, and winks at his friend.

Kitty loves Matt's laugh, rich and dark like chocolate.

A large and iridescent bird comes strutting out from among the weed-tangled rubbish dump, stares at the intruders with a scornful air and strides away, head high. Even in the dull light, rainbows shine luminously among his feathers.

'Wow, what a gorgeous bird. What is it?' Kitty cranes to get the last sight of the haughty creature before it vanishes in the undergrowth by the river.

'A pheasant, you ignorant townie,' taunts Matt.

'Gorgeous after being hung for three days then roasted with apple sauce,' says Tim.

'You wouldn't,' cries Kitty in outraged accusation.

'Would I? Would he?' laughs Tim. 'Your husband's a crack shot, darling. And the pheasants round here have been bred for only one purpose, to be shot by the likes of Matt and me.'

'In that case I won't agree to live here,' says Kitty sternly.

'There's a rough shoot over there.' Tim points. 'We won't shoot the one in your garden.' Kitty does not like the idea of any pheasant being shot, but at least feels calmed at the idea of this one escaping.

Tim opens the front door. The air inside is musty as though no one had lived there for years: Kitty follows the two friends and tries to swallow her apprehension.

Matt, looking back, half way up the uncarpeted, footstep-ringing stairs, sees her expression, says, 'Cheer up, Kits. Once you have got the knack of living in the country you'll love it.'

Kitty looks gloomily out of the stairway window to that dead scrambled place from which the pheasant emerged. Hankers for the sight of shops and traffic. A hum comes from a distant motorway that only comforts her a little.

Matthew opens the master bedroom window and leans out into the misty rain. He draws in breaths as though the air is nourishing him, sucking in great gulps through his nostrils. 'God, Kits, glorious, eh?'

'Why hasn't anyone bought it already if it's such a bargain?' asks Kitty sensibly. She is not often sensible, but the occasion seems to demand it. She sees the glance that passes between the friends and alerted, demands, 'You know something. Tell me. You've got to tell me.'

'Don't be silly,' he chides, shaking her

hands off. 'It's nothing.'

'It's ghosts, isn't it? The people here say it's haunted. That's why no one wants to live here.'

'Oh, don't be silly, Kitty,' says Matt once again. He gestures into the garden. 'If we buy I'll have that dying tree cut down.'

'Oh, the old pear tree. It's a landmark in the village. Someone told me there was another house here, over there, just beyond the pear tree. Where all that junk's been dumped. But the house was bombed by the Germans, blown up during the war. After the explosion had died away the only thing left standing was the pear tree.'

Kitty shudders.

Matt says, 'We can start our family here, Kits. This is the perfect place to bring up children.'

Kitty's heart leaps with hope. Suddenly the faults of the cottage fall away. A place to bring up children in. Matt's children. Her children. She puts her arms gently round his waist and hugs him.

'I love you, Matt,' she whispers.

'Come on, cut it out, you love birds,' says Tim. 'If you're really interested let's go back to the estate agent and make an offer.'

★　★　★

11

The sun shines, the day Matthew and Kitty move in to Waste Land Cottage. It all looks quite different, light spilling into the large windows, flushing the ceilings, making the linoleum glow.

'You see, it's quite modern, just the way you like things,' Matt says, as they go around among the movers, putting the furniture in place. 'It may not be very pretty, but it's well built and by this time next year, you'll see, it'll be really lovely when we've painted it, got some plants growing over it. And then, and then Kits, when we've got possession of that land out there, we'll have a great open glass conservatory here, get those trees in order, perhaps put a herbaceous border across there and from here get the full view of the river. Oh, Kitty Kitty, it will be like Heaven.'

'Yes,' says Kitty, her heart glowing, still remembering the way he had said, 'a good place to bring up children.'

'Look, lovely tiled floor under this ghastly lino.' Matt peels back the stuff. He thumps his hands against the cupboards, says, 'Strong wood, well made. Someone has put a lot of money into this fitted kitchen. You'll have fun making your cakes here.'

Kitty cranes on tiptoe to peer inside one of the cupboards. Some mouldering packets of food and a half full bottle of brandy lie there.

'A tramp got in and lived here for a while.' The gasman looks up from behind the stove he is reconnecting.

'What happened to the tramp? Why did he leave his things here?'

The gasman laughs. 'God knows. We heard an explosion one night. Really loud. As if the whole house had been blown up. Everyone in the village heard it. Anyway he came rushing out, yelling with terror and fell head first into the river. A couple of us had to jump in and pull him out in the end. Couldn't swim and even if he had known how, was so dead drunk that without us he would have drowned. He must have been pretty scared to have left his brandy behind and never gone back for it.' He fiddles with the pipes, tightens a screw, then says, 'I've never believed the village scaremongers who say the waste land's haunted. I still think it was something to do with a gas leak.'

'See, see, I told you,' cries Kitty.

'Oh, stop that,' Matthew tells the man.

The gasman packs his tools, shrugs, says, 'I'm only telling you what people say. I don't believe it. But there's people in the village that really do. Even the most daring of the village kids never play out there, on that bit of the waste land. And have you wondered why no one's ever built on it? They say that bad luck came to anyone who tried.'

Kitty shudders.

'Well, let's be thankful that it's not been built on,' says Matthew fervently. 'I wish the villagers would carry their prejudices a little further, though, and refrain from dumping rubbish on it as well.'

★   ★   ★

Kitty and Matthew have been living in the cottage for a week.

'See darling. Peaceful as paradise. No ghosts here.' Matt is still arranging his things, putting the furniture where he likes it.

Kitty smiles, happy to see him happy. Today she has actually tiptoed out onto the waste land to see if she could catch another sight of the pheasant. Walked softly so as not to wake any spirits, but gone there all the same. Then had stayed there for ages, enchanted by a little squad of ducks that had suddenly appeared along the river, and came up the bank to waddle among the rushes.

Matt shakes her out of her thoughts. 'Come on, you lazy lout. Don't leave everything to me to do. Help me get these things back in the cupboard. Tim's coming round in a moment. We're going out to try to bag a brace of pheasants for supper.'

'Don't go, don't leave me. I get shit scared on my own,' Kitty begs, clutching him by the arm.

'For Heaven's sake, Kitty,' he reprimands. He wags his finger at her, looks at her sternly over the top of his glasses.

Kitty still goes on holding him. She loves it when he talks to her as though he is her father. Or at least, since she never had a father, as she imagines fathers talk to their children. It makes her go goosey all over.

'It might be true, what that gasman said.'

'Even you don't believe it,' smiles Matt.

'But it's true nobody comes there. A perfectly OK man's bike was lying there the day we came and no one took it.' Kitty, whose eyes in London had always been kept peeled for the sight of an unlocked bike had stared at this one covetously. And if it had lain anywhere else would have snatched it up like a shot.

'I didn't see it,' says Matthew peevishly. 'You should have told me. You know how I need one. I'll get it now.'

'It's gone now. Someone did take it in the end.'

'There you are,' says Matt, cross and satisfied at the same time.

'Even birds and rabbits don't go in there so there must be something.'

15

'What about that pheasant, the day we came to look at the cottage,' laughs Matt. 'See how you contradict yourself, Kits.'

She laughs too. Her fears have ebbed really, but she is enjoying his chiding.

★ ★ ★

That night they hear a bird singing from inside the rubbish-littered undergrowth. Kitty and Matt, leaning from their bedroom window, drown in the sound of wonder from the small bird's throat.

Matt puts his arm round Kitty's waist. 'A nightingale,' he breathes.

2

A month has gone already and still Julia is no nearer to finding the place. She had a moment of hope when she found an old photo of the orphanage where she and her brother had been sent and actually found the place. But when she got there, turnips grew in rows where once there had been Nissen huts housing orphan children.

★   ★   ★

Tim is going to find Matt a puppy.

'I'll train him as a gun dog, and he'll be company for you in case I have to go away,' Matt says.

Aghast, Kitty cries, 'Why should you go away? I couldn't possibly live here on my own.'

Matt sighs, 'I have to get this business on its feet. It's my last chance.' He sighs and holds his temples in his hands, so that Kitty becomes overwhelmed with pity.

'How could Marion have done that to you?' She strokes his cheek. 'What a bitch she must have been. You'd think that by now she must be feeling sorry for hurting you so instead of going on getting more out of you.'

'She was bitter, Kits, because I never gave her children. And jealous because I made you pregnant.'

Kitty flushes, and her eyes go hot with tears gathering. She does not like talking about the banished baby. 'It's the wrong time, Kitty,' Matt had said. 'I must get my business established first, before we start a family.' He had paid for her to have an abortion but all the same had divorced Marion and married her.

★　★　★

'Shall we start our baby tonight?' Kitty says.

'Leave it a little while longer, love,' says Matthew, brushing his lips against her cheek. 'I need to get the business on its feet first.' He adds, 'By the way, an opportunity has cropped up which will mean me going away on a short business trip.'

Suddenly the sweetness of the night turns sour. 'Go? Go? Where can you go? I won't stay here by myself. I absolutely bloody refuse,' she shouts. The lilac withdraws its scent, the owl goes trundling back across the trees, seeking a more peaceful bit of sky in which to hunt.

Stroking her hair he soothes her, 'There there, Kits. It's only for a few days. You'll be OK. Tim will be in the village and you can ring him if you get into trouble. And he's getting the puppy before I go so you won't be alone.'

'Puppy, what the fucking hell am I going to do with a bloody puppy?' she bursts out. 'I never had a fucking puppy in my life and I don't want one now. I hate dogs.'

'There there, calm down,' laughs Matt, holding her tight like a therapist with a hyperactive child. 'Steady, steady, dearest girl. I want you to look after my puppy for me. OK? Keep him well and safe till I get back? Right? My pedigree gun dog. I don't want anything to happen to him. And I can't put off the trip. It's a big breakthrough, Kitty and I'll only be away for a few days.'

She grips his wrists fiercely but says nothing. He has suffered such a lot, wiped out financially by his two previous marriages. Who was she to prevent him trying to get back on his feet again for the third time?

'I'll stay here and look after your puppy, Matt,' she tells him with a hastily hidden shudder.

'There's my girl,' he says. 'There's my lovely girl.'

★ ★ ★

Kitty passes the village hall, and sees, among the several notices on the board, one advertising a course in Indian self defence called Danaveda. Kitty had been going to a keep fit class, in which fat middle-aged ladies waved their limbs weakly and there was no one of her age at all. This sounded more fun and rather exotic.

★ ★ ★

'You should keep your energy for cleaning the house,' Matt says with a mock frown. He says the words lightly but they sting at Kitty's heart.

'I'm doing my best, Matt. Honestly I am. I'm just not experienced with sweeping and dusting and things.'

'Well if you spent more time doing that, and less guzzling cakes and watching rubbish on TV you'd learn how.' Then seeing her fallen expression, 'Go on, ducky darling. Join the course. You might make friends there. People to talk to while I'm away.'

'I wish you weren't going.' She is in a panic.

'I have to. If it works out I'll come back rich, Kits. I'll take you to restaurants. I'll buy you gorgeous dresses.'

His eyes are sparkling. Kitty tried to subdue the pinch in her heart and smile as well.

3

Julia Pritchett has found the orphanage mother house, the place where she and Jem were eventually taken, but when she gets there, a notice outside announces, 'The Sunset Home for the Elderly'.

She expects nothing as she rings the bell, but when a nun opens the door, Julia experiences a shock of hope though she sees at once that the nun is too young to have worked in the wartime orphanage. She might be able to give Julia some sort of lead, though.

'Yes, I do remember some of the old nuns talking about an orphanage, and how all the children had been sent to Canada in nineteen-fifty-four, but that's all I know, really.'

'I am looking for my brother, Jem,' says Julia. 'He was adopted. Can I talk to some of the other nuns here? Perhaps they may remember something.'

'I am the only nun living here,' the sister tells her. 'The rest of the staff are lay professionals.'

'Where are the nuns that used to run the

orphanage, then?' pressed Julia. 'How can I find them?'

The little sister laughed. 'Darling, even nuns don't live for ever.'

★   ★   ★

Now, rather hopelessly, but not knowing what else to do, Julia is touring the countryside, looking for places she recognised.

Sitting on the top of double decker buses she avidly surveys the passing landscape, searching for anything that will jog her memory, watching out for a battered pear tree. There would be a river running at the bottom of the garden, and the corner shop would be visible from the road. Pathetic hope. Julia does not really believe, any longer, that she was going to find it. What pear tree would still be standing after all these years? The place would have been built upon by now. Blocks of flats or offices probably stood upon it.

★   ★   ★

Kitty is curled up in front of the TV when Tim comes in with the new dog.

'Matt's new puppy,' he cries triumphantly, as he plonks a small animal on her tummy. It struggles, sprawling, then creeps urgently onto her chest and cuddles against her body. Kitty stares, astonished. She had expected something bristly and ferocious, but this creature is very small, totally unalarming, has pudgy features, a hot loose skin and smells of dog milk, ammonia and pepper. It falls asleep as Tim goes upstairs, calling Matt to come and see. It lies against Kitty's bosom, its tiny snores making its whiskers quiver. If Matt had allowed her to keep that baby, Kitty thinks, it would have been bigger than this by now.

Matt is ecstatic. Snatching the puppy up he examines it from every side, running his fingers along its tail, pressing his thumb against its spine, holding it up to the light to see the formation of its hind legs.

Tim says, 'Both parents won prizes at Crufts. This fellow is OK.'

'At four hundred pounds he'd bloody well better be,' laughs Matt, sniffing into the valuable coat of his new purchase.

'Four hundred pounds, Matt?' gasps Kitty. 'I thought we were broke.'

'Not for long, Kitty love,' laughs Matt, swinging his puppy about in the air as though it was one of his bird corpses. 'If the Middle East deal comes off I'll be able to buy a dozen cocker spaniels.'

'It doesn't look big enough to carry pheasants,' says Kitty.

'He'll grow,' laughs Matt. 'And then he'll be responsive to my every gesture, obedient to my every whim. He will retrieve at the gesture of my hand.'

For the next few days Matthew constantly worries about the puppy. 'He's got outside. What the bloody hell did you have to go and leave the back door open for, Kitty?' or, 'If he's got onto the road he'll be run over in two minutes flat,' or 'For Heaven's sake don't take him so close to the water. He'll fall in and drown.'

Matt is due to leave for Waswar in three days' time. 'I wish we could have collected the puppy after I got back but as it is you will have to look after it while I'm away. Tim's going abroad for a year, some sort of exchange scheme with India. It's a damned shame. I would have been happier if he'd been on the end of the phone, so if anything went wrong with the puppy you could get him, but I suppose the chap that takes over from him will be competent. I'll only be away three days so hopefully nothing will go wrong in that time.'

'How will I know if it's ill?' asks Kitty, already chilled with the agony of his absence and worry of caring for this vulnerable and valuable puppy.

'Feel his nose,' says Matt. 'Healthy dogs

24

have wet noses. If it goes dry get in touch with the new vet.'

Cuddled up against Kitty that very afternoon, as she is watching *Neighbours* on the TV, Kitty touches the sleeping puppy's nose and finds it dry.

Tim and Matthew have gone out after rabbits. Kitty can hear the pops of their shots far across the fields.

Clutching the puppy to her chest she rushes out of the house and goes racing over the fields, shouting for Matt. Following the sounds of gunshot she finds them at last.

★   ★   ★

'He's perfectly all right. Fit as a fiddle,' says Matt with irritation.

'His nose is — was dry,' wails Kitty.

'Dogs' noses always go dry when they're asleep,' says Matt, 'You might have got shot, rushing up on us like that and you've scared away all the game for miles.'

'Sorry, Matt,' said Kitty, crestfallen. As she makes her way across the field she hears Matt tell Tim, 'Kitty doesn't know a thing about dogs.'

She trudges home with a heavy heart, weighed down by her terrible ignorance.

Matt comes home later, his mood cheery, spattered with the death of several rabbits and a hare. Swallowing her revulsion, trying to make up for her failure as a dog owner, she takes the heavy armfuls of dead creatures from him.

'Hang them in the larder, Kits. We'll live on them till I go.'

'Yes, Matt,' she says, swallowing. Anticipating all those nights and mornings where, going to get cheese or marmalade, or eggs to make a cake she would be confronted with the reproachful dead eyes of these poor wild creatures dangling there like dead men on a scaffold.

*　*　*

Kitty wants to stay with Gran while Matt is away but Matt won't allow it. 'I want you here, looking after my gun dog. I know your gran. She'll kill it with fudge and ginger cake. It's to have nothing but Pedigree Chum Puppy food. Do you read me, Kits?' He scowls at her, stern and firm, over the top of his glasses.

'Yes, Matt,' she says morosely.

*　*　*

He is leaving. Kitty has to bite back tears all the way to Heathrow. 'Be careful with the car

26

on the way home,' he tells her. 'I don't want to see a single dent when I get back.' Matt has only recently taught her to drive. 'I've aged twenty years,' he had said when she at last passed her test. He tells her, 'I've put in a offer for that piece of waste land beyond the cottage, Kitty. If I'm delayed you'll have to deal with it. It's absolutely vital that I get it. I've set my heart on it. Explain that to the lawyer. Look, here's his address.'

'Delayed,' screams Kitty. 'Don't you dare get bloody delayed.'

*   *   *

That evening is the first of the Danaveda lessons so at least Kitty will not have to spend it alone in a house without Matthew.

Mr Mitra, the tutor, turns out to be a small, thin, elderly Indian man in a floating white garment, so different to the husky muscular young men who had taught self defence in London, or the stocky local lady who had taken the keep fit class, that for the first few minutes Kitty thinks the whole thing is a joke.

There are two elderly ladies from Blenheim Terrace, several younger girls and one man, the bald-headed bespectacled manager of the supermarket. Apparently he has been assaulted several times by dissatisfied customers and feels he needs to know how to defend himself.

'Would it not be better to improve the quality of your merchandise, Mr Pearson,' one of the ladies from Blenheim Terrace suggests.

Danaveda, Mr Mitra tells them, has been practised in India for thousands of years. 'But we have brought it up to date. Tailored the ancient technique to suit modern requirements.' The Blenheim Terrace ladies wear thick track suits and health sandals, the young girls are dressed in bright lycra bodies that dart suggestively between their legs and on their feet wear bungy pristine trainers. Mr Pearson wears a pair of large and glossy shorts, a vest and tennis shoes. Kitty's feet are bare and she wears a tee shirt to hide her tummy. She keeps her toes folded under her feet to hide her toenails. 'Next time they'll be spotless, I swear,' she tells herself.

'Don't try, don't make effort, don't concentrate,' Mr Mitra tells them. 'Just let the flow of the Universe pass through you very naturally till you are connected with the Cosmos. Then you will be able to move a JCB with your mind.' This was his key phrase, his idea of bringing an ancient technique up to date. It always made his pupils giggle though he never knew why.

Waste Land Cottage is even darker, even colder, than Kitty had feared when she gets back. She opens the front door and shudders. Then feels tearful because she can smell a whiff of the minced pheasant pie she had made Matt for his lunch. But as she stands there miserably, out of the blackness comes the puppy, scooting and skidding, letting out little cries of delight. For the first time Kitty sees what Matt meant. It is nice to have the puppy there. It would have been nicer to have had Matt, but it is only three days and in the meantime the puppy is better than no one.

That night Kitty takes the puppy to bed with her, then remembering a song she had been taught at school, sings to it. 'There was a lady longed for a baby, so she took her father's greyhound and put it in the cradle-o. Bye, doggy, bow wow. If it was not for your wet nose I'd kiss you, ere now.' The singing makes her cry, but somehow comforts her as well, as though it is a magic spell which will undo something terrible that has been done.

She had thought she would lie awake, tense with terror, hearing every little rustle and imagining spirits, but the presence of the puppy soothes her and she falls into a comfortable and dreamless sleep quite quickly, and only wakes hours later to find the puppy nibbling at her ear. The sun has already risen and it is a moment or two before she remembers she is alone in the cottage and Matthew is in Waswar. She feels pleased with herself for having got through this night on her own and without torment. Only two more like this to go, and then he'll be back. She hugs the puppy gratefully.

After breakfast she pulls on her tee shirt and tights, and tries to remember what Mr Mitra had told them. After all, she has paid thirty pounds and thinks the Blenheim Terrace ladies are being naive if they think they will get their money back.

She gets her body into the position that she thinks Mr Mitra must have meant and as if her poised torso and hand holding the invisible bow has brought it about, there comes a thunderous roar from outside that goes on echoing for long moments.

Dropping unseen arrows all over the floor Kitty rushes to the back door and looks out, the puppy yapping and skidding after her.

The sky has become blotted out with a blur of smoke through which hurl ripped pieces of debris, as though some metal object is being town apart. Then Kitty sees something like a human body being hurled and her nostrils become filled with the smells of petrol and what seems might be human flesh scorching. She stands, frozen with horror as the rumbling roar reverberates through the summer air.

Then suddenly, as if she is no longer dizzy, the smoke and flying debris vanishes though Kitty can still hear the rumbling thunder of the explosion. The waste land becomes again a place of weeds and rubbish, Kitty can see bees buzzing over the weeds. She wonders if fear is causing her to hallucinate.

There comes another sound. Running footsteps and a small girl with a great mop of red hair, dressed in scarlet, screaming Mummy, Mummy, Mummy, goes trundling across the lumpy ground. She reaches the tangled centre of the waste land and stops, still sobbing. Then the little girl is suddenly gone, vanished as mysteriously as she appeared.

She must have jumped into the squalid centre of the weedly tangle and now be concealed by that old pram, thinks Kitty.

Creeping up cautiously, trying to ignore the rumbling of the ghostly fire, she peers through the weeds but can see no child.

Feeling shaky, wondering if she is having hallucinations or is going mad, Kitty runs quickly back to the cottage and dials 999.

The policeman comes at once and Kitty

tells him about the sounds of explosion and burning.

'I can't hear anything like that,' he smiles.

'That's because it's stopped now,' Kitty tells him desperately.

He looks at her dubiously, searches the waste land for a while, looks half-heartedly into the brambles, and before he goes pats Kitty on the shoulder and advises her to go and make herself a nice cup of coffee. As though she is ill, or has been drinking.

★ ★ ★

Julia Pritchett is losing heart and sometimes she doesn't look around her at all, but stares sightlessly ahead, lost in her own gloomy thoughts as the bus trundles along the lanes. She is losing hope of finding Jem. Soon she will leave, never come to England again and that will be the end of it. She will return to Canada. Not home. She has never thought of Canada as home. Just the place she has been forced to live for the last twenty years, after escaping from South Africa. She has booked her flight already.

The bus climbs the hill and she looks wearily around her. Her heart lightens a little at the sight of a river, fawn like milky tea. Had she been along this road when she was

32

little? She tries to scrunch her mind up into remembering, but nothing comes. Now Julia is looking down on a village. She can see another stretch of the river. Something stirs inside her mind, a feeling that she has been here before. But she has had this feeling often already and each time has found she has been kidding herself.

The bus begins descending and the feeling of familiarity grows. Excitement starts to tingle through her. But then ebbs as the bus moves through a row of houses where, if it had been the right village, there should only have been fields. But wait, these houses are new. Perhaps they have been built here since Julia's childhood.

She lets out an audible gasp as the bus turns the corner and passes a corner shop. So loud that people turn around to look. The river, beyond, has willows along it as she remembers.

The corner shop. It's called Patels instead of Roses but otherwise looks much the same. She is filled with certainty. It's it. One more turn. Unbelievable. Julia Pritchett feels the hair on her head and neck start to prickle with total recognition. The pear tree, shrunken and old now, but surely the same one. The place where her home had been, now a lump of tangled weeds and bushes into which people had been dumping rubbish.

But then passing round the trees her hopes fade again as she sees the hideous little cottage standing on the place where she thinks her father had had his vegetable garden.

Then as they come closer she realises that the cottage is fairly new, built in the last twenty years by the look of it, made perhaps from the material of her parents' blown-up house, and feels again, with a great surge of joy, that this is, after all, the place. It must be. It is more like it than anywhere else she has seen. She gets off in the village centre, feeling more and more certain. She is sure this is the pub where her father sometimes used to go for a pint in the evening. And the hotel called the Blenheim Arms looks like the place where her mother used to meet friends for morning coffee, though it has been tarted up now.

She books herself into a B and B, asking the landlady, as she signs the register, 'Do you remember a family called Pritchett who lived in the village during the war? Over there, by the river?'

'I've only been here six years,' the woman says. 'Ask at the pub. They might know.'

The pub, the Golden Pheasant, has a low doorway. She has to duck her head to go in, and has a sudden image of her father stooping like this, too. Of course she and Jem had never been inside the pub with him. Children had not been allowed, but they had waited for him on a bench till he came out again, carrying crisps and bottles of fizz for them.

Inside, in the sudden, smoky dark, she asks around among the older people, 'Do you remember the Pritchetts? A family with bright red hair?' One old man said he remembered a red-haired family, but they were not called Pritchett.

'Over there, where that pear tree is. On that bit of waste land. I'm sure that's where the house stood.'

'That house was bombed during the war, but I don't think the family who lived there were called Pritchett.'

An old lady said she thought she remembered some Pritchetts, but they did not have red hair.

'Are you sure?' urged Julia.

'Sure, love. They were negroes.'

'Mr and Mrs Rose ran the corner shop,' Julia tried.

'Ah, yes. The Roses.' Several people remembered them, though none knew were the Roses were now. 'Dead and buried, poor dears, no doubt.'

She has lunch in the Blenheim Arms and finds one old man who remembers the house that had been blown up during the war. 'A pretty old place, with a lovely garden,' he says.

'Who lived in it? Can't you remember that?' urges Julia.

The old man waits, lost in thought. Shakes his head. 'It was wartime. Everything was upside down. I was in the army then. Sorry, my dear, but I just can't recall the name. The parents were killed by the bomb. I remember that. And the kiddies were taken away to an orphanage. It was so long ago, and my memory's not what it was.'

'Was their name Pritchett?'

'Could have been,' says the old man. 'Yes, could have been. In the village they say that bit of land's got a curse on it. Anyone who tries to build there comes to a bad end, they say. One firm went bust. The last builder had a stroke. Now they just let it lie fallow.'

Julia pinches back a satisfied smile. Of course it was haunted. The ghosts of her own past, her parents' ghosts were there and protecting her property.

She buys herself a pair of garden gloves and a little trowel. The land with the pear tree on it did not seem to belong to anyone now. She would go and dig there. Who knows, she might come upon her mother's metal box in a moment.

* * *

Two more days. Two more nights. Then Matt really will be back.

That night Kitty wakes suddenly to hear a sound outside.

Fear jerks you out of sunken relaxation in a moment. Makes every bit of your body and your mind scrunch into tightness.

It is dark now.

Kitty clutches her own drying throat with one hand and the eager puppy's body with the other. Holds the creature against her walloping heart and does not feel the least bit calmed by it. The puppy wiggles, nibbles, and squirms, and Kitty's body undergoes the wave of falling caused by terror.

The sound is not explosion, not weeping, but it seems to Kitty worse, the scrape scrape against the ground. The sound of skeletons getting their bones together before they come, clacking and clattering, to find Kitty in her isolated cottage.

Silence falls at last but Kitty cannot sleep. She lies there in the terrifying dark, her faith lost in the dog, who seems to have nothing more subtle on its mind than romping and chewing the bed clothes. And peeing. Nothing in the whole world would have persuaded Kitty to take the puppy to the garden now. She would rather the cottage became awash with pee. And it very nearly was.

The shudders of horror rattling through Kitty make her hungry.

She opens the fridge and hauls out a bowl of trifle left over from the last lunch with Matt. She has fought the temptation to eat from it a hundred times in the last two days for she has promised God that if He brings Matthew back the day after tomorrow she will not eat a mouthful but keep it for their first supper together again. Now she gobbles down the sherry-wet cake, puppy wrestling at her throat for falling dribbles and tries to get her mind off the sinister noises but in the end, trembling with horror, hugging the trifle bowl to her chest, she goes upstairs and stands at the bedroom window where she hears again, the crackle and scrunch from the waste land. She feels dizzy with fear as she eats the trifle.

*   *   *

A spit of fire shoots up out of the dark. Kitty flinches wildly and drops the bowl. Wet cake and whipped cream go shooting round the walls. The puppy scampers yelping with shock and at the same time tries to gobble up the flung food.

Kitty stands staring into the red-sparked night, to the wavering lick of flame. Half fainting in her fear yet unable to take her eyes off she sees the flame illuminate a face. Not a child's face but a grown woman's.

Then the flame is out leaving only a dancing red eye to punctuate the darkness.

Kitty sinks down again onto the chair and feels the great tide of terror ebbing. She begins to breathe. Her shuddering subsides.

Ghosts don't smoke cigarettes.

4

Julia leans back and inhales the smoke. She is exhausted. The old man said builders had tried to work here again and again, always ending with disaster. But all the same probably one of them, years ago, had taken that box.

Julia has thought about this moment for so many years. She had imagined coming instantly onto the thing that will give her back her identity, restore Jem to her, make it possible to give him back his property. It has been the thing that kept her going.

But now, in this nippy dark, after hours of digging she has found nothing.

In her dreams golden undefined objects have risen out of earth that is always soft and friable. Dream certainties have emerged out of the trunks of trees that had been saplings when she was young. But now faced with reality she finds the earth as hard as stone. It had not been like this then, surely, or her father could not have grown lettuces in it and her mother raised roses. Nothing left of either, now. Well, you would not have expected lettuces to last for sixty years, but there might have remained a rose bush or two, enormous, scrambling over the trees. Perhaps those thorny bushes sprawling everywhere were roses, she suddenly thinks. She does not know much about British plants.

The cheap trowel she bought is inadequate, its tip bending if any force is used on it, blistering her palm with a badly designed handle.

She tries to build up her optimism. All these years she had feared finding a weight of brick and steel, stone and cement smothering this ground, so that when she found a little area of wild land with nothing built on it and the pear tree still standing, she had been euphoric, thought the battle won, the task done, the prize won. But hours later she is still scratching miserably into ground that is revealing nothing.

She had bought new clothes the day she found the village. She had gone through the local shop, county and expensive, feeling hopeful, seeing in the good wool skirt, the lambswool sweater, the tweed coat, the first sign of her new identity, the true Julia Pritchett. Almost as though she was trying to prove that such a person existed. She had stood before the mirror and thought that the reflected Julia, thin, tall and smart in well-cut tweed, looked less haggard. There had even been a bit inside her which tried to remember the red coat she had worn the day they had sent her away. But no matter how hard she pressed down her mind, tried to see that seven year old, no picture came. She had no photos. They had probably denied her these on purpose too, as they had denied every other thing that had created her.

The new clothes are quite wrong now, though. They are not meant to be knelt upon. They are not designed to keep out the wind. They hardly keep out the cold. She wishes she had bought one of those dowdy windproof anoraks instead of the tailored suit.

Her body is not used to heavy work. Her back aches but she only has a little time and so knows she must thrust on.

Even though she is engaged in frantic exercise her finger tips are numbing and her toes seem to have gone missing. After a while she has to rest and leans against a tree, wants to smoke again, opens her last packet of cigarettes. She is almost out of money. When this pack is finished she will have to think twice before buying another. She handles the pack regretfully, as though it is a symbol of bereavement.

Several times her heart begins to beat faster

as she sees something glint or strikes something that makes her trowel blade ring, but each time it turns out to be only a bottle top, a coke tin, a broken part of a dog's lead, a bit of foil off a crisp packet. Nothing that could have been lying there for nearly sixty years. Sometimes she feels into the ground with her fingers, thinking that perhaps they might remember something her eyes have forgotten. Once she gives a small cry of joy when she comes across a coin and remembers getting Jem to help her bury a penny.

'So that we can go shopping when we are big,' she had said. She holds the coin up to the light. The date on it is nineteen-sixty-nine. Years too late.

She is momentarily shaken by the emergence of a pink limb, which, in the misty torchlight, had for one second seemed as though it could have been her mother's arm. Her senses clear instantly, as she realises it is only a six inch limb of plastic from a broken doll. A modern doll. They did not make that sort of plastic when she had been a girl.

The church clock strikes midnight, the hours echoing through the foggy dark. This is when ghosts are supposed to walk, thinks Julia, and sitting back, wills them to come. Ghosts and shadows are all she owns now and even the ghost of pussy, who died in the blast, would do. Probably, unless she finds something soon, ghosts, shadows, memories would be all she will have for the rest of her life.

* * *

Kitty watches from her bedroom window, panic flowing out of her with a crinkly feeling, like paper being uncrumpled because, out there in the waste land, it is not a ghost but a real person smoking a cigarette.

Next day the woman is back on the waste land. Kitty can see her properly now, thin, wearing slim, smart clothes, not what you'd expect. The woman looks cold. Her long, narrow face looks pinched with it. Kitty wonders if she ought to do something.

But Matt will be back soon and he'll know what to do. She goes to the supermarket and loads her basket with ingredients to make Matthew a welcome-home cake, stocking up for his return with ham, bacon, pork pie, the things you can't get in Muslim countries. Tomorrow he is coming. Only one more night now.

* * *

Matthew rings in the afternoon.

Kitty can hardly hear him because she is so

sure he is going to tell her he's been delayed. She's eaten all the trifle in spite of her promise to God. God had to punish her. He couldn't possibly let her off after that.

'What? What?'

'Be at Heathrow to meet the plane at three.'

Oh, thank God. Happiness whizzes through her system with a feeling like wheels being turned inside her.

★   ★   ★

The puppy shoots out of the door as Kitty is emptying the kitchen bin into the dustbin. Dusk has already fallen. She stands by the back door, looking into the waste land, which is opaque with river mist and calls, 'puppy, puppy, puppy,' in a hopeless way. The puppy has never come when it was called yet, so there was no reason why it should do so this evening. She has to go out after it in the end, plunging her legs into vapours contaminated with ghosts. Only the certainty of Matthew's return, and the value he puts on the animal, gives her the courage. When she reaches the dark and tangled place where she encountered the ghostly child, she lets out a shriek of terror as a dark figure looms out of the gloom.

In a moment she realises it is only the

digging lady, but still her heart is hammering.

'Here,' said the woman. She has the puppy in her arms and thrusts it towards Kitty.

Her legs still shaking, Kitty takes the proffered dog.

'Thanks,' she says, her voice muffled with the flurry of slapped-on puppy kisses.

'What do you call him?' asks the woman.

'Ouroborus,' says Kitty.

'Oh, yes,' said the woman. 'The snake of ancient Greek and Egyptian myth that holds its tail in its mouth and continually devours itself and is born again.'

'My husband called the puppy 'Our Rob or us' because it kept biting its tail and going round and round in circles and knocking things over.' Kitty had thought it a silly joke at the time but had laughed because Matt had seemed to like it.

5

Next day Julia begins to explore the cracks in the willows, prodding through the sappy crevices, poking among spider webs and ancient foliage and her hopes are raised for a moment by something shining. The silver salt cellar? The last time her mother had used it was a month before the bomb, when Uncle Glossy had come to dinner. He lived in a distant town and often used to visit her parents and sometimes even stay a few days. When Julia pulls it out it turns out to be only a piece of crumpled foil, but her mind goes back to that happy evening of long ago.

It was down in her diary, the description of that last dinner party.

*   *   *

Uncle Glossy was my father's best friend. Jem was asleep, but I crept out of bed and tried to listen to the grown-up conversation from the upstairs landing, and revel in the smells, lit candles, baking, herby ones of my mother's special cooking. Even though it was wartime she had always managed to produce something delicious, flavoured with the herbs she grew in a little plot by the back door. Smells of spam fritters frying wafted up to me. I could hear the sound of the silver cutlery tinkling, the sounds of their chairs being drawn over the carpet, the exciting laughing ones of adult conversation which, mostly, I did not understand. Then their voices seemed to go serious as though they had started talking about something sad.

I heard my mother ask, 'Will you go back to Poland, Glossy?' and Uncle Glossy reply, with his funny accent, 'Yes. I leave tomorrow. I shall join up on arrival.'

There fell a little silence and then my father asked, caution in his tone, 'I hear the Jews are not being treated very well.'

'Don't you worry about me, Charlie,' said Uncle Glossy. 'I shall be all right. Don't listen to those rumours. People do so exaggerate.'

★   ★   ★

No salt cellar. Only a piece of silver paper from a cigarette packet. She comes, instead, across a dirty length of dark string with a shattered lump adhering and is flooded with the memory of her father skewering a hole through chestnuts, threading them with string and teaching her and Jem the game of conkers.

She holds the little thread reverently, filled with a sense of grateful security, as though, in spite of its not being silver, at last here among her fingers is a real and tangible piece of her missing past.

She stands up, straightens, rubs her aching back and catches sight of the girl with the puppy peeping from the kitchen window of the cottage. Julia's scowl tightens. The girl is a trespasser and she plans to get her property back from this girl. But then she sighs. More than half her life is gone and she should have concentrated on making the best of what was left of it instead of wasting her years on hunting for things and people that she would never find. Perhaps she had invented them. Invented her family, her home, even Jem. Otherwise why was it that no one in the village, even those who had lived here during the war, could remember the family called Pritchett?

She had been to a psychiatrist in Toronto a couple of years ago and he had said that it was possible all her childhood memories might be figments of her imagination.

'You were not much more than a baby, after all.' He had told her of his own impossible childhood memories, hens flying out of wardrobes, frogs filling the bath. 'People need a sense of being connected with their past and if this has been taken from them imaginative people often invent.'

'You are part of the conspiracy!' she had said coldly.

'Imagining conspiracy is a symptom of a mental disorder,' he had told her. 'Why not just drop the matter and get on with your life?'

'I cannot do that till I know who I am,' she said furiously. 'I have not even been able to marry, for I have never been sure any man is not my relative.'

'Very unlikely that such a thing should happen,' the psychiatrist had smiled.

Julia had raged at him. 'You have no idea what it feels like to be me. Not knowing who you are.'

★   ★   ★

Wearily she starts to dig again, this time near the pear tree, amazed again that they have not cut it down. It is so old and gnarled that one might have expected some government official to declare it a danger to the public.

If this was the one.

She remembered how the wasps had wobbled as they staggered out of the alcoholic pears that lay splatted among the maids-a-milking and ladies' slipper.

My mother was putting the lardy cake into the oven. My father took Jem and me into the orchard to look at the wasps. He squatted between me and my brother, Jem, she had written of that day. Grass seeds tickled our chins that had been made golden by the reflections from buttercups. Above us pollen like snow drifted down from the cow parsley and midges sparkled in the shafts of sunlight among the apple trees.

My father had changed out of his army uniform and had put on grey flannels and an open-necked shirt but still smelled of deserts, guns, and military polished buttons. I can still remember that.

As we crouched watching wasps, a thrush was singing in the pear tree. I could see his shining beady eye watching us through the laced branches. My father leant back against the gnarled trunk of the tree and said, 'Just listen. I dream about the song of that fellow when I'm in the desert.'

Shining beads of water hung on the leaves from a recent shower and the whole world seemed to be going silently round and round while the clouds stood still. The thrush sang his song twice, carefully, as though practising.

Daddy laughed and said, 'This is what life

is meant to be about. The smell of moist earth filtered up through the grass and the smell of Dorry's baking wafted from the kitchen. A thrush singing above us.'

'And the pears have got a funny smell too,' said Jem. He was four. His chubby grubby knees were pressed against his lips so that his words came out muffled. His ears stuck out on either side and the setting sun glowed pinkly through them.

'It's alcohol,' I told him, proud to know. 'Like Mummy and Daddy and Uncle Glossy had last night.'

'Why does Jewel know things and I don't, Daddy?' grumbled Jem. He was resentful instead of impressed because of wanting my father to admire him.

'You know quite enough for four,' laughed my father and put an arm round him. Jem and I leant against Daddy's knees and Jem twitched and jerked away when a wasp came too near. Jem had been stung the day before and his lips had swelled out till he looked like a circus clown so now his shoulders were tight with fear and his jaw became rigid. Only my father's presence gave him the courage to stay.

'It won't hurt you if you don't hurt it,' Daddy whispered. 'If you are gentle you will be treated gently even by wasps.'

'Even by people?' asked Jem.

'Specially by people,' said my father.

'If you are gentle to the Germans will they stop trying to kill you, Daddy?' asked Jem. I felt my father's body stiffen but he said, 'Don't you worry, old man. I'm not going to let them kill me. I expect to be a grandad in due course. I might even be a great-grandad if I'm lucky.'

★　★　★

The memory of those words causes a wave of such bitterness to rise up in Julia that she can almost taste it. Like when you are eating a rosy apple and suddenly your mouth is filled with the terrible dark flavour of worm invasion.

★　★　★

'Will Mrs. Rose's evacuees stop throwing conkers at me if I don't throw things at them?' asked Jem. 'Is that what being gentle means?'

Daddy laughed and hugged him. 'Try it, old man,' he said. 'Though having seen Milly, Fred and Will I fear they may be the exceptions to the rule.'

Three London children had been evacuated to the country and billeted with Mr and

Mrs Rose of the corner shop. I and Jem hated them. They were afraid of dogs, wouldn't enter fields of cows, ran screaming when they heard the buzz of bees. Jem was training himself to stop flinching from wasps so as not to be like them.

The boy called Will had pushed Jem into a cowpat on the lane to the farm, then laughed and shouted, 'Now you stink as shitty as everything else in this village.'

He had had spots and wore glasses stuck on with elastoplast, Julia remembered. He must be nearly seventy by now, she thought, and found the idea unbelievable.

★   ★   ★

Jem had hidden behind the chestnut tree till the evacuees went by, then thrown a conker. The evacuees rushed at him yelling, 'You stink and your village stinks.'

I shouted, 'You shouldn't have pushed Jem over and you shouldn't say our village stinks.'

'We'll say it because it does,' yelled Milly. 'It's a horrible place and we wish we'd never come here.'

'If you like London so much, go back there,' I retorted. 'Why did you come here if you hate it so?'

'Because,' said Milly smugly, 'Our parents

didn't want us to be killed by bombs. That's why.'

'That shows it's better here,' I said. 'We don't have bombs.' I would remember those words later. Oh God, how I would remember them.

★ ★ ★

She had been standing over there when she had shouted that to Milly, Julia thinks. There had been cowslips there then. And shrub roses. Both flowering at once. That's what she remembers, anyway. Couldn't be right though because even she knew that the two flowered at different seasons. That is the trouble with all her memories. She cannot be sure of any of them.

The road had not been tarmac then, though. She feels sure of that for she can remember pushing her sandalled feet through little golden dust clouds and her mother saying, 'Don't, Jewel. You'll ruin your new shoes and we haven't got any clothes coupons left.'

Julia tries to catch her mind unawares, to catch a glimpse of her mother's face before it realises what she is up to.

The track had been knee-deep in mud in winter. She can still remember the feel of suck and splot as her wellies went in and out on her way to the farm that was now a BP garage.

Whenever she passed the evacuees, ploughing their way through the mud, Mrs Rose's milk can lugged among them, they were always squealing with disgust and holding their noses. They would have liked it now, thinks Julia. They would have been happy that the cowslips and the grass, the hedges and the lane have all been transformed into traffic-heavy roads and lines of houses.

* * *

My father got up at last and said he had to mow the lawn before tea. When he tried to start up his mower engine, nothing happened and he shouted, 'damn blast hell bugger.'

My mother called out from the kitchen, where she was laying the table for our tea, 'Really, Charlie, in front of the children.'

My father turned the handle once again and got it going.

Jem went running over the lawn shouting, 'Daddy, Daddy, I want to push it.'

'Come on then, you little imp,' laughed my father. He had a streak of black oil right across his face and he was happy now.

My mother called through the open

window, 'He heard every one of those bad words of yours.'

'I knew them already, Mummy,' Jem shouted.

'Who told you them?' demanded my mother leaning out across the still, her face rosy, her hair tied up in a headscarf.

'Jewel.' Jem was gripping the lower part of the mower handles while Daddy steered with the upper. He did a skip or two so that his body rose in the air and was carried along on the mower for a little way, hanging in a storm of chopped grass that enveloped him like green snow.

'And who told you, naughty girl?' laughed my mother.

I was sitting on the lawn trying out buttercups on different bits of me. 'You, Mummy.'

'Me?' said my mother. 'I never use such words.'

'Yes, you do, yes, you do,' I told her. And Jem who had done a whole round of the lawn by now joined my chant of, 'yes, you do.'

'When?' demanded my mother.

'When you tried to open the treacle and the lid came off suddenly and treacle went over the floor,' I said.

'I only said damn,' sighed my mother.

'You said bugger when Pussy knocked over

the treacle, ran in it, then jumped onto the sofa, though,' cried Jem. 'I heard you.'

Pussy heard her name and leaping from the sill arched her body purring against Jem's knees.

My father finished the last of the grass and we all went inside to wash our hands, Pussy following us because she knew it was tea time.

That was when my father noticed the candlesticks were gone. He would have gone out then, and dug the box up if my mother hadn't said he should do it after tea because we'd all just washed our hands. So we sat down at the table instead, Pussy winding herself round our legs, and my mother, her face flushed with steam and pride, took the big lardy cake out of the oven and put it on the table. She was just about to start cutting it when the air raid siren began to sound.

'Oh, bother,' said my mother, jumping up. 'What a moment. Come on, children. Quick, down to the cellar.'

We came reluctantly, feeling we were being done out of our tea. I grumbled, 'We've been down there lots of times and no bombs have ever come.'

Jem said, 'I expect there aren't really any bombs but the Jerries are just pretending.'

My mother said, 'Don't be silly. You both

said it was fun down there.'

It was fun in the middle of the night when we sat up playing draughts and drinking cocoa but this was a glorious warm late spring afternoon and we had been just about to tuck into hot lardy cake.

After we had been there ten minutes during which we heard birds sing outside and no enemy planes at all Jem said he wanted a wee.

'You've got to hang on till the all-clear,' said my mother. We waited there for another quarter of an hour, with Jem getting more and more desperate till at last Daddy told him to do it behind the sacks of coal.

'Suppose it doesn't do an all-clear by bedtime, then what will happen?' asked Jem.

'Then Daddy will have to concentrate on us instead of the silly old garden,' laughed my mother. 'He will have to tell us a story.' Then she remembered her cooking. 'I hope the all-clear comes soon or the lardy cake will be stone cold,' she said.

'That would be disaster,' laughed my father. 'All that mowing has made me ravenous.'

Then we heard the sound of planes droning at first far away but gradually coming nearer.

'They're Jerry ones, they're Jerry ones,' cried Jem.

'You're just pretending,' I said.

'I think he's right,' said my father and to Jem, 'Perhaps you'll be an airman when you're grown up.'

'If it is really German planes coming I've got to rescue Pussy,' I said, leaping up.

My father seized me by the ankles and pulled me back.

I began to howl, 'Pussy might be killed'.

Jem who copied me in most things began to howl as well.

Mummy said, 'If you make such a din we won't hear the all-clear.'

My father said, 'Cats know how to protect themselves when bombs fall.'

'But she was in the kitchen when we started to have tea,' I sobbed.

'All the same,' said my father keeping his tight grip on me.

At first, over the sound of the planes' engines I could still hear the thrush singing but as they came closer the noise drowned the sound of the bird. Then the planes came so near that they seemed to be right over the house and made a sound like a million saucepans being crashed about together in the sky. The noise became so loud that Jem got frightened, stopped shouting trium-phantly 'Jerry planes' and threw himself into my father's lap where he buried his head between Daddy's knees. When the planes seemed to be overhead, the house gave a shudder. And a moment after, a second shudder more violent than the first. My mother let out a scream and said, 'We've been hit, Charlie.'

We all sat, hands over our ears waiting in a sort of terrified tingly silence while the Jerry plane sound receded into the distance. But no great explosion came. No vast bang obliterated our home.

After ten minutes like this the all-clear went.

'It must have been a shock wave or something,' said my father. He sounded doubtful. We all started scrambling up then. I had pins and needles in my feet. Jem was white. My father said his knees had gone numb from Jem squashing them for so long. My mother shook dust out of her skirt and said, 'There, that's over, thank God. Now we can have our tea at last.'

Upstairs it seemed astonishingly bright after three quarters of an hour in darkness. The thrush was still singing.

Jem asked, 'Don't birds' voices ever get tired?'

My father said, 'Thank goodness little boys' voices do or none of the rest of us would ever get a word in edgeways.'

My mother began to cut the lardy cake.

'It's still quite warm,' she said.

Daddy said, 'What are we going to have with it?'

My mother stopped cutting, knife in the air, went red and said, 'Darling, I'm sorry. Because the children don't like jam and you were away I didn't have any in. I'll go to the shop and get some this minute.'

'No, no, Dorry, don't be silly,' laughed my father pulling my mother back into her seat again. 'I can go without jam this once.'

But my mother's mood was spoiled. 'Let me go, Charlie.' She tried shaking his arm off. 'I want to get it for you. This is your last tea.' Her eyes were starting to fill with tears.

'I'll go,' I said getting up. 'You be pouring the tea, Mummy.' Our little corner shop was only a few minutes away. 'I'll be back before you've finished doing it.'

'You are an angel, my little jewel,' said my mother.

'Mrs Rose's home-made plum,' said my father, licking his lips with anticipation. 'Here, how much will it be?' He handed me the money.

'I want to go with Jewel,' Jem began to shout as I made for the door.

'Sit down and drink your milk, Jem,' ordered my mother weakly.

But Jem was already scrambling after me. 'I

won't be good in the next air raid if you don't let me.'

My father said, 'It'll take even longer for my plum jam if there's an argument.'

My mother sighed then said, 'All right. Run along. Do as Jewel tells you. Take care of your little brother, Jewel.' She was already pouring the tea.

Those were the last words she ever said to me.

★ ★ ★

The girl from the cottage drives out of her garden and heads for the road. Julia can hear the puppy squealing with loneliness inside the cottage.

The brief glimpse Julia has had makes her think the girl is going somewhere nice. She is smiling, looks radiant with expectation, looking as though she is not going to be lonely very much longer. She seemed frightened yesterday, but now the fear has left her. Julia goes over and looks into the kitchen window of Kitty's cottage. The puppy stops scratching at the door and rushes, skidding over the kitchen, towards Julia. It leaps onto the sill and, in an ecstasy of hope, tries to burrow its way through the glass and into Julia's arms.

Inside it looks chaotic but cosy and homelike.

6

Kitty reaches Heathrow with half an hour to spare. She is loving the anticipation of Matthew's arrival and would have got there even earlier if she could. She is comfy in modern, shiny places, she revels in tubular steel and vinyl grandeur. She enjoys airports, feels stimulated and excited by the international crowd and the sparkling sensation of coming and going. She loves the atmosphere of easy movement round the world and is quite happy now, sitting, drinking Coke, munching Mars, watching the announcement boards, tingling with excitement because Matt will soon be here. God has answered her prayer even though she ate the trifle.

The plane is on time. She finishes her Coke as the announcement comes on to say that the plane had landed. Just enough time, she thinks, to go to the loo and make herself beautiful.

Her reflection, there, looks fat. She will have to suck her tummy in when she meets Matt. Later, in his happiness at seeing her he will, hopefully, not notice. She practises, pulling in all the possible bits of her, till she feels she is going to pop with effort. She decides to concentrate on her hair, the one bit of herself that seems not to need too much embellishment. Dragging off the multitude of little plaits that Gran so laboriously created for her a week ago, her hands quivering with spasms of panic in case Matt is already coming out, in case she misses him, she spins it into an explosion of black, like a dark celebration firework then stabs it through with a shimmer of rhinestone combs. She arranges her six-inch-long Oxfam skirt till it hangs in a glittering frill above her aubergine tights and glistening jelly boots and inserts earrings that flash with watch-battery powered lights. She loves sparkle though the beads and tinsel that she glues to her clothes with Copydex tend to drop off leaving a sparkling snail-like trail in her wake. She examines herself on all sides then lets out a howl of anguish because there's an inexplicable ladder in the purple tights. Of course she has forgotten to bring the nail polish so will have to let it run. Also there's a smudge of choccy on the nipple area of her tee shirt. Now she will have to keep her right breast away from Matt as well as her left leg. And suck in her stomach. The posture is more complicated than anything she has had to learn in the Danaveda class.

'Luggage in hall' has come up when she goes hobbling out.

Kitty joins the crowd at the arrivals barrier and watches the passengers emerge with their luggage-loaded trolleys.

Till suddenly Matthew is there.

Forgetting all about the posture that hides the stomach, the stain and the ladder, she rushes forward, her breath fast, her heart hammering.

★   ★   ★

No, it isn't Matt, but another man carrying only his hand luggage. Another man looking trendy, smart, cool like Matt will be when he emerges.

Kitty's excitement recedes and she returns to her state of expectation. Anyway it is too soon for the passengers from the Waswar flight to have come through, she decides.

★   ★   ★

One by one passengers emerge looking a little shy to be suddenly confronted by the pack of expectant faces. After half an hour the emerging passengers begin to look Chinese, and all the people who had been waiting with Kitty have gone and been replaced by a new lot. Kitty cranes to see from the luggage labels where the passengers have come from now. A plane that had landed half an hour after Matt's.

She waits another hour before going to the information desk.

'He must have missed the plane,' says the girl.

She waits for the arrival of two planes from Dubai, for you never know, he may have gone direct from there. But he is not on either.

She has the Waswar hotel number Matt has given her and rings it from the airport.

A man answers. 'Mr Wing checked out this morning.'

★   ★   ★

Again and again throughout that evening and night Kitty asks for an announcement to be made. 'Will Mr Matthew Wing, arrived from Waswar, please come to the information desk where his wife is waiting.'

Kitty buys four KitKats, two doughnuts, and a packet of crisps and eats them on the way home. Her mouth is smeared with chocolate and sharp with sugar grains by the time she is half way there.

Matt must have gone to an unexpected business meeting. He has tried to ring her at home, but of course, silly her, she has left early. There will be a message from him on the ansaphone.

As she approaches the village, an hour and a half later, she begins to feel quite calm again. Even a little bit cross that now she will have to make the trip all over again, probably tomorrow. The thought of the message that will be waiting for her even drives away her fear of another night alone with the ghosts on the waste land.

It is nearly midnight by the time she gets home. She rushes the car into the garage, nearly hitting the doors. Without locking the car she dashes for the cottage. As she scrabbles with the key the puppy can be heard squealing and clamouring inside. She bursts open the door and tangles her ankles up with a hurl of happy puppy. He has already done a couple of pools on the floor and a worse thing too, and now pees again in his happiness at seeing her back. She hardly notices.

There are no messages. Kitty stares at the machine in disbelief. Then decides it must be broken. At midnight she rings Gran. Gran answers cheerily. She has reached the stage and age where time is of no significance. She can sleep as easily at midday as midnight, dine as easily at four in the morning as at four in the afternoon. Kitty is weeping by the time she gets Gran to understand.

She puts the receiver down and waits. After a few moments the phone rings three times, then she hears her grandmother's voice say on the ansaphone, hopefully, 'I suppose you've got nits then? Is that why you phoned me?' There is nothing in the world Gran enjoys more than a good nit hunt. She deplores modern hygiene which has almost eradicated them. Kitty knows the ansaphone is working — and feels like howling aloud.

She sits by the phone till dawn breaks, staring at it as though it is someone dying and she has to be in attendance at the final moment.

★   ★   ★

Julia has seen Kitty coming back, no one with her in the car, her expression desperate. She recognises desperation. She has experienced a lot of it since the day she went with Jem to the corner shop to buy plum jam for her father's tea.

★   ★   ★

The corner shop was almost at the end of our garden, she had written. Otherwise our mother would never have let the two of us go there alone. No cars were coming as we climbed down from the bank and carefully crossed the road.

The shop bell rang with its lovely singing echoing, a sound that even years later I continued to associate with warm cakes and jelly babies. Inside it was cool and dark and full of its own special smells, the strong salty one of bacon, the butter one of Cheddar cheese, sugary smells of sweets in glass jars, a small whiff of paraffin which was much stronger in the winter when Mrs Rose had a heater on and overlaying all these the smell of strong yellow washing soap. I often thought how strange it was that all these smells could be experienced separately.

'Hello, my duckies,' said Mrs Rose coming out, wiping her fingers on her apron. 'What do you want, my darlings?'

She took down the bottle of plum jam with mittened fingers. She wore full gloves in the winter and ones out of which the pink tips of her fingers peeped like mice in the summer, I suppose because no matter how warm the weather the flagged stone floor of the corner shop never warmed up.

'We'd better have a small one, Mrs. Rose,' I said. 'Daddy's only back for the weekend and then he's going abroad.'

'It's secret,' Jem announced huskily.

Mrs Rose wiped the jar with a clean cloth and handed it to me.

Just as we were going out Jem suddenly stopped and pulled back. 'I want an ice.'

'Oh, come on, Jem,' I said trying to pull him.

'Do you, ducky?' said Mrs Rose.

'There's not enough money left, Mrs Rose,' I told her counting up the coins in my hand.

Mrs Rose opened up the fridge, winked at Jem and said, 'Lemon?'

Jem shook his head and laughed because she always played this game with him. She knew perfectly well which he wanted for he never chose any other. Jem watched, his fingers gripping the counter like another set of even smaller mice, his nose squashed up against the counter top, his eyes wide with expectation as Mrs Rose's mouse fingers groped among the oranges and greens, the purples and white. 'Peach?' she laughed. Jem was giggling too now and breathing fast with the excitement of suspense. 'Blackcurrant?' Then at last the great moment came as it always did, Jem relaxed and his breathing went to normal as Mrs Rose said as though the idea had only just struck her, 'I know, you want a -' and then she and Jem said together, as again they always did, 'A cherry.'

71

She handed Jem the bright scarlet triangle of water ice and gave me an orange one. I was too old for jokes. 'Your Daddy can pay me next time,' she said.

Sucking our ices we went out of the shop. To this day I can remember that cardboardy taste mingled with the orange. The cold shudder against the tongue. The sharp cardboard corners against my palm.

'Hold my hand. Watch out for a car,' I warned Jem as we started to cross the road. Jem's face was already smeared with red, his lips making sucking popping sounds, his attention entirely on the ice. He held my hand tightly and trotted along at my side, his cheeks pushed out so that he looked like one of the blowing cherubs that held up the little lampshades in my parents' drawing room. I took his ice and held it for him as we climbed back up onto the bristly verge. From the top I could see Mummy standing in our open kitchen door. She began to wave at the sight of us. The thrush was still in the top of the pear tree, still singing. I suppose the wasps must still be getting drunk in the pears down below. Later I would wonder what had happened to them.

I was saying, 'Come on, Jem. Eat that later,' when the explosion came. For one second the house seemed to rock into the air a little. The last thing I saw was Mummy sort of jerking upwards as though she was one of my dolls being thrown. Then there came the most enormous roar. With a scream, because Jem was even afraid of the sound of balloons popping, my brother threw himself down among the hog weeds. Sharp, heavy, hurting things began to crash around us as the roar went on and on. When I peeped out through the grass I saw that in the place where our house had been, now there was only a great ball of smoke and dust out of which suddenly licks of fire began emerging.

Jem, beside me in the grass, found a voice at last and began screaming, 'Mummy, Mummy, I'm frightened.' He got up and began running towards the burning gap that had been our house. I rushed after him and grabbed his hand. Peering through the billow of flame and smoke I tried to see where Mummy was, while Jem clutched my hand with all his might.

'Mummy, Mummy, Daddy, Daddy,' we sobbed as we stood staring with streaming eyes and choking breath into the ball of fire that a moment before had been our home.

I heard a voice behind me screaming out, 'Children, come back,' and saw Mrs Rose running towards us. Her eyes were wild with horror.

The heat was scalding my face. I could smell my hair burning. Red hot flaring things began to fall on my clothes, on Jem's clothes, hurting us. Jem was screaming, smacking at his skin, leaping up and down as Mrs Rose caught up with us and grabbed us.

'I don't want you, I want Mummy,' Jem yelled, struggling away from her. She tried to pull us away but we were desperate to get to our home. Jem was trembling just like the day the wasp had stung him. His jaw was shaking.

'Come back to the shop, darlings,' she begged.

'We must go home,' I said. 'Mummy will be wondering where we are.'

'Yes, we've got to go,' said Jem, who had become calmer.

'Deary, it's a bit dangerous over there at your home,' said Mrs Rose. She still held me. I began resisting and, looking and looking through the veils of smoke and plaster dust, tried to catch sight of my mother and father. By now they must be running to find us and soothe us after the shock of the explosion.

'Just come into the shop a little while,' Mrs Rose said in a shaky whisper. 'Just come in and sit down while we sort things out.'

'Daddy is waiting for the jam,' said Jem.

'Were they in the house when you came here?' asked Mrs Rose.

I nodded.

'Come.' Tears were pouring down her face.

The chill that had been licking round my heart seemed to give a sudden bite into it.

Inside the shop I felt my legs go weak and had to hold onto the door-post to stop myself falling.

'I'll give you each another lolly,' said Mrs Rose. When she reached up for the jar her hands were so shaky that twice she almost dropped it. In the end she had to take her mittens off to get the lollies out. Silently, not playing a game, she handed Jem an orange one.

'Cherry,' said Jem, shocked. 'You know I always have cherry in everything.' His tone was reproachful.

As though she had not heard she thrust lollies into our hands. It seemed as though she was trying to compensate us for something.

I took mine with numb fingers. Suddenly I had lost the appetite for lollies. A great tightness was arising across my throat and chest as though someone had tied a rope round me. When I tried to breathe I found the air would not come. I felt as if I was choking. Mrs Rose put an arm round me and hugging me said, 'There, there, darling, there, there, darling.'

'My Mummy will be able to cheer Jewel up,' said Jem. 'So thank you for the lolly. We had really better go now.'

'I think your Mummy might have gone away,' said Mrs Rose desperately.

'Of course she hasn't,' said Jem in a shocked voice.

'She might have had to go to . . . ' Mrs Rose paused, then finished quickly, 'to hospital.'

'She wouldn't ever just go off and not say goodbye to us,' said Jem. 'Anyway Daddy's there.'

'He has gone too,' said Mrs Rose. 'Come into my sitting room while I try to explain.'

Her sitting room was very small and filled with chairs covered with lace mats. There were lace mats on the tables too, dozens of clocks and it smelled of wood polish, lavender bags with a tiny little whiff of soap and bacon from the shop added on. It was much warmer in here than in the shop.

'Sit down on my knee, Jem. Sit here, by me, Jewel. Your Mummy and Daddy have been hurt by that big bomb you heard and the doctor might have to take them away to hospital to get them better.' I knew from the way her voice kept fading and her eyes filling with tears that she was saying something she did not believe. 'They might be away a long time,' she added. 'They might not ever come back.'

Mr Rose came rushing in. He was the postman and his hands shivered as he pulled the strap of the post bag from his shoulders. 'They've both been found,' he said, shaking his head. 'Shattered.' His face was white.

Outside we could hear the sound of firemen, the squirt of water, the banging of ladders. He shook his head sadly, and repeated the word, 'Shattered.'

Our maid had broken a china jug that had once belonged to my grandmother and that had been Daddy's favourite. I remember my mother saying, 'Don't worry, Charlie. I'll glue it together for you,' and my father replying mournfully, 'Throw it out, Dorry, it's shattered.' Shattered meant past repairing. Shattered meant being scattered in little bits all over the room.

'Heaven help the poor souls,' said Mrs Rose.

'But at least the kiddies are all right,' said Mr Rose again. He looked from Jem to me and from me to Jem. There was worry in his glance. 'I had letters to deliver for . . . ' Mr Rose paused, and looked back over his shoulder. 'I don't know what I'm meant to do with them.'

Mrs Rose shook her head in a sorrowful

way and said nothing.

'Well, at least the kiddies are OK.' He did not seem to realise that this was the second time he had said it.

'I want to go back to my mummy but Mrs Rose won't let me,' said Jem.

'I've tried to explain to him,' whispered Mrs Rose. 'But I can't get him to understand.'

'Your Mummy and Daddy have gone to Heaven,' said Mr Rose. 'Do you understand that, Jem?'

Jem nodded.

Mr Rose took Jem and me by the hand. 'Let's go and look at the fire engines.'

'Oh, Bill,' cried Mrs Rose. 'Do you think it sensible. They might see . . . ' Her voice trailed away.

'They've been taken away,' said Mr Rose. 'Let the kiddies see that the house and everybody in it is gone. It will make the next stage easier.'

My legs were shaking as I took Mr Rose's hand and set off out into the road with him and Jem.

'Where's our house?' asked Jem when we got there. He stared at the smoking, steaming tumble of debris where it had once stood.

'It got exploded in that big bang, Jem,' I said.

'All our house?' said Jem. 'What exploded it?'

'It was a bomb, dropped by the Germans,' said Mr Rose. 'The firemen said it had fallen onto the thatch where it must have been while you and Julia were going to the shop. Then it must have rolled down onto the ground.'

'Where's Pussy?' said Jem. 'Did she get exploded too, Mr Rose?'

Mr Rose nodded his head sadly. 'I think so, Jem.'

Jem put his thumb into his mouth and stood looking thoughtful. After a while he pulled the thumb out with a pop and said, 'Now I know why Jewel keeps crying. But you don't have to be sad, Jewel. Daddy will buy you another Pussy and then you will be happy again.'

7

Kitty takes the puppy with her when she goes back to Heathrow next morning. Its hot, soft body and unafraid expression seem to be the only glimmer of comforting she can see anywhere around her.

Last night she had not gone to bed but sat, her head on her arms, at the kitchen table waiting for the phone to ring. She has rung Heathrow twice.

'I am being silly, I know I am,' she tells herself sternly when daylight starts flooding in again. 'He has been held up, couldn't get to a phone and will be on today's plane instead.'

★　★　★

The puppy is not a success in the car, scrabbling at Kitty's knees, trying to sit in her lap and lick her face as she drives, then as though in revenge for being rebuffed, doing a pool all over the back seat.

She makes a new promise. I won't eat anything at all till he arrives.

She has left the cottage at a swift run to

avoid eating breakfast. The worst thing was having to feed the puppy without eating anything herself. See, God. Look. I'm feeling ravenous, so now you've got to do your part.

By two her mouth is tingling with the need for food.

She has bought the puppy a hot dog and has not eaten a single crumb herself. Fried onion has encircled her finger like a wedding ring and she has shaken it off into the ash tray instead of eating it.

Kitty's shock when Matt does not arrive today either is total. She stays, staggered in disbelief for an extra half an hour after the information desk tells her the last passengers from that plane had gone.

She hangs about for ages, certain it's hopeless now but not knowing what else to do, and in the end drives home very slowly because there is nothing to hurry for.

She feels thin already because it is so long since she had eaten anything but the feeling gives her no satisfaction. Worried thoughts go whirling through her mind, and to drive them out she turns on the car radio.

It is the news headlines.

'We have just been informed that a British business man has been kidnapped in Waswar. It is not yet known who is holding him. He was travelling to the airport, apparently, when a black car came out of a side turning and stopped the one in which Mr Wing and his driver were travelling. According to the driver, four armed men came up, ordered Mr Wing out, then told the driver to continue. The driver saw Mr Wing being bundled into the other car and driven away. The only reason for his kidnap seems to be that Mr Wing was in the wrong place at the wrong time.'

★ ★ ★

It cannot be true. Such a thing cannot possibly happen to Matt. Feeling as though she is in the middle of a nightmare from which she will soon wake, Kitty drives waveringly the rest of the way home. As she comes into the house the phone is ringing.

Putting the puppy down she rushes for it, grabs up the receiver, shouts, 'Matt, darling.'

A strange man's voice says, 'This is the Foreign Office. Am I speaking to Mrs Wing? We are very sorry to inform you — '

Kitty drops the receiver, leaves it dangling on its cord and sinks onto the sofa. Dimly, through her shaking, Kitty can hear the voice calling, 'Mrs Wing? Are you there?'

★ ★ ★

Julia has seen Kitty come back alone for the second day, has watched, from the waste land, her rush to the phone. Can see her now slumped, the phone dangling. Recognises misery. You have to learn to cope, she thinks. There is no point in succumbing to it. Misery is life's main ingredient and the sooner one learns to accept the fact the better. Another person, she thinks, would have gone in and tried to comfort the girl. Well, Julia knows all about that, and how useless it is. Strangers had tried to console her and Jem and they had not been comforted.

$$\star \quad \star \quad \star$$

After looking at the fire engines for a while, Jem and I went back with Mr Rose. 'The wife will give you supper. You can spend the night with us while we work out what to do,' he told us.

'And then will Mummy and Daddy be home from Heaven?' Jem asked.

'Jem,' I told him. I remember how my heart seemed to almost shake inside me as I spoke. 'People never come back from Heaven so you will have to be very brave and bear it. I will always look after you so you won't have to worry.'

'You aren't being brave, Jewel,' he said.

'You keep on crying.'

'I'm sorry, Jem,' I told him, squashing my mouth up to keep the crying in. 'I won't cry any more, I promise you. And you have to promise me to be a good boy and do what I say.'

He nodded solemnly and although he did not actually make the promise I trusted him.

Mrs Rose cooked Welsh Rarebit for supper. 'Your Mummy told me it is your favourite, Jewel,' she said, serving a bubbling golden slice onto my plate. I stared at it with no appetite at all and thought to myself, from now on, for the rest of my life, whenever I smell toasted cheese I will feel miserable.

Mrs Rose put her arm round my shaking shoulders and said, 'There, there, Jewel dear. Leave it if you like. I won't mind.'

'What's she carrying on for?' asked Milly. Over my head I felt Mrs Rose do a shake as though she was sending out some silent signal.

Jem told Milly, 'Pussy died in the bomb. That's why Jewel's sad.'

'You don't understand anything, Jem, you stupid little fool,' I screamed suddenly.

'Hush darling, hush darling,' soothed Mrs Rose rocking me back and forth in her arms.

★ ★ ★

Later that evening the policeman, Constable Toms, came round to talk to me and Jem. We both knew him well for he often stopped by our house to talk to our father and after the war started he had shown my parents how to do the blackout. His face was all red and concerned as he asked me, 'Do you know anything about your relations?'

'Relations?' I repeated. I did not understand the word.

'Grandparents, dear. Aunties. Uncles. Do you have cousins?'

'We've got an Uncle Glossy,' I said.

'Do you know his surname?' asked the policeman.

I thought for a moment, then said, 'That is his surname.'

'Glossy?'

'We couldn't pronounce the real word,' I said. 'Because he's Polish.'

Mrs Rose said, 'Do you think it the right time to be asking the poor child all these questions, Percy? Should she not be left in peace at such a time of grief?'

The policeman shook his head sadly and said, 'We've got to find some relatives, Jessie. Otherwise what is going to happen to them?' He sighed and asked me, 'Apart from Uncle Glossy is there anyone else?'

'I think my Daddy had some cousins in

South Africa,' I said. 'But I'm not really sure.'

The policeman said briskly, 'Well, let's concentrate on Uncle Glossy for the moment. When did you last see him?'

'Last night,' I said. 'He came for supper.'

'I remember him,' smiled Mrs Rose. 'A tall foreign gentleman.'

'He said he was going back to Poland but he told Mummy he was coming back in a month.' Suddenly I realised there was no house, now, for him to stay in. Turning to Mrs Rose I asked, 'Could he stay here when he comes, Mrs Rose? He won't be any trouble.' I remembered Mummy always said that about me and Jem when she was persuading people to have us to stay with them. 'I will look after him. I know all the things he likes to eat.'

As soon as Uncle Glossy came, everything would be all right.

That evening the evacuees began yelling, 'Jewel's hair's on fire,' and threw a bucket of water over my red hair while Jem stood tremblingly watching. Turning on him, as I shook the water out of my eyes, I shouted furiously, 'Why didn't you stop them?'

'How could I?' he whimpered. 'They're bigger than me.'

'You could tell them not to,' I said angrily. 'I always stick up for you.' I knew I was being unreasonable. I had never really expected Jem to protect me. I suppose I was just not used, yet, to having no one to defend me.

Mrs Rose found me shivering and dripping.

As Jem and I lay in bed we could hear Mrs Rose scolding the evacuees and telling them to be especially kind to us because of our tragic loss.

In the morning my shoes had disappeared. As I went hunting and scrambling under the beds looking, the door opened and Milly, Fred and Will stood there and began to chant, 'Tragic loss, tragic loss, tragic loss.' Something seemed to break inside me and I went for them, punching, kicking, biting, as though they were the people who had dropped the bomb on my home and killed my mummy and my daddy.

★　★　★

Mrs Gill came to see Jem and me next day. She was a large lady with enormous teeth and very reflective spectacles so that you could see your own face when she was talking to you. She was, my mother had told us, a do-gooder. Whenever there was a crisis in the village she was there first. She had been waiting with blankets the day one of the cottages caught fire, ready to wrap them round the trembling occupants when they were rescued. She was first on the spot of a car crash in the High Street, ready with Dettol and bandages. When our river rose and flooded the streets and lower cottages Mrs Gill appeared with sandbags and mops. She was, my mother said, a miracle of concern.

'Why don't you like her then?' I had asked. My mother had flushed and said, 'Of course I do. Everyone likes her. She is such a kind lady.' But I knew from my mother's voice she was not telling the truth.

Mrs Gill wrapped her arms round Jem in a huge muffling embrace, until only his legs wiggling wildly for escape, could be seen.

'My poor, poor little man. I was not there when it happened. I was visiting my sick sister in town. What a tragedy.' I thought she meant the tragedy was her not being there when the bomb fell, because Mummy had once said that she liked to be in the thick of disasters.

'Now what is going to happen to them, Mrs Rose?' she asked, putting Jem down. He looked red-faced and cross as he tugged his clothes back the right way round.

Mrs Rose sighed. 'They have an uncle. In Poland. But we don't know his address.'

'Well, at least that's something,' Mrs Gill boomed, grinning her huge teeth smile. Then

88

to us, 'In the meantime hop into my car, the pair of you, and I will take care of you until the relatives are found.'

It took Jem a moment to understand then he caught hold of Mrs Rose's hand and clung to it, looking panicky.

'Come on, don't be silly,' said Mrs Gill, trying to tug him away.

'Perhaps you'd better leave them with me for the meanwhile, Madam,' said Mrs Rose. 'They have had a shock, and need some kind of stability.'

'You want to come and stay in my house, surely,' pleaded Mrs Gill getting down on her knees so that it seemed she was imploring humbly. 'It is too much to ask Mrs Rose to take any more needy children now that she has all those evacuees. Five children and a shop. That is too much to be asked of any woman.'

'Well, Madam, it's all right,' said Mrs Rose, but she spoke hesitantly, and I realised in a moment that having us had been a lot of trouble for her.

8

Mrs Rose came to see me and Jem the day after we were taken to Mrs. Gill.

'I want to come back and live with you,' Jem wept, clinging to Mrs Rose as though she was now his mother.

Mrs Rose looked embarrassedly at Mrs Gill while she patted Jem, saying, 'There, there, darling. You come and see me whenever you like but sleep here in Mrs Gill's nice house, where those naughty evacuees can't taunt you.'

Mrs Gill, smiling enormous teeth, said, 'Don't you worry about this little pair, Mrs Rose. They'll soon settle down. I've had great experience with troubled people, as well you know.'

'You are a saint, Mrs Gill,' said Mrs Rose. 'But I have some good news.' She held out a letter. 'This is from Uncle Glossy for the children's mother. It came to my husband for delivery. His address will be in it.'

I began to jump up and down in my excitement. Once Uncle Glossy came Jem and I would be somebody's children again.

'Open it quickly and read what he says,' I urged Mrs Rose.

Mrs Rose carefully slit the envelope, and began to read. 'He says, 'Thank you for a good visit. I shall remember, for a long time, our meals under the pear tree and the sweet thrush singing'.'

'That's just how he talks,' I said.

'Will he come today?' asked Jem.

'He doesn't yet know about your parents ... ' She could not complete the sentence. Wiping away a tear she said, 'But I'm sure that as soon as he hears what had happened he will do his best to get to you.' She went on with the letter, ' 'I am looking forward to seeing both of you and the sweet children soon, though with this dreadful war it seems as though it may be some time before that happens.' And here is his address. Now we know where to contact him.'

Everything was going to be all right, I thought, warm with hope.

* * *

Life is better without hope, thinks Julia. Then you can't get disappointed. She wishes she had not had so much hope of finding the metal box, for now the failure was even more bitter.

The kitchen door of the cottage suddenly opens. Kitty stands there. She looks dishevelled, her face red from steam, her eyes red, perhaps from crying, a white pout of whipped egg on her stomach and two large ladders in her tights.

'Would you like to come in and have a cup of tea?' she asks.

Julia feels panic. The girl is going to ask her for help, for consolation and Julia has never even managed to solve any of her own problems. But the desperation in the girl's eyes makes the invitation impossible to refuse. Julia goes in reluctantly.

'I'm making meringues,' said Kitty. 'Do you like them?'

'No,' says Julia. 'I find them too sweet.' When she was young, after she left Dikkers, people would tell her, 'You should eat more sugar,' but she had stayed as sour as that first orange she had eaten on Dikkers Rhodesian farm all those years ago. Dick had laughed at the way she had screwed up her face after sucking into that first Dikker orange.

'Give them another month, Jewel. They'll be lovely then,' he had told her. And it was true. A month later the sun had sweetened the oranges. It would have done it to Julia too, if life had allowed it. Sun, love, Dikkers, Dick. Sweetness ended after that.

'Anyway they take four hours to cook,' says Kitty. 'And I don't expect you've got so long.'

'No,' agrees Julia.

'The good thing about meringues is that they need lots of beating,' says Kitty.

'Is beating a good thing?' Julia asks.

'It keeps your mind off.'

'What happens when you run out of things to beat?' asks Julia.

'I cry,' says Kitty. The puppy wakes and resumes his attack on her laces. 'And I'll beat you if you go on doing that,' she tells it.

Later, saying, 'The news,' she switches on the TV and sits on the edge of her chair, plate balanced on her knee, an éclair from an earlier baking half way to her mouth, staring attentively into the screen.

Matthew's face appears suddenly. Kitty lets out a little yell and drops her plate.

'There has so far been no news about the latest kidnap victim, Mr Matthew Wing, who was abducted on his way to the airport yesterday. He was married six months ago and lives near Portsmouth.'

A photo of Kitty and Matthew on their wedding day.

'Oh,' says Julia.

9

Kitty reaches out and switches the TV off in mid-sentence, then ignoring Julia, turns and stares out of the window into the black waste land. Her shoulders are shaking. The machinery is off but the tragedy is only silent. Still there. Misery unaltered.

Julia waits awkwardly.

'We were happy,' says Kitty after a while, her voice muffled.

Julia shrugs. She knows all about that, happiness snatched away. 'Haven't you got any family?' she asks. 'Anyone you can go to?'

'My grandmother. In London,' said Kitty. 'But she's a bit, you know, away with the fairies.'

The puppy lets out a little cry in its sleep and its legs twitch with some dream of running. Julia looks down at it and feels despondent.

Kitty, following her glance, says, 'It's Matt's. He's going to train it to bring back pheasants. I didn't want the dog at first but now I'm glad. It's the only thing of Matt left at the moment.' She looks away and her shoulders start to heave again. After a while she asks in a choked voice, 'How long do you think they will keep him?' as though Julia is an expert on hostage taking.

Julia shrugs, then sighs. 'I had better go,' she says, getting up. 'Ring your granny, or something.'

She goes over across the room, she reflects that the floor is very solid and if the box is under it she will never find it. As she opens the back door to go out the puppy dashes past her and vanishes into the night.

For the next half an hour Julia and Kitty go striding over the coarse grass in two directions, calling, 'Rob, Rob, Rob,' and, 'Puppy, puppy, puppy.'

'He might have fallen in the river,' Kitty calls weepily through the blackness. Once or twice they think they hear faint and distant yapping.

They return to the cottage at last, no sign of the puppy. Kitty sits on the kitchen step and begins to cry, not soft weeping sniffles, but open mouthed howling. Julia turns away and pretends she has not noticed.

Kitty gets up at last, and still sobbing goes with Julia into the kitchen, The puppy is under the kitchen table, collapsed, tummy pink and wide, surrounded by meringues in all stages of half eaten and half sat upon. He looks shyly triumphant as though aware that he has outwitted them. He is, it seems, too full and tired to bark.

'Where do you keep your cleaning things?' asks Julia.

★ ★ ★

As Kitty crawls by Julia's side, swab in hand, clearing the mess, she experiences a small feeling of comfort, a relief at not being alone. The woman has thin shoulders, haggard features and is someone who does not eat cake, but she is here.

'We've got a spare room,' murmurs Kitty as they collide under the kitchen table.

The puppy is yelping with bad dreams brought on by indigestion.

Julia shakes her head. The solidity of the kitchen floor has disheartened her. She wants to get away soon. She is putting on her coat when Kitty starts vomiting.

'My God, I am sorry,' she gasps through spasms, while Julia, cursing herself for not having left quicker, turns her head away and holds her breath. 'I always eat too much when I'm unhappy.'

'Shall I ring a doctor?' asks Julia. 'I can't really leave you like this.'

'I haven't got one yet. Matt and I haven't signed on with anyone.'

Julia goes through the Yellow Pages, Kitty protesting that she is all right now, then she is sick again.

By the time Julia rings several, listens to messages advising the caller to try again in the morning unless it is an emergency in which case an ambulance should be summoned, leaves a message of her own on a couple of the machines, asking the doctor to call back, Kitty has fallen asleep on the sofa.

Julia goes upstairs, finds a duvet on top of the wardrobe and bringing it down spreads it over Kitty. Kitty does not stir.

Worn out, Julia climbs the stairs and lies down on Kitty's bed without even taking off her shoes.

She does not sleep that night, but looks out into a dark that she longs to remember.

Next morning Julia comes down and finds Kitty wildly waving a grubby tea towel at a cloud from burning toast.

'I'm bloody sorry about all that,' she says when she has got the flames out.

Julia does not know if she is referring to the night before or to burning the breakfast.

Kitty looks as though she had not slept much either.

'We'll have to have cornflakes and they're stale,' she tells Julia.

10

' . . . *a video of the British hostage,*
Matthew Wing . . . '

The cornflakes fall from Kitty's spoon as she stares at the TV screen. Her hair crest, held up with a cord pulled from Matt's pyjamas to remind herself of him, topples like the tail of a stricken dog.

Matt, haggard, eyes red-rimmed, unshaven, holds yesterday's newspaper, the date foremost. The paper quivers with his hands' trembling.

'The slimy scum.' Kitty leaps up, strides up and down the kitchen letting out inarticulate shouts, clenching and unclenching her fists, imagining her knuckles cracking into hostage-takers' mouths.

Julia says cautiously, 'What can I do to help?'

Kitty does not hear her.

⋆   ⋆   ⋆

Years ago Julia had written, Mrs Rose tried to help Jem and me, tried to console us, tried to make up for a loss that nothing in the world could make up for.

She brought cardboard suitcases for us when we were at Mrs Gill's.

'You won't be here for ever so they're to pack your things in when you leave,' she said.

'Everything of ours got burnt in the fire,' cried Jem. 'We haven't got nothing to pack.'

Mrs rose put her arms round Jem. 'I've popped a few things in for both of you, darlings, so that you won't be without.'

The cases felt quite heavy and when we looked inside there were clothes for both of us, a doll for me, a tin train for Jem and lollypops, lots of them, although sweets were rationed.

'Perhaps Mrs Rose is really a fairy in disguise,' said Jem, awed by so many lollypops at once.

★ ★ ★

Mrs Gill was not used to children. At first she tried being heavily kind to us, thrusting spoonfuls of rosehip syrup at us and saying, 'Drink this, dear. Good for you. Yum yum yum,' or giving us drinks of blackcurrant puree mixed with water. 'Now drink this up at once. It's full of vitamins. Make you strong.' I tried to gulp all these things down just for the sake of peace but Jem, who had always been fussy about food, adamantly kept his lips tight and refused to swallow. Then she and Jem would get locked into what looked like a test of strength, Jem with his jaw clamped so tight it made the veins in his neck stand up, Mrs Gill ramming the spoon hard against his teeth and trying everything. 'Be a good boy and I'll give you a sweetie after,' then, 'I'll give you a real good whacking if you don't drink it,' while I danced around them begging, 'Please drink it up, Jem. It's too little to be worth making such a fuss about,' and 'He's not really a naughty boy, Mrs Gill, but he isn't used to being forced to eat and drink things.'

'A child who disobeys an adult by refusing to drink what is given to him is what I look on as a naughty child,' said Mrs Gill.

Mrs Gill's approach was so challenging that Jem fought, in the end, more out of pride than distaste.

As the days went by I could see that although she was trying terribly hard to be kind and sympathetic she was getting more and more irritated with us. We left grass stains and mud on her pristine carpets when we came in from the garden. All the time we played out there I was aware of her looking at us from one window after another, worrying that our ball might fall among her flowers, or that Jem would scuff holes in her turf with his boots. Jem had already banged against one of her wobbly little statues and it had smashed. Jem told me later, 'I think the statue must have been Mrs. Gill's mummy in disguise and that was why she was so upset when it got shattered.'

'We must try to be more careful,' I told Jem. But it was really difficult. There were so many things and the gaps between the furniture were so narrow that we were constantly afraid of breaking something else, getting my nerves constantly on edge. Jem added to my anxiety by constantly asking, 'When's Mummy coming?'

At first I would say, 'She's dead, Jem. Don't you remember?' and he'd say, 'I know, but when's she coming back from dead,' until in the end, just for peace, in the end I said, 'tomorrow.'

For the rest of that day he stopped asking me when she was coming and instead toddled peacefully around humming little tunes under his breath as though he was thinking about something happy.

Next morning he woke up and shouted, 'Tomorrow's come, Jewel. Where's Mummy?'

I tried and tried to explain that I had only said it to get peace, but he wouldn't listen.

'You said tomorrow, Jewel, and it is tomorrow.'

'I know,' I said. 'Let's go home and leave a letter to the fairies asking them to send Mummy and Daddy back to us.'

Jem and I had often written to the fairies asking them for things and they had always given us what we wanted. Almost what we wanted.

'Dear fairies, please send Jem a real train engine that he can get into,' I would write at Jem's dictation. Or, 'Dear fairies, please send me a real live baby donkey.'

We used to leave the letters in the under-stairs cupboard before we went to bed and next morning, quivering with excitement, we would peer into it. The present would always be there. Almost there. The live donkey had been a stuffed one and the fairies had pinned a little note to it. 'Dear Jewel, we are very small so can't bring you a full-sized donkey, but we hope you will like this one. His name is Neddy.' The train had been a toy one with a similar explanation attached to it. Once Jem asked for a seaside in his garden, and the fairies left only a letter saying, 'Dear Jem, a lot of other people wanted to use the seaside too, so we didn't bring it. But we have asked Mr Philps, the builder, to make a paddling pool for you in the garden when the summer comes.' They always answered our letters, always explained and no matter what they sent us we loved it, because the things were fairy things. Jem had been so awed by his fairy train that instead of playing with it he had made Mummy bury it in the tin box with her precious things.

Even though I thought it might be very hard for the fairies to really bring our parents back I felt sure that when they found out what had happened to us they would think of something to make things better. We asked Mrs Gill to let us have a pencil and some paper. 'So we can practise our school work,' I said.

Mrs Gill looked delighted at the idea of us sitting quietly for a while. When I had finished writing we fell asleep feeling much better.

In the morning, gently, so as not to wake Mrs Gill, I shook Jem. We tiptoed out of the room and down the stairs without putting on our clothes or even our shoes.

'Won't Mummy be cross if we go out in our pyjamas?' said Jem. He looked very small and vulnerable in Fred's baggy pyjamas. I thought what a huge job I had ahead of me looking after him.

But I told him this was an emergency and, if we changed, Mrs Gill might wake up and stop us going.

We tiptoed through the house, creeping carefully past all Mrs Gill's rattling ornaments and complicated brass fern holders. Jem and I, clutching our letter, crept out of the front door, being careful not to let it click shut, so that we could get back in again.

'We might not have to come back here if the fairies send Mummy and Daddy back quickly,' said Jem.

As soon as we were out of sight of Mrs Gill's house we ran as fast as we could, jumping over the verges, leaping the drainage cuts, both of us feeling quite hopeful that we had thought of the way to solve all our problems.

As we crossed the road, me holding Jem carefully by the hand, the milkman drove past, the bottles jingling in time to the trotting of his pony. He looked at us with an expression of pity, said, 'Hello, kiddies,' and as though we embarrassed him, urged his pony on down the street and past the place where our house had stood without stopping.

Jem said, 'I expect Mummy's note for how many pints got burnt in the fire and that's why he didn't leave us any milk.'

Clutching each other's hands we climbed through the fence and stood inside our orchard. When we turned in the direction of the house it was as though a fog had hidden it, for all you could see was sky now, with a wisp or two of smoke still coming up from the remains of what had once been home. On the place where our house had been there was only a great big heap of twisted, wetted, blackened wreckage.

The thrush was back in the old pear tree, singing loudly. I felt a little shocked, as though it was somebody being happy at a funeral.

I turned my back on the vanished house and looked only at the orchard and the stream, the bird singing behind us. I kept my mind fixed on the things that the bomb had not changed and was comforted for a moment.

Jem started crying.

'We could pretend Mummy is in the kitchen cooking lardy cake,' I told him.

'What happened to the lardy cake, Jewel?' Jem wept. 'Mummy said she was going to give it to us for tea but she never did. I was telling lies when I said I didn't like lardy cake, Jewel. It wasn't true that I only liked ice lollies. Do you think Mummy knows?'

'She knows everything because she is in Heaven now, Jem,' I told him.

'She'll come back when the fairies get our letter,' said Jem. 'But how are we going to find the under-stairs cupboard?'

'Perhaps we could find the tin box of valuables and put the letter into it,' I suggested. But everything was different in the garden and though we searched for half an hour we could not find the place.

*   *   *

How strange, Julia thought, that sixty years later she is still hunting for that box.

*   *   *

In the end we pushed the letter into the fork of the pear tree. 'I expect the fairies will find it all the same,' Jem said. 'They're supposed to be clever.'

*   *   *

When we got back to Mrs Gill's she was outside in the drive, looking furious. As soon as she saw us she began shouting.

'You naughty naughty children, how dare you go out without permission. And leaving the front door open. Don't you know my house is filled with precious things. A thief could have come in and stolen everything.'

*   *   *

For the rest of that day Jem and I waited for the fairies to get our letter. During it we kept hearing Mrs Gill talking and talking on the telephone. We knew she was talking about us, telling people how bad we had been.

That night we could not go to sleep for ages, hoping and hoping that the fairy letter would have worked. As soon as daylight came we rushed over to the window and looked out onto the road expecting to see our parents coming along to get us. But all there was out there was a single ginger cat.

'Do you think that cat is Mummy in disguise?' said Jem. 'Its hair is just the same colour as Mummy's. And yours, Jewel.' But I knew that even he did not believe that.

By lunchtime we had lost hope. Jem began to weep, saying that the fairies must have all been killed in the fire.

★ ★ ★

After lunch next day Mr Rose arrived in his jeep. Mrs Gill rushed out to meet him as though he had come to save her from something.

'I'm really sorry about it,' Mrs Gill told him. 'I have tried my very best, but they are totally disobedient. Uncontrolled. Do you know what they did yesterday? I am sure they will be better off in the Home where they will get proper supervision until their uncle is found.'

Mr Rose said to us, 'Come on, kiddies, get packing. We're off to your new home.' He sounded worried.

As I came down the stairs I heard Mr Rose tell Mrs Gill, 'We managed to get someone to take a message to the uncle's house, but it seems he is no longer there. All the Jews have been taken to live somewhere else, apparently. But we are still trying to contact him.'

Jem said, 'We've got to stay here, actually, Mr Rose, because the fairies are getting Mummy and Daddy back for us. We left a letter for them.'

Mr Rose looked suddenly very sad, and said, 'Tell me where you've left the letter, and I'll go every day and see if there is an answer. But you have to come along with me now.'

'I'm sorry, Harry. I really am,' said Mrs Gill. 'You know how much I love little kiddies usually but I have to think of my blood pressure.'

'That's all right, Mrs Gill,' said Mr Rose. 'You did your best. We all know that.'

Mrs Gill clasped Jem to her bosom as we were leaving, and hugged him while he kicked and wriggled to be free. After she let go of him I saw her give Mr Rose a meaningful look over Jem's head.

I thought of explaining, 'It isn't that he doesn't like you, Mrs Gill. But just that you are squashing him.'

★   ★   ★

Julia puts down the diary and thinks, I was always a liar. Even now I tell Kitty, 'I can be helpful to you. You need someone at a time like this,' when really I am hoping to see some way to take her home from her.

★   ★   ★

Before I had time to say anything Mrs Rose, who had come to see us off as well, hugged Jem and he did not wriggle once.

Mr Rose drove us away from our village with Mrs Gill and Mrs Rose standing in the road and waving and waving. Jem and me twisted round in the jeep and waved back as hard as we could.

'My waves are only for Mrs Rose,' said Jem sternly.

Mr Rose pressed his lips together as though something was hurting him inside and said, 'Now listen, my darlings. I am taking you to a place with lots of other children and some kind nuns will be looking after you.'

'Till Uncle Glossy comes?' I said.

'Till Mummy and Daddy come,' corrected Jem.

'It may be,' said Mr Rose cautiously, 'that you will have to live in this children's home for quite a long time because at the moment it is very very difficult for anyone to find Uncle Glossy so you must do your best to settle down there.'

'But I thought you'd found his address,' I protested.

Mr Rose pinched his lips tight and did not answer.

'I don't want to go in a children's home,' wailed Jem. 'I want to go back to my Mummy.'

I sighed. 'I've tried and tried and tried to explain it to him, Mr Rose, but he just won't listen.'

'It's a hard thing for a little boy to have to bear,' said Mr Rose softly. Then to Jem, 'Now be a good boy and stop all that racket and at the next chance I'll buy you an ice.'

Jem stopped crying at once and instead began bouncing up and down, shouting, 'A cherry ice, a cherry ice.' Then suddenly he stopped and said, 'Jewel, where's my ice you bought me in the corner shop the day our house blew up?'

'Come on, kiddies, enough of that. I'm

going to buy you another.'

We drove for a long time. We seemed to be getting very far away from home and our letter to the fairies.

'You are going to a lovely place by the sea,' said Mr Rose. 'It will be just like a seaside holiday there.'

11

We reached an empty bleak landscape of rough grass, bushes, and some Nissen huts surrounded by barbed wire. Over rusty gates was a painted sign with the words, 'Convent of the Holy Mother,' and underneath in smaller letters, 'Suffer the little children to come to me.'

Mr Rose slowed up, then stopped the jeep and stared. He didn't say anything but I could see from the way his jaw had gone tight that he was upset.

Wind was pushing down the bushes and grass against the ground, and making a wailing noise like a sad animal. Everything looked grey and cold. There was no colour anywhere.

'Where's the sea? I can't see the seaside,' cried Jem bouncing up and down, and peering in all directions.

'It must be over there,' said Mr Rose, pointing. I noticed that his hand was trembling. 'Now sit still and wait while I open the gates.'

As we drove into the wire-surrounded area he said, 'The convent was evacuated here to get away from the air raids. As soon as the risk of bombs is over they will be going to a nice house with a lovely garden. You two won't have to stay here for long.'

'When is the war going to end, Mr Rose?' asked Jem.

'Soon, darling, soon I hope,' said Mr Rose. There was a shaky sound in his voice as though he was nearly crying, but I knew it could not be so. Men don't cry, do they.

We had reached the first of the Nissen huts, on which a sign was hung stating, 'Main Office.' Mr Rose stopped the jeep and tooted his horn.

The door opened with a whine of hinges, and a tall nun, a white wimple fixed very tightly round her red face, came out.

'Ah, Mr Rose, you have brought our new little residents, I see.' The chill wind was billowing out her black habit, making her look like a black ship sailing.

Mr Rose lifted us out one by one, greeted the Reverend Mother then said to her, 'It's a bit grim, isn't it. It looks more like a prison than a children's home.'

'It's the best we can do in the circumstances,' said the nun firmly. 'We must thank God for whatever we can get.'

'Be good children and do as Reverend Mother tells you,' Mr Rose told us. 'And Mrs

Rose and I will come and visit you whenever we can.'

'There. That's nice,' said the nun, taking up our cases. And to us, 'Now come along you two. I'll show you your quarters.' I took hold of Jem's hand and the two of us crept along the concrete path. Ahead of us the nun seemed to fill the whole horizon with an enormous black presence. Our clothes felt thin and inadequate in the wind.

★ ★ ★

We kept looking back and waving till Mr Rose was out of sight and we were alone with the nun.

She turned, said, 'Now do hurry up, you two. Come along,' then as though seeing me properly for the first time she gave a little gasp, reached out and taking hold of a handful of my hair said, 'Heavens. We shall have to have that off.'

'What do you mean?' I said, clapping my hands protectively over my mass of flaming curls. Everybody in our village had admired my hair. My mother would run her fingers through my hair saying, 'Gorgeous, glorious.'

'We can't have hair like this in the orphanage,' said the nun. 'We'd have nits all over the place if we allowed hair like that.'

'Where's the seaside?' demanded Jem, as the nun led us towards one of the Nissen huts.

'Oh, we can't go there. It's covered with defences,' said the nun. 'Don't dawdle, child. Come along do.' Then to me, 'This is the girls' dormitory. This is where you will be sleeping, young lady.' She flung open a door and put down my case. I saw lines of camp beds each with a blanket folded at its foot. 'We have no room for private storage space so for the moment you will have to keep your box under the bed. Your bed will be that one at the far end. Come on now, little boy, I'll take you to the boys' dormitory. What is your name?'

Jem seemed too frightened to reply. He flinched and grabbed my hand, half comprehending.

'Jem,' I said, adding, 'Jem and I always sleep together. He mustn't go to a separate room.'

'We don't have girls and boys together in this home,' said the nun, distaste in her tone.

Jem clung to me. 'Jewel promised to never leave me,' he said.

The nun tried to pull him. He grabbed hold of my legs and hung on.

She began shouting, 'I will not tolerate this sort of behaviour. Obey me this minute.'

115

Jem howled louder.

'Please let him stay with me,' I said in a trembly voice. There was something quite frightening about this nun, with her huge angry voice and scarlet face. 'He is only little.'

'Absolutely out of the question,' said the nun, still dragging at Jem.

He got his arms round my waist now and screamed, 'You got to stay with me, Jool. You promised you would for ever.'

Suddenly something seemed to break inside me. All the tears I had been bottling in so long came rushing out. I just stood, my face flooded with crying, my body shaking with it, my little brother clinging and screaming.

'You'll have your meals and lessons together.' The nun had to shout to be heard over Jem's cries. She let go of him and said, her voice a little gentler than before, 'We have rules here and they must be kept, but you'll meet during the day.'

'May I come with him to his room and settle him down,' I whispered.

In the end they made a bed for Jem at the top end of the boy's dorm and mine at the bottom so that there was only a thin wall of plywood between them.

Through it, that night after we had gone to bed, I whispered, 'Have you brushed your

116

teeth, Jem?' and heard his little hoarse voice whisper back, 'Yes, Jewel.' After a moment's silence he said, 'Don't be sad Jewel about breaking your promise because I know it wasn't your fault. But we ought to have run away when the bomb came and not let those grown-ups catch us.'

With a dandelion bitterness rising in my throat I thought that he was right, that we had been wrong to trust any of the adults, even Uncle Glossy. Even Mr Rose had betrayed us. There was no seaside here.

★   ★   ★

Julia gives a start and feels a scarlet guilt when Kitty finds her poking into the lawn.

Kitty has brought Julia tea and stands there with the mug steaming in her hand.

'Whatever it is I'm sure you won't find it there,' she says. 'Matt laid that lawn only six months ago. He dug the whole place up. If only you would tell me what you've lost I might be able . . . ' Two huge safety pins hold up her tassel of tulle that answers for a skirt. Following Julia's gaze she says defensively, 'It shrank in the wash. It was OK when I bought it.' It had cost her twenty pence in the village hall jumble sale.

Julia makes sandwiches for lunch for both

117

of them, later, but Kitty is feeling sick again and cannot eat.

For a day or two Julia makes plans to leave, booking herself onto Canadian flights, then cancelling them. She feels like a gambler who is sure that the next dice throw will be the winner at last. One more thrust of the trowel and she will find the box. One more day and all her troubles will be over

Just when she has completely run out of money she sees a temporary and part-time job advertised in the local library, goes for the interview, gets the job.

She keeps staying on encouraged by the little income and the access to Kitty's garden.

The two fall into an uneasy routine. Julia furtively searches Kitty's soil, and, to justify her presence in Kitty's house, helping with the housework.

Julia washes the kitchen floor then gets cross when the puppy piddles on it.

'I don't mind,' says Kitty. 'It only takes a sec to wipe the puddles with a tissue.'

'I saw you use the tea towel that is meant for drying the dishes we eat from.' Julia makes a big thing of wiping the puppy-soiled area with disinfectant. Kitty scowls and feels criticised.

Julia begins to train the puppy.

Kitty is pleased at first, but after a while

and a lot of slaps and shouting from Julia, Kitty begins to feel that the puppy's craven obedience is humiliating. 'It's making him sad,' she protests.

'You can't have an untrained animal round the house,' Julia says firmly.

'My house,' says Kitty.

The puppy, in spite of Kitty's feelings, seems to like Julia more than Kitty. Kitty feeds it, romps with it, cuddles it and yet it seemed to prefer to be with Julia who is constantly hectoring it. It follows Julia round the garden as she works with her trowel and the metal detector she has hired, diving gleefully into the little holes Julia makes when she gets a beep. Digging joyfully, sending up sprays of earth into Julia's hopeful face as she looks into the cavity. Kitty feels neglected, tries to trick the puppy, with pretend scratching motions, into believing there are bones buried under the sofa cushions. But the puppy gets bored of the game. It prefers Julia's earth.

Kitty knows she is being unfair and jealous when she turns on Julia, shouting, 'It's my bloody dog, not yours.'

The ducks start coming into the kitchen in a great waddling crocodile. Kitty is delighted and throws them bits of bread ripped from the new loaf Julia has just brought back from

Patels. They waddle after it, quacking and splatting out river-white droppings.

The puppy, who is smaller than the smallest duck, wanders among them, amazed, looking ardently into the down-turned duck faces. Then Julia spoils it all, rushing in and shooing the ducks out.

'Don't, don't,' Kitty cries, but the ducks have lost their comfy momentum and are already skidding for the door.

'Sorry,' says Julia. 'Didn't see you,' which Kitty feels sure is a lie. 'But look what a filthy mess they've made on my clean floor.'

* * *

'My brother and I used to play here as children,' Julia tells Kitty. 'We told each other that if ever we get separated we will leave messages for each other here. In a tin box. I thought there might be something hidden round here that will help me find him.'

Once or twice she digs up things that set her heart racing, a little toy car, a scrap of paper scrawled with childish writing. But it is a modern car and when she and Kitty dry the paper they find the words, 'Tracy loves Mark for ever' written on it.

'Chuck it in the fire,' says Kitty. 'It's probably infected with AIDS.' She is getting irritated with Julia's foolish search. 'If I was you I'd do something about my life now instead of hankering after the past all the time.'

'If I was you I would take control over my own life instead of waiting for a man to come back and look after me,' retorts Julia, knowing she was being unfair. 'If I was you I would do something positive about getting my husband back instead of sobbing all day and guzzling cakes and letting me do everything.'

They face each other, eyes flashing with fury.

'You are fucking right,' says Kitty. 'And the first thing I can do without is you.'

'I wouldn't stay here another minute, anyway,' shouts Julia grabbing up her things. 'And I hope you don't think I have to be grateful to you for letting me stay here because I consider I have done more for you than you for me.'

'I know why you stay here.' Kitty shouts, Her hair sprout quivers in the violence of her outrage. Her safety pin pops, she pulls the poke away from her skin and holding the skirt up with her fingers rages on, 'You're up to something. You're trying to get something over me. It's not true about looking for a note from your brother. No one would be so stupid as to think a bit of paper would last for so many years. You have been lying to me, and you are trying to trick me. My grandmother thinks that too.'

'How dare you,' breathes Julia, with the anger of the guilty.

★   ★   ★

Julia packs and comes downstairs.

Kitty is unconcernedly dusting icing sugar over fairy cakes.

'I hope the ghost child gets you. I hope you get blown up in the ghost explosion,' she says.

12

Kitty's words bring Julia up short. 'What ghosts?'

'A child. And a fire.' Kitty puts down the sugar shaker. She shouldn't have reminded herself. Suddenly she is afraid to be left alone again, wants Julia, however nasty, to stay.

'What happened? Tell me what happened.'

Alarmed, Kitty tries to back away. 'I just thought I saw a ghost, but of course I couldn't have, because they don't exist, do they? I mean, I wouldn't have told anyone except Matt and even he doesn't believe me.'

'I believe you,' growls Julia. 'So go on and tell me.'

Reluctantly Kitty drags the story out.

'How old? How old was the child?' cries Julia when she had finished.

Kitty shrugs. 'It was all a bit hazy. She had red hair, though. I'm sure of that.'

'What was the girl wearing?' whispers Julia, raising her hand and touching her own head.

'Red,' says Kitty.

'A red coat,' breathes Julia.

* * *

Julia and Kitty are going to London, Kitty to visit her gran, and Julia to see the lawyer.

Kitty wears a voluminous patchwork quilted jacket just covering her bottom and on her legs spangled orange tights through the ladders of which white skin shines. Patent leather boots up to her knees, so close fitting and shiny that it looks as though her legs have been dipped in oil. On her huge flare of hair Kitty has pinned a flopping pink velvet hat, where it dangles like a faded poppy in a bramble bush. She looks, thinks Julia, like a gaudy lollypop.

Kitty senses criticism. 'It's what people of my age wear.'

Julia is smartly dressed because she wants to assure the lawyer that she can pay the bill, though she herself has doubts of this. Her tights are without blemish and her brogue shoes well polished. She has pinned the brooch Dick gave her for her seventeenth birthday on the lapel of her narrow-cut navy Jaeger coat and skirt. A gold baboon. He had it made specially.

When they get onto the bus there were no two seats together and each is relieved to sit separate. They are not friends. They have nothing in common. They have been thrown together by a dice throw of fate that each of them might be growing to regret.

Julia has secretly used Kitty's phone when Kitty was taking the puppy for a walk to make her appointment with the lawyer. A walk. Kitty carries the puppy, won't let it down on the ground long enough for it to even do a poo.

'That's why it shits all over,' says Julia savagely.

'Its legs will grow too long, Matt said,' Kitty tries. 'And I like the feel of it.'

'You ought to have a baby,' Julia says.

* * *

They reach Marble Arch and Kitty gets off ahead of Julia, then staggers, dizzy.

'I feel sick again,' she says.

Julia bites back irritation, tries to be patient. 'You'll be OK in the fresh air.'

But the girl walks unsteadily. 'I've never felt like this before,' she says.

Julia takes her to a café and orders coffee for two. But when the coffee comes and Julia pours it Kitty reels back.

'Fucking hell, it stinks. What's wrong with it?'

'Nothing,' says Julia sipping her own grimly. 'It's very nice. And for God's sake don't talk so loud. Everyone heard.'

'Sorry.' Kitty pushes her cup away.

125

Julia sighs. 'I suppose you want a cake,' she says, trying to keep the sarcasm out of her tone.

Kitty stares into Julia's face with anguished eyes, and shakes her head dumbly. 'I don't know what's wrong with me. I don't think I could even eat a cream puff. I couldn't even choke down a chocolate brownie.'

'Heavens! You must be ill,' says Julia, pinching a smile away.

★   ★   ★

'I can do nothing without proof,' the lawyer tells Julia. He is young and blond and has a slightly sneery way of talking. 'Thinking the land is yours is not nearly good enough.'

'I am in the process of looking for proof.' She tells him about the box her mother buried.

He tells her that if she finds that, and provided her parents have not officially willed it to someone else, if she can prove she is the daughter of the owners of the waste land then she is entitled to a share of the property. 'You will need to find your birth certificate, though. Nothing can be done unless you have that, for otherwise even if you find these papers, what proof have you that you are the daughter of the owners of this land? You need proof that this is the same land, proof that you are who you say you are, and once you have these we can go further. It looks complex though, will probably be expensive and it may be too late'

'And it may not,' says Julia savagely, visualising suing a long-dead Reverend Mother, who, in the interest of her starting a new fresh life in Rhodesia, had destroyed all her papers.

★ ★ ★

Julia goes to Kitty's gran's house in the evening.

Kitty's gran is enormous, reminding Julia in both shape and colour of a dark barrage balloon teetering on its tether. She has tiny feet for such a huge woman and as she offers Julia a giant, much-ringed hand to shake she totters like a circus lion balancing on a ball. She wears men's clothes, a vast, patched and filthy old tweed jacket pulled inadequately across the biggest, lowest, softest bosom Julia has ever seen. If Gran's necklace broke, the beads would vanish among the folds and billows of that mighty breast and not be found again for months, thinks Julia. Gran wears pinstriped trousers that have obviously been discarded from some outsize city gent.

The trouser cuffs are tucked into a whiskery pair of woollen socks. On her head is a knitted wool cap, brilliant coloured, of a type worn by Rasta men. Her fingers, nails thick as hooves, emerge out of battered mittens and look like rhinos instead of the mice of Mrs Rose.

The room is small and packed with extraordinarily gory and gaudy pictures of Christian saints. The Sacred Heart dripping blood, Saint Catherine dying piously on her wheel, Saint Sebastian, looking heavenwards and stuck all over with blood-dripping arrows. One saint holds what at first sight appeared to be two apples on a plate, which on further scrutiny turn out to be her amputated breasts. Julia is briefly and gloomily reminded of Mrs Gill's over-ornamented house. But the granny's things are not genteel but outrageously vulgar.

The granny's hand presses Julia's so hard that it hurts and she stares inquiringly into Julia's face. 'What do you want of my granddaughter?' Her voice is as deep and resonant as that of a large man.

'Gran, Gran, don't,' wails Kitty.

'I have to ask. It's the duty of a granny. I hope you wish my granddaughter well, for she needs another woman to be looking after her at this special time.'

'Special time?' asks Kitty.

The gran turns to Julia. 'I am unable to give my granddaughter proper care because she lives so far away, but as you are staying with her, Mrs Julia, I hope you will look after her. It will be best if she has a girl for I am bored of males, Mrs Julia, but all the same we must make do with them on occasion.'

Kitty gasps and sits down suddenly as though winded.

'Are you saying Kitty is pregnant?' Julia asks.

'Well, can't you see it? I would have thought it was obvious to anybody, especially a woman.'

13

It is too late now for Julia to have children. That chance is lost, like all her other chances. She had written, in her diary, Jem is the only child I have ever had to care for and after they put him in another room from mine, with a plywood wall between us, that first night at the House of the Holy Mother I tried not to sleep so that I would hear him if he called me. I thought morning would never come, and when at last it did I wished it hadn't.

I looked down the long room where dozens of other girls began wriggling out of nighties and into day clothes.

A nun came and stood over me.

'I am The Girls' Sister' she said. 'And you are,' she looked at a paper in her hand, 'Julia Pritchett.'

I shook my head. 'That's not right,' I said.

The nun frowned and looked closely at the writing. 'That's what it looks like,' she said.

'It didn't sound like that when my Mummy said it.'

'Pritchett is what's written here,' said the nun firmly, as though once something was written it made it a fact.

'Sometimes they called me Jewel Trinket,' I said cautiously, trying to be helpful.

The Girls' Sister laughed. 'No one is called Jewel Trinket. That is what is called a nickname, dear. We don't want to get things muddled, by starting with the wrong name, do we?'

'It's what my Mummy and Daddy called me,' I said. Thinking about my parents made me nearly start crying.

'Do you know the story of Saint Julia?' the nun said, and when I shook my head, 'She was tortured for her faith. She was hung by her long hair till she died. Your name is not as important as that, now is it? I hope you will be a good brave girl like her and put up with pain and loss for the sake of the Lord.'

I put my hand up to my hair and nodded shivering. Suddenly what I was called seemed to hardly matter at all in comparison with being hung by your plaits till you were dead.

The nun thrust a small bundle into my hands. 'Now those are your vitals, dear,' she said. 'You will be fitted with your uniform tomorrow. I will take charge of the stuff you have brought with you.' She made a sort of disgusted face as she gathered up all the nice clothes that Mrs Rose had given me. Then she said, 'Put all your other things in the box under the bed. I don't want to see anything left out except family photos, which go on that table over there.' There were dozens of framed photos standing on the table she pointed to.

'I don't have any photos,' I whispered. 'Everything like that was burnt when our house got bombed.' I was still trying terribly hard not to cry, trying to be brave like Saint Julia.

'Well, that's another cross you will bear with fortitude for the sake of the Lord,' said the nun and turning to the girl in the next bed said, 'Emily, show the new girl how we get into our clothes, here, without exposing our bodies.'

After the nun had gone, I opened the bundle and found three pairs of inner white knickers, two pairs of outer dark blue bloomers, a liberty vest, and a face flannel. Everything was marked in big black letters with the words, 'girls' dorm'.

All around me, other girls were bouncing and laughing and looking at me with curiosity. Someone chucked a screwed up bit of paper at me and began to make noises like a fire engine rushing to a fire. I knew the next thing would be water over my head if I didn't act fast.

'Red-headed people are very dangerous.

You have to be careful how you talk to them,' I said, trying to look much calmer than I felt. I could see I was going to have to keep myself very safe if I was going to be able to look after Jem from a distance like this.

The girls stopped bouncing around and looked at me more closely this time and without such jeering expressions.

'My brother and I shall not be here long,' I said. 'Uncle Glossy is going to come and get us at any moment. He is a Polish soldier and he is very fierce.' This was not really true. Although Uncle Glossy was big, he was gentle and funny.

One asked in quite a friendly tone, 'What's your name, new girl?'

I was pleased to see that she did not call me 'firehead' or anything like that.

'I'm Jewel,' I said.

'Hello, Jewel,' came a chorus from round the dorm. Then I was showered with so many names that I could not remember a single one except the girl in the bed next to mine, whose name was Emily.

I was desperate to see if Jem was all right so still in my nightie I went to the Boys' Dorm.

Jem was gripping onto his sheet and a nun was trying to get it away. Jem's face was white, his expression frantic. Several giggling boys had gathered round.

'Jem, Jem,' I shouted.

The nun seemed horrified at the sight of me. 'Go out of here at once, girl,' she shouted. 'This is the boys' dorm. It is absolutely forbidden for girls to come in here.'

Jem dropped his sheet, scrambled out of the bed, came racing towards me, threw himself into my arms and clung there, sobbing. His pyjama bottoms were sopping.

★ ★ ★

It's a month since Matt was taken. Julia, with the puppy scooping enthusiastically alongside, has dug a vegetable garden with Matt's garden fork. 'It'll be good for you and the baby to have fresh vegetables,' she says.

'Or are you just taking the opportunity to see if there is a message from your brother in the soil?'

'That's a nasty thing to say,' cries Julia, scalded by the truth. She finds a coin later that day, dark with burial. Date blurred and indecipherable. Almost.

'Kitty, with your young eyes, what do you think?' She puts it on the table, where Kitty is twining brandy-snaps, lace thin, still pliable from the oven, round the handle of a pudding spoon.

'Let me finish these before they harden,' she says. 'Then I'll look.'

It's a new phase of their relationship. Julia has never asked Kitty for help before.

'My brother and I buried coins when we were children,' Julia says.

From the hesitant and cautious way she speaks Kitty knows that Julia is hiding something. She puts her thumb over the penny as though holding it hostage till she gets the information she wants.

'Where is he?' asks Kitty. 'How did you lose your brother?'

'It is all written down,' says Julia. 'One day I will let you read it.' She is lying. She does not intend to share her secret childhood with anybody, let alone this plump girl who is probably illiterate.

'I'd like to,' says Kitty. But she's lying too. She wants Julia to tell her things, not read them.

* * *

The Boys' Sister became increasingly angry with Jem over the bed wetting. I suppose she had too much work, and too little time for all us children. I heard her tell the Girls' Sister, 'I can see that Pritchett boy has been terribly spoiled. He needs a firm hand,' and the Girls'

Sister answered, 'Poor children. They are suffering from the loss of their parents and every other stable thing in their lives,' then she saw me listening and said in a brisk voice, 'Now come along, Julia. Don't stand there dawdling. Do up your shoes and hurry off to your lessons.'

I went on slowly lacing up my shoes while the Boys' Sister said, 'We've got twenty kids who have lost their parents and Pritchett is the only one carrying on like this. Unless he pulls himself together we're going to have a hard time placing him.' Then to me, 'What are you up to, big ears?'

'This is the boy's sister,' said the Girls' Sister.

The other nun did not answer, but just gave a sort of snorting noise, and strode away carrying Jem's wet sheets.

★   ★   ★

That night I asked Emily what 'placing' meant.

'It means getting adopted,' she said. I looked at her blankly. 'You get a new mummy and daddy,' she said. 'Which won't ever happen to me because I've got epilepsy.'

'I'd hate to have new parents,' I told her fiercely. 'Anyway Jem and me don't need them because Uncle Glossy is coming to get us.'

'It's better than staying here until you're grown up like I'm going to have to,' said Emily sadly.

She was my best friend. I couldn't bear to see her sad. I said, 'When Uncle Glossy comes I'll tell him he's got to take you as well.'

Emily's eyes filled with hope. 'Oh, do you think he would?'

'Of course,' I said. 'He's the nicest person you ever saw. He'll love you, I know he will.'

'But what about the epilepsy?' sighed Emily. I had seen her have a fit once, rolling round the floor, the whites of her eyes showing, spittle frothing from the corners of her mouth, nuns reaching into it to grab her tongue in case she swallowed it, but all the same I said firmly, 'Uncle Glossy won't mind. I know he won't. He's not like other grown-ups.'

*　*　*

Most of the children had no visitors at all but once a month Mr and Mrs Rose came to see us. They brought enough apples for all the children once, and another time a huge bag of sweets so that every child had one.

'How are you, my darlings?' they would

say, and hug and kiss us as though they were our parents. I used to long for their visits, enjoying the feeling of their arms round me even more than the presents they brought us. No one in the home ever held us children. Sometimes children would pretend to fall down so as to get one of the nuns to pick them up and carry them. Us children would often hug each other. Emily and I would secretly cling to each other, holding our bodies tight together, feeling each other's hearts beating inside our uniforms. Knowing that Jem must be as badly in need of hugging as I was I would kiss him and caress him whenever I got the chance and though, in the old days, when we were at home with our parents he had wriggled and tried to escape if I caught and kissed him, now he leant supine and happy in my arms, letting me run my fingers through his hair, and press my lips to his hot red cheeks. The Boys' Sister always put a stop to it if she caught me, saying, 'Unhand that child this moment, Julia Pritchett. You are making a monkey of him.'

'Why are they so cross about us kissing each other?' I asked Emily.

'They are terribly frightened of sex,' she said ambiguously.

★ ★ ★

The next time Mr and Mrs Rose came I refused to see them. I had done a lot of thinking since their last visit. I had understood about the treachery of adults.

The Girls' Sister tried to persuade me. 'They have come a long way and they are so fond of you.'

'I am too busy. I've got too much homework,' I said. They had sent me and Jem away and kept the evacuees. They had tricked us into coming here. They had pretended there was a seaside. By now the fairies must have sent an answer to my letter and Mr Rose had not even gone to look. He said he went but I knew he was lying because otherwise why hadn't we heard from the fairies who had always responded to our letters before?

★ ★ ★

After six months in the Nissen huts we were taken to the Mother House in Sussex.

14

Kitty is four months pregnant and the baby is starting to show.

Matt had said, you are young. You'll have other children. But now she feels a new grief for the lost baby, as though she had deprived her unborn daughter of a brother. Or her unborn son of a sister. Whichever.

Matt has been on TV three times, each time looking more haggard, and now has a beard.

Kitty feels shocked and horrified, and also excited. Discovering something new about him even now, even from so far away and under such unimaginable circumstances. The beard is thicker and fairer than his head hair.

Once his lips, snuggled inside that amazing tangled, soiled beard, struggle to twist into a little smile and he says, 'Hello, Kitty, my queen. I hope you are listening.' His body gives a little jerk as though someone out of sight has pulled him away from the camera but those words, that smile, lights a little spark of hope and warmth in Kitty.

'It's going to be OK,' she tells Julia. 'He is a sturdy bugger. They won't break him.'

★ ★ ★

Julia is hoeing round her vegetables, amazing herself by the sight of them, brilliant green, crisp, tender. She had not expected real vegetables to materialise out of her excavations and haphazard plantings. When she strikes something buried, tin, rusty, deep, she feels a momentary spurt of annoyance at what damage this buried metal chunk might be doing to the celery. It takes long moments before the idea of what it might be leaps into her mind and the hammering of the heart, the drying up of spittle, the shaking of the legs overwhelms her body. She thrusts her fingers into the tilled soil and touches the rough sharp corner. She lets the anticipation take over, digging no deeper, looking no further, not wanting to discover it is a false hope, yet.

She gets up, groans from the pain in her knees and goes towards the house, walking unsteadily, her legs weak as though she has just been ill, or had a shock.

Shedding mud and weeds, she pulls off her gumboots at the back door, the puppy, now three-quarters grown, prancing round her, trying to grab her socks.

In the drawing room Kitty is watching the TV, looking traumatised.

She leaps up, swings round to face Julia,

her face ablaze with excitement. She waves her arms wildly and shouts, 'They are letting him out. They are setting him free.'

'The British hostage, Matthew Wing, is to be released in the next few hours,' the voice comes from the TV.

★   ★   ★

Kitty dances round the house shouting, 'He's coming home, he's coming bloody home,' putting water in a vase, starting to put flowers in, leaving them lying while she rushes off to the corner shop to buy butter for a cake, beating the sugar and butter then dropping that because he would like his clothes, that had lain in the drawer all this time, ironed.

'Oh, and his shoes need polishing,' she remembers.

'I'll do that,' says Julia. She is pleased that her voice comes out calm and steady. But Kitty is too excited with her own good news, at first, to notice anything shaky about Julia.

But then Kitty stops her wild dashing. 'What's the matter? You don't seem thrilled.'

'Of course I am thrilled,' says Julia.

'You don't have to go.' Kitty has suddenly seen something from Julia's point of view. 'You can stay and live with us.' Her tone is doubtful.

'I wouldn't dream of it,' smiles Julia and sees Kitty's shoulders sink with relief.

The puppy, the puppy, Kitty remembers suddenly. She had promised Matt to brush it every day and because it wriggled so and bit the brush and because her mind had been so taken up with misery she has not brushed the creature for weeks. Desperately she gets out the brush and pinning the dog against the back of the sofa tries to draw the bristles through its coat. Already the coat, which Matt had said should have been soft, silky, flowing, golden has turned coarse and orange because of Kitty's carelessness. She struggles with the brush, but nothing will bring the sheen and waviness back.

The Foreign Office rings and Kitty forgets her failure.

'He will be taken to an RAF camp in Waswar,' says the official. 'He will probably be there tonight. If you like we can make arrangements for you to be flown out in the morning to meet him.'

'Oh, God, I can't believe it. It's too fuckin' wonderful for words.' Tears of happiness are running down Kitty's face as she replaces the receiver. 'This time tomorrow. I wonder what he will think when he sees this.' She pats her stomach.

'I'll stay here and look after Rob till you get

back,' says Julia. It's the least she can do.

'Thanks.' Kitty is not thinking about the dog.

'Are you supposed to fly? Isn't it bad for a pregnant woman?'

'Come on,' cries Kitty. 'I'm only four months. Do you think I should wear this . . . or this?'

'Haven't you got anything to hide the bulge?'

'Hide it?' cried Kitty, amazed. 'I want to show it to everybody. I want Matt to see it the second he sets eyes on me. It's the first sticking out tummy I've ever liked.'

She would be away several days. Perhaps as long as a week.

Julia is glad that Matthew is coming back. She will feel less treacherous taking Waste Land Cottage away from Kitty now.

★　★　★

The moment Kitty is out of sight, on her way to the airport, Julia rushes back into the vegetable garden and begins to work at the box. She has to pull up several cabbages as well as the celery in the end.

The box has been buried very deeply and subsequent topsoil and builders' rubble dumped on it. It takes her the whole afternoon to get it out.

The metal has rusted and is as frail as wet cardboard. Once or twice she puts her fork right through, the metal crushing like egg shell, but at last she frees it and pulls it into the open.

She has dug a hole deep and wide by now, with the puppy digging wildly alongside, convinced that all this effort must be leading to something delicious.

It lies there at last, like the heart of an artichoke, her life, her identity, her property. She does not recognise it as the box her mother buried, but then she was only little and the box is orange with decay. Gently she probes inside through a rusted hole and feels the mackintosh material. It must be it, it must, it must, it must.

Her hands are shivering as she starts to withdraw the bundles that will give her back her childhood, her parents, Jem, her identity. Perhaps, in spite of the waterproof canvas, the contents are deteriorated beyond legibility. Even the papers were probably decayed. Jem's tin toy train surely was.

★　★　★

When Jem had said, 'Put my fairy train in, too, Mummy,' my mother had tried to argue,

145

to explain that only important things that would affect our future lives must go in this to-be-buried box but in the end Jem's whining had made her give in.

After we got to the children's home, Jem began to cry for his fairy train, till the Boys' Sister ordered him to shut up and never mention the matter again. After that, although he did not talk about it, I knew he was longing, in his heart, for his buried fairy gift.

He was still crying about it as we drove in the convent van from the Nissen huts to the Mother House. Then, with a sudden shock, I saw we were going through our village. We turned the corner and there was the horrible piece of land with piles of shattered masonry on it.

I shouted, 'Please stop, Sister.'

The van stopped with a jerk and the Boys' Sister said crossly from the front, 'What's the matter?'

'That's our home,' I told her, pointing a trembling finger at the ruin. 'And Jem's left something there. And we want to get it.'

'Don't tell lies, Julia Pritchett,' the nun said. 'Sit back in your place this moment and let's have no more of this naughty nonsense. Drive on, please.'

The van started up again. We passed the corner shop and I caught a glimpse of Mrs Rose cutting roses in her garden. We drove over the bridge crossing the little stream that ran at the foot of our garden. I looked back, and the last thing I saw as we hit the open road again was our pear tree.

I whispered to Emily, 'That was my home whatever she says.'

★   ★   ★

The Mother House was big and grand. We entered up marble steps, among marble columns. The windows were huge stained glass, the roof high and ornate. It felt as if we were going into a cathedral.

We came into a huge hall and looking up I saw, far above us, a high coloured glass dome. The sunlight pouring through it was reflecting on our faces, making Timmy green, Alice yellow, Emily crimson, Jem purple. We milled about letting the different colours spill on us. We began laughing and running around. The hugeness of the place made our voices echo and sound far away. Jem forgot his train and said, 'It sounds like the seaside.'

The Boys' Sister came in bringing luggage. 'Come on you children, enough of this romping around. Go and get the hand luggage in the back and then Mother will show you your dorms.'

We were put in a long room, rows of beds

with little cubicles, no need for boxes under the beds. A nun called Sister Patience, round rosy cheeks and a plump figure, was our house mistress. 'You can come to me if you have any little problems, children,' she told us kindly.

On our first morning at the Mother House we were all made to stand in rows in the hall, while the new Reverend Mother addressed us. She told us we must be obedient, clean, quiet, work hard at our lessons, pray with pure hearts, and added, 'I have heard that some of you children are not house-trained. I will not stand for anything like that in this convent. Any child who filthies their bedding will be punished. Do you understand me?' There came a nervous mutter from among us children. After, when we were allowed out into the garden to play Jem rushed up to me, his face white, his teeth chattering.

'What shall I do, Jewel? I can't help it.'

He had got used to sleeping on his own, without my bed near his, but ever since we had first gone to the home six months earlier he had wet his bed every single night.

'Don't worry, darling,' I told him. 'I will go and explain to the Reverend Mother.'

'Thank you, Jewel,' he said, and clung to my hand as though I was saving him from drowning.

'I want to tell the Reverend Mother

something,' I said to Sister Patience.

'You tell me, dear,' she said. 'Reverend Mother is much too busy to talk to children.'

'It's about my brother, Jem,' I said. 'He wets his bed.'

'Oh, dear,' said the nun. 'He'd better put a stop to that quickly or Reverend Mother will have his skin. Be very cross, I mean.'

I told the nun, 'I think it's because he is frightened because he never did it before the bomb. Could you explain?'

'Of course I will, dear,' she said, smiling. And added, 'He is a lucky little boy to have a sister who cares so much for him.'

'My mother told me I had to look after him,' I said.

Next morning we all stood in the assembly hall with the coloured lights from the roof dome glimmering over us. After the prayers and the hymn were over and Reverend Mother had given us a talk she said, 'There are some children among us who, in spite of what I said yesterday, have persisted in their filthy habit of urinating in their beds, children who have been too lazy to get up in the night and go to the lavatory. I will name these dirty children and we shall wait here while each comes forward.' Then she recited a list of names and to my horror among them was Jem's.

Sister Patience was standing next to Reverend Mother. She looked at me, went red, looked away, but said nothing to the Reverend Mother.

One by one the guilty children came shuffling forward, their faces red, their heads down, the others jeering, whistling, aiming little kicks and punches. Jem stayed where he was. I had never lied to him and he still trusted me.

'Where is the child, Jeremiah Pritchett?' roared the Reverend Mother. 'Come out at once.'

I pushed my way through the other girls. 'Jem is my brother. Sister Patience said he didn't have to . . . ' I began to stammer.

'Get back into your line,' the Reverend Mother said and then, 'Jeremiah Pritchett, come out this moment.'

Jem crept out. The jeers were twice as loud for him as for any of the others. He stopped when he reached me and, his eyes wide with fear, whispered, 'Save me, Jewel.'

The Boys' Sister came striding across the hall and grabbed hold of Jem. Wildly, Jem seized me round the waist. The nun jerked him easily away and holding him by the shoulders propelled him towards the Reverend Mother.

* * *

In the days that followed Jem stood in the great hall with the other bedwetters, shamed, holding his wet sheets for all to see. I could not swallow the blackcurrant juice they gave the rest of us. My throat was too tight and dry to eat the biscuits.

15

Jem and I were going to be adopted. Well, some people were going to try us out and see if we would do. We were to go to tea with them. On the morning of the day, a very old nun called Mother Philomena caught me gently by the sleeve and whispered, 'A word of warning, Julia, dear. When these people take you to their home, try to subdue your own strong personal loyalties and allow them to like you, for I know that really you are a good and nice little girl, in spite of what the other sisters say of you.' She spoke in a very urgent voice, as though telling me something of terrific importance.

We were told we had to call the kind people Uncle Harry and Auntie Joan.

'For the moment,' Reverend Mother added.

'Suppose we don't like them?' I asked.

Reverend Mother glared at me with flared nostrils. 'The very fact that they have the generosity of spirit to adopt a pair of ill-behaved older children instead of a baby shows that these are people of great virtue.'

'Jem and me are going to be adopted by

people of great virtue,' I told Emily.

She began to cry. 'Then you'll go away and leave me. You're my only friend and I'll never see you again,' she wept.

I hugged her and promised, 'I will ask Uncle Harry and Auntie Joan to adopt you too. Reverend Mother says they have generosity of spirit, so probably won't mind about a bit of epilepsy.'

'Oh, Jewel,' gasped Emily, her tears drying. 'Will you really ask them?'

'I'll tell them that if they don't have you they can't have me either,' I told my friend sturdily.

Jem and me were dressed up in our best clothes for the outing. As we sat waiting in the nun's parlour Mother Philomena looked round the door and said, 'Now remember to behave like perfect darlings.'

★   ★   ★

Uncle Harry and Auntie Joan arrived in a pony cart. All the boys and girls and even the nuns stood watching and smiling as Jem and I were put on a seat and the shiny black pony trotted us away. My last look back was to see Emily's face, pinched with longing, watching us go. The excitement of the pony cart was so great that it took some time for Jem and me to take our attention off the bouncing trotting bottom of the harnessed pony, the clip-clip of the pony's feet on the tarmac and the great thin wooden wheels turning so near to our faces. Uncle Harry was driving and had his back to us, holding the reins in one hand and a whip, with which he just tickled the back of the pony as though giving it signals, with the other. But he kept looking round at us and smiling encouragingly.

Auntie Joan sat facing us and kept smiling too, as well as saying over and over, rather breathlessly, 'Isn't this exciting. Isn't this exciting.' She sounded as though she was shy of us.

Jem, thinking she meant the pony cart was exciting said, 'I have only ever seen one before and that was the Ennyoliron man's one.'

'Oh, tell me about that, dear,' said Auntie Joan. I was relieved that she had a reason to stop saying 'Isn't this exciting.'

'He's got a huge big cart and a fat horse with lots of hair on its legs and when he goes round the village shouting, 'Ennyoliron' people sell their old bits of iron to him,' explained Jem. 'Once my daddy gave him a kettle but my mummy went and got it back because she said there was a man who could mend the hole. But the Ennyoliron man never let Jewel and me ride in his cart.'

The seats of the pony cart were high and slippery, so that Jem began slithering forwards and nearly falling off. Auntie Joan reached out to hold him, but I quickly got my arms round him first.

'Would you like to sit on my knee, Jem?' Auntie Joan asked.

'It's all right, Auntie Joan,' I said. 'I am holding him tightly.' Remembering what Mother Philomena had said I gave her an enthusiastic smile, so that she would not think I was being bossy. Auntie Joan did not return my smile.

★　★　★

It took us nearly an hour to reach the aunt and uncle's house and then Uncle Harry handed the reins to his wife and came round to the back of the cart. He held out his arms and cried, 'Come on, kids. I'll catch you. Jem first.'

I steadied Jem.

'He's all right, Julia,' said Uncle Harry. 'Leave go of him. Come on, old chap. Hop into Daddy's arms.'

Jem wriggled out of my grasp and jumped. When he was on the ground he asked Uncle Harry, 'Are you really my daddy?'

155

'I hope I'm going to be,' said Uncle Harry. His voice sounded happy.

'And are you my mummy?' he asked Auntie Joan.

She nodded silently. For some reason her eyes were filled with tears.

'You see, Jewel,' my brother said to me. 'The fairies did give us our parents back after all. You said they had forgotten us but they had remembered all the time.'

'Uncle Harry and Auntie Joan aren't our real parents, silly,' I told him. 'They are still dead.'

Jem looked doubtfully at the aunt and uncle but before he could say any more Uncle Harry picked him up and walked away with him towards the house. He did not look back at me.

★　★　★

Auntie Joan was already laying lunch. 'I've done sausages and mash, kids,' she said. 'And jelly to follow. How's that?'

'Wow, scrummy,' shouted Jem enthusiastically.

'Come and sit down then. You there, Julia, and Jem here by me,' said Auntie Joan.

'Where is your bathroom, Auntie Joan?' I asked politely. 'Jem has to wash his hands before we eat. Our Mummy always said we must wash first.'

'How silly of me, I forgot that,' laughed the auntie. 'What a good little girl you are. Come along.'

I followed her feeling pleased that I was doing things right, just as Mother Philomena had told me.

* * *

When we got back to the Orphanage that evening Mother Philomena asked me, 'Did they like you, Jewel?'

'I don't know,' I said.

'Think hard, dear. And if there are things about you which displease them, do try to change them.'

'What sort of things, Mother Philomena?' I asked.

She paused, looked at me closely, and said, 'Let them look after Jem from now on. Let them take over the responsibilities of parent.'

'I can't do that, Mother Philomena,' I told her. 'I've got to look after him for the rest of my life.'

Mother Philomena sighed and looked distressed. 'Sometimes, in this life, my dear, the right thing to do looks like the wrong one. Do you understand what I am saying?'

The phone rings. The sudden shock makes Julia flinch. Rob leaps up barking.

At first all Julia can hear are sounds of wheezing gasps. 'Hello, hello, who is it?' Through the cacophony of miserable sounds she hears Kitty sob, 'He never turned up. We waited and waited but he never came.'

16

Three days later Kitty is back, a tiny person shrunk round an enormous stomach. She approaches slowly, holding the arm of the man who has brought her.

Julia had planned to talk to Kitty about the new-found documents the moment she got back, but things are different now. Julia had been thrilled at first, when she began to look through her mother's box and came upon Jem's toy train, horribly rusty now, but then she found that the candle sticks were gone, showing that someone had got into the box after all. They must have decided the accompanying, almost unreadable, documents useless. Perhaps they were. The only thing Julia has managed to learn from them so far is that her name is not Pritchett. An expert would be needed to decipher the important ones.

As Kitty staggers forlornly along the path, clinging to the man's arm, Julia wonders if she will bother to get it done. Anyway, this is certainly not the moment to prove that she, not Kitty, owns the Waste Land.

★ ★ ★

The man from the Foreign Office asks Julia, 'Are you her mother?'

'A friend,' says Julia, getting the words out fast before they grate against her throat.

*   *   *

Kitty throws herself into the sofa and puts her feet up on the coffee table after the man has gone. There are long pink rifts up Kitty's stockings and a tear in her skirt, but Julia does not comment. Making no protest about her shoes on the table Julia goes into the kitchen and makes cups of tea for both of them. When she gets back Kitty has not moved. Julia sets the cups on the table, alongside Kitty's shoes and says, 'Tell me about it.'

Kitty's voice is low and expressionless as though nothing she says matters any more. 'There was the smell of fucking gunpowder everywhere.' Her voice is shaky. 'Even the bloody food tasted of gunpowder. And huge explosions every night making me wake suddenly. Making the brat inside me wake. He would suddenly start kicking. I used to dream he was jumping right out of me.' She opens her mouth and begins to howl, childlike, tears and snot running down her face.

'It's probably only a hitch,' says Julia.

'Don't bloody give me that. That's what the plonkers said there, as well. But they don't know a bloody thing. No one does. The hotel manager said, 'You will be all right here, Madam, because we are protected by the military.' You should see the fucking soldiers, the military. They don't half make you confident. They're more bloody dangerous than the fucking bombs. Well, for a start they looked more like kids than adults. Fucking children armed with loaded Kalashnikovs. Imagine.' She stops for a moment and stares at some inward horror. 'The soldier kids drive armoured cars round and round, guns pointing out in all directions, just firing for the heck of it. They seem to just shoot things for moving. Once I saw the buggers fire through the windows of a house and then there came a whole lot of screaming from inside. Then all these women covered in blood and clutching bleeding children came rushing out. The soldiers were laughing as they shot them down. The bloody little murderers giggling as the women and children, splatting blood, fell into the dust.' She shuddered. 'Sometimes you would see some soldier kid staggering along on his own, looking sort of dizzy, just shooting at anything, cats, pie dogs, crows, the rats that crawl over the rubbish piles. But when I told

161

the plonker of a hotel manager that I had seen drunken soldiers he said it was impossible because they were Muslims and never took alcohol. Later some prat from the Foreign Office said they might have been drugged on opium. Matt is being held by psychopathic and drugged children.'

Julia shivers.

'Nobody's got no mercy in that bloody dump. There was this donkey. It had its front legs tied together with a bit of wire that had cut right into the bone. It was sort of hobbling along like that when one of those infant murderers held out a piece of mango for it. I thought, well, perhaps the filthy little bastards aren't as bad as all that after all. But then this juvenile psychopath sticks his gun into the moke's forehead while the donkey goes on nibbling at the fruit. The sick bastard pulls the trigger and the donkey's head explodes like a fucking melon. The soldier, laughing and waving his gun goes staggering off along the road as though he's a hero.

'Those plonkers at the FO got me onto Waswar TV and told me to say I was preggers with Matt's kid. I said it, but I knew it was bloody useless. Those mother-fuckers don't give a damn about anything or anyone. They'd stick a knife into a pregnant woman just for the heck of it.'

Rob thrusts his nose into Kitty's lap. Kitty stares at him, aghast. 'My God, Julia. He looks like a fucking donkey with spots. What the hell you been feeding him on?'

Julia strokes the dog and smiles ruefully. 'He's not exactly a spaniel,' she says. 'His father was very likely a Great Dane. Your Matthew was done, I'm afraid. But he's a nice dog all the same.'

'Matt paid four hundred quid for a bloody gun dog. Nice won't do for him. Nor four hundred quid neither,' says Kitty. 'You just get fucking swindled all the time.'

'I'll make supper. You stay there and have a rest. You look done in.' Julia goes into the kitchen and takes out a cook book. She studies it, searching for something simple.

Rob has followed her and stands by the kitchen table. His head is higher than its surface. You couldn't leave any food around, no matter how high up, without him being able to get at it.

Julia has stopped trying to discipline Rob. She feels she no longer can cope with it. The dog is too big and its desires too strong. She gives the dog what he wants when he wants it. He has an almost inexhaustible appetite. Julia sometimes thinks that however much food is put before him he will eat it all. She has never known him to leave anything.

She settles on tinned soup, cheese on toast and salad from the garden for her and Kitty. As she works, spreading bread, slicing tomatoes, the silence from the other room starts to worry her. She opens a tin of tomato soup and putting it to heat on the hob, goes through.

Kitty is sitting crouched on the edge of her chair, hugging her knees, cowering like someone outdoors in icy weather. She is shivering silently. 'The fucking bastards,' she mutters. 'The bloody bloody bastards.'

'You mustn't get into a state,' says Julia.

'Why?' says Kitty.

Julia sits beside her. 'Because it is not only you any more. You have to look after Matthew's son till he gets back.'

'Some bloody if,' says Kitty.

'We've got to work hard to see that it's not if but when,' says Julia.

'We?' Kitty asks the question dully.

'I will try to help you get him out, Kitty. I swear it,' said Julia.

The words pop out unbidden. She had been on the verge of leaving and now here she was making an offer that might take months. Years. And she'd made one of those promises which she might not be able to keep. Well, too late now. It was out and already Kitty was looking brighter.

'There, drink the soup while it's hot. I'm sorry I'm not a good cook like you.' She has never said sorry to Kitty before. 'You are going to need all your strength. Come on. Chin up. Drink up.'

Then the hope fades out of Kitty's face again and she shouts, 'You have no idea what's happened or you wouldn't be talking such fucking trash.' She rises suddenly, knocking the soup to the floor. Cream of tomato shoots out, dimming the shine on the furniture and squirting scarlet over the carpets. She goes over to the drinks cupboard and pours herself a gin.

'Kitty, don't. Please. Think of the baby.'

Kitty goes on grimly pouring.

Rob goes slithering over the floor licking wildly.

'It's dead,' says Kitty. 'The little bugger is dead.'

Julia stares. 'Did you see a doctor?'

Kitty shakes her head. 'There's no fucking need.'

'How do you know it's dead, then?' asks Julia.

'How do I bloody know?' shouts Kitty. 'How do you think I bloody know. You haven't ever had children so you wouldn't even fucking understand if I told you.'

'Try me,' says Julia softly.

'It doesn't move any more. That's how I know it's fucking dead,' roars Kitty. She gulps her gin and pours another. 'I'm taking this to bed with me,' she says. 'I expect you'll be glad to be rid of me.'

After Kitty has gone Julia feeds the dog for the fifth time that day, washes up, cleans the kitchen floor, doing everything flat out so as to avoid thinking. She has always found that doing housework soothes her.

★ ★ ★

I tried to do lots of housework for Aunty Joan, seizing the brush away from her and sweeping the stairs myself. Eagerly clearing the table almost before they had finished eating. I kept saying, 'I'll do it, I'll do it,' and telling Jem, 'Look, Auntie Joan is carrying a tray. Go and open the door for her, Jem.' Or 'Don't let Auntie Joan have to keep going to get things for you, Jem. You get it yourself.'

'I like getting things for him, dear,' Auntie Joan said. 'And perhaps you would like to call me something else instead of Auntie Joan.'

'What shall I call you then?' I asked her.

She looked at me cautiously, as though she was nervous. 'Do you think you could possibly call me, Mummy?'

'Oh, no,' I said, shocked. 'I've got a Mummy already, even though she is dead.'

Auntie Joan sighed as though I had disappointed her.

We went to lunch with the aunt and uncle every Sunday for the next three weeks and when we got there they played games with us, pushed us on a swing that they said they had bought specially for us and took us for walks over the fields. Uncle Harry knew the names of all the wild flowers and each time we went out he showed us new ones, picking one flower from each plant for Jem and me to press. Auntie Joan played nursery games with us like 'Here we go round the mulberry bush' and 'Ring a ring of roses.'

'It must be lovely to have people of your very own,' sighed Emily, 'When are you going to ask them to have me, Jewel?'

I felt my face go red because I had been having so much fun with the aunt and uncle that I had forgotten to say anything about Emily. 'Next Sunday I will, I swear,' I told her.

'You said that last Sunday, too,' sighed Emily.

On our third visit Uncle Harry called me into his garage.

'I have got a present for you,' he said. He flung open the garage door and there stood a lovely shining bicycle. 'It belonged to our little girl but she died and now it is yours.'

I remember standing in that garage doorway staring at the bike in disbelief. Then I told him, 'But I don't know how to ride a bike, Uncle Harry.'

He put his arm round me and gave me a hug. 'I'll teach you, Jewel,' he said.

'My mummy had started teaching me, but before I had learnt how, that bomb came and . . .'

Till this moment I had never talked about my mummy, as though I wanted to keep her to myself and Jem, as though I want to keep her as our own precious secret. I loved to talk about her to Jem but, until this moment, refused to discuss her with anyone else at all. But something about the way Uncle Harry had talked to me and had put his arm round me made words come tumbling out.

'Your mummy must have been a lovely lady, Jewel,' Uncle Harry said when I had finished talking. 'Otherwise she would not have had such nice children. Jem is a great joy to me and Auntie Joan.'

'And me? Aren't I?' I said.

He hugged me a second time and said, 'Jem is a baby and you are a big girl.'

'My mummy only ever called me a big girl when I was naughty,' I told him. 'Then she would say, You are too old to do silly things like that.'

Uncle Harry spent all afternoon teaching me how to ride the bike, holding onto the back of the saddle and running round and round, steadying me and saying, 'Pedal, Jewel. Pedal faster,' till at last I suddenly got it and for a few yards actually pedalled on my own before crashing into the flower border.

I thought this was a good time to ask about Emily.

'She's my best friend, and she wants to be adopted too,' I said. 'She's really nice and if she gets epilepsy I'll look after her.'

A dark red colour flushed over Uncle Harry's face and when he spoke the words came out stammering, as though he was embarrassed. 'We have quite a lot of problems to sort out, what with this and that,' he said. 'It's all rather complicated. One of the nuns is going to talk to you about the whole matter in due course,' he said.

When I got back to the orphanage Emily was waiting, looking hopeful. 'Did you ask them, Jewel?'

I nodded.

'Well?'

'I'm not sure if he said yes or no. But he said he's going to talk to one of the nuns so perhaps it means he's going to beg them.'

Even as I spoke, though, I had a feeling of fear. I had never seen Uncle Harry awkward like that before.

The following Sunday, as we were going back to the orphanage, Uncle Harry said, 'Goodbye, Jewel, dear. You may take the bike back with you. Look after it, won't you, for it once belonged to someone very precious to me and Auntie Joan.'

I felt sure the nuns would not allow me to bring the bike, but to my surprise they were really nice about it and even gave me a place in the wood shed to keep it.

'You will be the only child with a bike, Jewel,' Sister Patience said. 'So you will have to share it with the others.'

'OK,' I said. 'But I won't be here for long. I'll be living with the aunt and uncle soon.'

Sister Patience did not answer, but instead looked quickly away as though she was hiding something.

17

A few days later I came into the refectory and saw that, sitting in the place by me, was not Jem but another little boy called Anthony. I strode through the tables and grabbed the child by the back of his collar. 'You can't sit there,' I said. 'That's my brother's place.'

The little boy dangled, looked white and afraid, and said in a husky whisper, 'Sister told me to sit here.'

Sister Patience said, 'Oh, Julia dear, I've put little Anthony beside you because you were so good with Jem. I hoped you'd be a good influence on this little chap as well.'

'Where's Jem?' I demanded. I could feel my heart beating heavily against my chest.

'Calm down, calm down, dear,' said the nun. 'He's gone to Uncle Harry for the day.'

'What about me?' I yelled.

'Reverend Mother felt that all the disruption was having a bad effect on your school work, so decided you should stay here for the moment, dear.'

My heart pounded even more furiously, as fear and anger thundered through me. 'Why didn't you tell me?' I shouted. A silence fell throughout the refectory.

'Because it is none of your business, child,' the nun said gently. 'Now sit down and eat your breakfast before it gets cold.' She clapped her hands and shouted to all the other children, 'Everyone stop staring and get on with your meal.'

The clatter of cutlery against china instantly started up again.

I stood rigidly, staring defiantly at the nun. She said softly, 'Please don't make a fuss, Julia. He'll be back by supper.'

I couldn't eat any breakfast and felt shivery inside all morning as though I was getting a fever. All day I counted the hours till Jem came back again and worried that he might not be wiping his feet on the doormat, saying 'thank you' properly, or washing his face after meals. I kept think over and over how much rather I would be there, with the aunt and uncle, eating Auntie Joan's apple pie, being taught to ride my bike by Uncle Harry. I longed to be far away from all these other children, away from the nuns, and with the aunt and uncle where I felt like a real child with a real mummy and daddy. When we knelt for prayers that morning I begged, 'Please God let Auntie Joan and Uncle Harry adopt me soon. Even if they don't want Emily please let them send for me really quickly.' I knew I was being treacherous, but I could not help it, I longed for it so much. As I sat over my cooling porridge, feeling waves of longing pour through me I heard a soft hissing sound from beside me. It was Anthony. He was crying, almost silently.

'What's the matter?' I asked sharply. I resented the nun thrusting the responsibility for this boy onto me. The Girls' Sister was not my mother.

'I want my mummy,' wept the little boy.

I suppose I was a hard child, as now I have become a hard woman. But for one moment then, my guard slipped down. I understood exactly what he was feeling, because I had felt it so much myself. As though he had been Jem I put my arms round him and held him tight. I held him till the shuddering sobs eased. I knew that misery does not get better because someone else hugs you. But I knew too, that it does give a little comfort.

* * *

As we left the refectory I passed Mother Philomena. I got the feeling, from the expression in her eyes, that I had disappointed her.

'Uncle Harry gave me a bike,' I told her. 'So it shows he likes me.'

'Yes,' she said, but there was something sad in her tone.

* * *

All that day, as I waited for Jem, Anthony followed me crying out, 'Jool, Jool, I love yer.' Once I was even in the toilet when I heard his voice close to the door shouting, 'I love yer, Jool.'

The Boys' Sister heard him and shouted, 'You are a disruptive influence, Julia Pritchett.' I did not know what I had done wrong.

* * *

Jem arrived back at supper time, in Uncle Harry's pony cart, looking jubilant, his cheeks scarlet, his eyes shining, his hair on end from the wind.

I rushed up as Uncle Harry helped him down. 'Look how untidy you are,' I scolded, smoothing his hair with my hands. 'Now say a nice 'thank you' to Uncle Harry.'

* * *

'We had raspberries with cream,' Jem told me breathlessly as we went into the convent. 'And then me and another boy called Freddy

174

whose mother is Mummy's friend came, and we played in the sand pit, and Daddy is going to get me an absolutely new bike. And my room's going to be blue with pictures of hippos on the curtains and planes on the walls -'

'Wait, wait, Jem.' That rapid hammering breathing was starting up again in me. 'Why are you calling the uncle and auntie Mummy and Daddy?'

'Because they told me to,' said Jem. Then without a pause dashed on, 'And Daddy is going to make me a tree house and Mummy said I can have a puppy of my own — '

Suddenly the Boys' Sister appeared out of the convent and pounced on Jem. 'Now come along in, young man.' To me she said, 'Shouldn't you be in your dorm, getting ready for bed, Julia?'

I crept off to my dorm feeling terribly left out. Even my bike, that had seemed so wonderful, seemed less so now that Jem was going to get a brand new one.

* * *

Next day Anthony was put beside me and Jem was seated at a distant table. Nothing I could say to the nuns would persuade them to change the arrangement.

175

'You know he gets miserable if he's away from me,' I said.

'Look at him,' said the nun, pointing. Jem was laughing and romping, and did not look the smallest bit miserable.

★ ★ ★

Three days later I looked across the refectory and Jem's seat was empty.

'Where is he?' I asked the nun who was serving out our porridge.

'I can't really say, dear,' she told me mildly. 'A little more?'

I caught up with the Boys' Sister after breakfast. I was afraid of her but had to know.

'He's gone to Uncle Harry's,' she said. 'I would have thought even you would have understood that.' She tried to stride away from me as though she was escaping.

I raced after her. 'When will he be back?'

She did not answer.

Waiting for him that day was not so bad as the first time, as though I had got a little bit used to him being away and me left out. But all the same as five o'clock came nearer and the time for Jem to come back approached I stood by the front entrance, watching the road for the first sight of the pony cart, straining my ears for the first sounds of the

176

clopping hooves and grinding wheels. I kept looking at the clock in the hall and felt amazed at how slowly time seemed to be passing.

At half past five, though, he still had not come.

At six the bell for supper rang and still no Jem.

Now I was starting to get really worried and thought that perhaps the pony might have bolted and the cart crashed. I thoughT that Jem and Uncle Harry might be lying dead in some ditch and no one even knew.

I heard all the children shouting and laughing as they went into supper, but I stayed where I was, watching the road for Jem.

Then just when I felt despair I heard the sound of horses' hooves, and the creaking of a cart. Relief flooded over me like waves of warm water. It approached very slowly. It took ages, ten minutes perhaps before it came into view. And then it turned out not to be Uncle Harry and Jem at all, but the coal man with his big flat cart and shaggy piebald horse.

Sister Patience came out and found me there, tears of disappointment running over my face.

'Jem hasn't come back, Sister,' I gasped. 'I

think he must be dead.'

'No. He's quite all right, dear,' she said. Her tone was very calm. Taking my hand she said, 'Now come and have your supper and I will tell you all about it.'

As we went along the corridors to the refectory she said, 'You have to be very brave, Julia and understand that this is for the best. You must think of Jem's happiness before your own.'

'I always do,' I said, but fear was drying up the spittle in my mouth.

'Jem will not be coming back here,' said the nun. 'Uncle Harry and Auntie Joan have adopted him.'

★ ★ ★

At least they had told her the truth that time. For once, thinks Julia, as she stares out of Kitty's kitchen window.

The lies she told Dick. That she was marrying and going to Canada. Lying about her name because if she was discovered, Dick would know she had not really gone away at all.

Not lying to herself, though. That was her only truth. Her love. Her still strong, no longer hoping love.

She touches her face with a finger that is

marked with the freckle-browns of age, patchy patterns, not at all like the sunny specklings that had spattered her skin in her youth in Rhodesia.

The skin of her hands is wrinkly. She hates that, the plump plum bloom lost for ever so that if ever she meets Dick again, which of course she won't, he will see an old woman.

She would not be Jewel of the flaming hair, tight and rosy skin, clear eyes, but grey-haired and shrivelled. Altogether someone else.

And Dick. He does not exist either, she decides. Because who could imagine him walking slow, bent on a stick, false teeth, hard of hearing. Dick who had moved like a dancer over a sprung floor as he strode across the veldt.

Because Africa has a deer called dikdik, Julia can never go back to Africa. She dare not go to a country that has, running loose on its veldt, a deer called that. People in Canada never talk about dikdiks and that is why she can tolerate living there.

★ ★ ★

But now a baby has been conceived on this land of hers. And has been growing in the body of a woman who had seen the waste land exploding and a little girl in the red coat,

179

running. She would never have children of her own but Kitty's baby seemed to be very near to being hers. You are doing it again, she tells herself crossly, wanting something that belonged to someone else. But all the same, because of these things, getting the baby's father back seemed the right and only thing to do.

At first Julia had wondered why Kitty had not seen the little boy as well, then a cold fear had gripped her that it was because Jem was dead. Perhaps you can only be a ghost when you are alive. But she has to keep on hoping about Jem, otherwise despair will overwhelm her and she will be unable to continue her search. Perhaps Kitty cannot see him because he is lost to Julia. Yes, that must be it.

Julia has questioned and questioned Kitty about her vision. Yes, Kitty thought she had seen a body flying in the air, but could never be certain of that. So much in the way of bricks and bushes were flying up that she had been unable to see properly.

'Two bodies?'

'Only saw one.'

'A woman?'

Kitty shrugs. 'Looked like a man.'

But it must have been my mother, thinks Julia.

'And a machine,' says Kitty.

'A machine?'

Kitty shrugs. 'I dunno. Bits of metal. Wheels.'

The car. Daddy's precious car.

'Yellow? Was it yellow?'

Kitty shrugs.

Everyone in the village had teased Julia's father about his yellow car. They had not even been able to drive it much because of the petrol rationing. But every time he came on leave he polished it as though it was a racehorse, cleaned the pistons and the carburettor, recharged the battery, pumped the tyres.

All that work for nothing, thinks Julia. Gone up in an explosion of chaos. So much love lost and wasted in that one eruption of destruction. Getting the baby's father back might make up for some of the suffering and loss.

But the baby had turned out to be a lie as well, for it no longer existed. Julia wonders if, now that the baby is dead, she is freed from her promise to help save Matthew Wing.

18

For two days Julia tries to bring herself to tell Kitty that she owns Kitty's house and land, but cannot do it while Kitty sits slumped on the sofa, pushing the food away that Julia makes for her, shouting angrily if Julia says anything comforting.

'Oh, don't fucking worry about me. I'm bloody done for.'

She shouts at Rob, too, when he thrusts his nose into her lap, thumps his paw on her knee.

'Get out, you fucking donkey.'

She says to Julia, with a bitter laugh, 'When that creature was little I used to carry him in my arms as though he was a baby. Funny.'

'Funny,' agrees Julia. Her fingers are tingling. It's something that sometimes happens to her. She stands by Kitty, opening and closing them.

Dick used to say, 'Your hands don't fit you. They are too big, the wrong shape, as though when you were made you were given the wrong pair. The hands of a workman.' Once Dick laughed and said, 'The hands of a sculptor.'

Creativity in Julia's hands sometimes itched so much that no amount of scratching eased them. It would wake her in the night. She had learnt, after ages, that her fingers were informing her. They knew things her mind did not.

Quietly sitting down by Kitty, she says, 'Let me feel your stomach.'

'Don't be bloody stupid,' Kitty rages, thrusting Julia's hands away. 'If there was the slightest chance do you think I would tell you the little bastard was dead?'

'Let me feel all the same,' Julia urges.

'Do you think a woman wouldn't know if a brat inside her was dead or alive,' storms Kitty, but she rolls up her jersey all the same.

'You are bigger than ever.' Julia is impressed.

'It's a corpse inside there,' Kitty roars. 'A great fat fucking corpse, going rotten inside me. Like a maggot.'

Julia puts her tingling hands on Kitty's stomach. It is the first time she has touched Kitty on purpose. She lays her palms, cupping them across the tight mound. Kitty closes her eyes and keeps a scornful expression on her face.

They remain like this for some long moment, during which Rob watches with interest, occasionally thumping his tail approvingly against the ground. It looks like a friendly episode and Rob likes friendliness.

Julia can feel the deathly stillness in Kitty's womb. The child, whose kicks Julia had seen through the cloth of Kitty's dress, does not stir now.

Kitty forcefully shoves her away. 'Oh, fuck off,' she says. 'Leave me alone.'

But Julia's hands are quivering like a hazel dowser over water. Julia's hands have a wisdom of their own and she has learnt never to ignore them. She holds them tight against Kitty's belly. Kitty pushes at her once or twice then gives in, lies supine, angry, her huge, still belly jutting hopelessly.

Julia stays like this for what seems like silent ages.

Even Rob sits still and watches, awed, sensing something important might be happening.

Then, with a gasp of excitment, Julia feels a tiny movement tickle against her hand. 'There, what was that? Did you feel it?'

'It was your own hand,' says Kitty without opening her eyes. 'Take your fucking hands off me now.'

'Oh, yes, it must have been.' Julia says, but keeps her hands clasped over Kitty's stomach, determined not to give up the final hope so quickly. And feels the movement again.

'I told you the thing is rotting in there and

falling apart,' says Kitty. 'That's gases, like you get in stagnant water.'

The next movement was a sudden thump which even Kitty is forced to acknowledge.

She sits upright, her expression less grim.

'That's not gas,' says Julia.

'Could be. What the fuck do you know about rotting babies,' scowls Kitty. But her tone lacks the conviction of anger.

Another series of vigorous thumps, the strong kicking of a healthy foetus.

'He's alive,' Kitty,' whispers Julia. She is as awed as Rob.

'He's alive,' agrees Kitty and reaching out to Julia, puts her arms round her. 'You're a fucking witch,' she says in a furious voice.

Julia's mouth twists in a sour smile. It is not the first time someone has called her that.

Kitty suddenly doubles over. 'Now the little bugger's behaving like a bucking bronco. He's kicking my insides to smithereens. How did you do it?'

'I think I must have comforted him,' says Julia. 'You mustn't let him sink in despair again. Now eat up what I've cooked and then go to bed.'

★ ★ ★

Kitty was to be on television. 'They have asked me to make a plea for Matthew's release. I told the prats that Matt was being held by murderous children who didn't know the word compassion but they said if I care about Matt I should do it.'

★ ★ ★

Julia, sitting in the cottage, Rob's head on her lap, watches Kitty. On screen Kitty looks like a small and spherical child, tucked among large adults. Her deep hoarse voice clearly takes them by surprise. Her vivid use of language, requiring a multitude of censor blips must, thinks Julia, have made them regret they'd asked her.

But Kitty, instead, is a media success. Most morning papers have her on the front. She is in demand. Some of her less awful language is let through. In the end it is Julia, and not the mother-to-be who prepares the layette, decorates the nursery, buys equipment for the baby. Kitty becomes busy with fighting to get Matthew out.

She has, 'Free Matthew Wing' groups from the Highlands to Brighton by the end of that month. A month after that people by the thousand are signing petitions demanding the government do something firm and immediate to get the young father back to his pregnant wife. No kidnap victim has had so many yellow ribbons tied for him. Kitty herself has climbed a ladder and tied a thousand, one by one, all over the pear tree on the waste land, Julia holding the ladder and begging her, 'For God's sake, Kitty, be careful. You are eight months pregnant. This is the last thing you should be doing.'

'Don't fucking fuss,' commands Kitty.

★   ★   ★

In the late summer evenings Kitty and Julia sit under the fluttering yellow ribbons drinking Kitty's screwball made from gin and home grown blackcurrant juice to celebrate. Julia has given up suggesting, 'Why don't you keep off spirits till the baby's born.'

'What do you do together in the evenings?' Kitty is asked on a radio programme, the question's tone implying they are lesbians.

'Screw balls,' says Kitty, joyfully.

★   ★   ★

Searching Kitty's recipe books for easy bakings Julia bakes a stodgy, high Madeira.

Kitty takes a bite and doubles over gasping.

'It's not as bad as all that, surely,' says Julia, offended.

'Ow, ow, ow,' yells Kitty, unable to reply.

187

First babies are slow in coming. Julia has a lot of time to think, as she waits in the cottage, for the phone to ring. Kitty's granny is at the hospital. There is nothing for Julia to do there, and, dry spinster that she is, she feels ill at ease in maternal situations.

'You stay at home in case it's Matt,' are Kitty's last words as she gets into the ambulance. When it rings, Julia knows, it will either be news of Matthew being freed, or his son born.

★ ★ ★

Julia can hardly bear the waiting. There seem to be interminable hours ahead before she can see the baby which, by now, feels almost as much hers as Kitty's for not only did she bring it back to life, but she also knitted many of the little garments and bootees herself and even decorated the nursery.

★ ★ ★

She had been only three when Jem was born, but she has the faintest memories of the day. He had come into her life with such ceremony and gone out with such silence that

188

he had stuck like a hurting thorn in her consciousness all these years. Perhaps, she thinks, if she had had a chance to say 'goodbye' to him, she would have found it easier to give him up. As it is she is still straining for him, still unable to let him go.

★   ★   ★

I went wild after they said he was never coming back. I went running towards the wood shed. Anthony came after me, shouting, 'Where are you going, Jool? I love you, Jool. I want to come with you.'

'Go away, clear off,' I yelled at him, but he just wouldn't leave me. When he caught up with me I grabbed hold of his collar and shouted into his face, 'Get out, you filthy little beast.'

He stared at me with horror in his eyes. They began to fill with tears as he said, 'I love you, Jool.'

'I hate you,' I yelled, and slapped him hard across the face.

I did not even care when he began sobbing, 'You hurt me, Jool.'

'Go away or I'll do it again,' I bellowed. He gave me one terrified look and went scuttling away. He looked back at me twice as though he could not believe what was happening. I raised my fist threateningly at him and with a gasp of fear he ran on, and vanished round the corner.

I went into the wood shed where my lovely bike was kept. I took the chopper that was used for cutting kindling and brought it down heavily on the frame. Flakes of red paint flew off like blood. I raised the heavy axe high above my head and brought it down onto the ringing metal and dead rubber again and again. The air went out with a hiss as the blade burst the tyres. I smashed spokes, shredded the saddle, gouged into the pedals. I did not cry. Tears dried up in me. I don't think that in all the rest of my life I have ever cried again. I beat at the bell till it shattered in two parts which rolled tinklingly over the stone floor. And as I hacked there was a roaring in my ears as though waves from a great ocean beat inside my head. When my bike was just a heap of jumbled metal, rubber, leather and cloth, I set upon the others, the orphanage bikes. I beat them all to bits. I smashed up the pedal cars, I spintered the buckets and spades. I destroyed the wooden bricks, the dolls prams and the rocking horse. There were no toys left by the time I had finished with my chopper. When the nun came in and found me there I raised my chopper and I saw her flinch as though she was afraid, as though she thought I was going to attack her. I had made a grown up frightened of me. I was pleased.

*   *   *

Later the nuns tried to get me to say sorry but I refused. They tried punishing me by sending me to bed, by not allowing me any supper, by leaving me alone in the home when the other children went out on a picnic. I did not care. I did not want anything from them.

*   *   *

All of us were taken to the seaside shortly after Jem vanished. I was told that in spite of my wicked behaviour I was being allowed to go as a special concession, but I knew they were really sending me to try to bribe good behaviour out of me. I said nothing and looked scowling. I was not at all excited about the outing, for I knew it would not be the same as when I went with Mummy, Daddy and Jem.

*   *   *

But as the day of the seaside outing approached there gradually grew up in my mind the idea that Uncle Harry and Auntie Joan might have taken Jem there at the same time. This thought made me start looking forward to the trip, until the scowl on my face got less, and the nuns started saying things like, 'I am very glad to see you behaving so much better, Julia Pritchett,' or looking at each other knowingly as though they had handled me cleverly.

As the days passed I grew more and more excited about the outing, till I worked myself into a state of certainty that Jem would be there.

We travelled in the convent van, driving over grassy hills on which sheep grazed. I knew the sea was coming long before we got in sight of it, because my Daddy had showed me how the colour of the sky changed, grew lighter, sharper, over the sea. Then as we came even nearer I began to smell the familiar sea air, fishy and salty and I heard the first cries of the gulls, shrill and wailing, like sorrowful children. I remembered how, it seemed like years ago, I had heard this sound as Mummy drove us to the beach. 'What is it,' I asked her, and she had answered, 'Sea girls.' Well, I thought she had said that. I never forgot my disappointment when we turned the corner and Mummy pointed saying, 'Look, there they are.' And they were not mermaids at all, but ordinary white birds. But now I was happy to see them because they were bringing me nearer to Jem.

We had a picnic lunch on the beach, the nuns making us children sit in a neat circle round several large rugs. Then they walked round giving out sandwiches. While the others munched eagerly I held mine and looked up and down the beach, hunting for my brother. The air was stinging and strong, the light bright, the waves roared soft and rhythmic in my head. I felt a little dizzy. Sister said, 'Stop day dreaming and eat up your lunch, Julia.' I raised the sandwich to my lips and was about to bite when very far away along the beach, silhouetted against the glistening sky, I saw my mother and my father and Jem.

19

I leapt up and began to run, the soles of my sandals smacking like webbed feet against the sand. I dashed among boys playing cricket with a stick and a rubber ball. I trampled through their three-stick wicket, and ran on. My lungs began to scald, my chest ached, but I knew I must never pause till I reached my family as though, if Sister caught up with me first, my family would cease to exist.

The boys yelled with rage and threw sand at me as I rushed past, but I did not pause. I could hear Sister's footsteps coming after me now, heavy as though she was shaking the beach. I looked back and the wind had filled her black veil and habit making her look terrible and enormous. Because of her heavy shoes, starched veil and gown I thought I had a chance of getting to my family before she grabbed me.

She was shouting as she ran, but because of the blood hammering in my ears and the noise of wind and sea I could not hear her words, though I knew they must be angry and threatening. Sweat, or was that wetness tears? was starting to run down my face so that my distant family became blurred. But they were getting nearer and I knew that in a minute or two I would be back with my parents and Jem, and stop being Julia Pritchett. In a minute I would become Jewel Trinkett and once again live in a pretty Sussex cottage with a mummy who loved me. This very night, I thought, I would be back in my flowery bedroom with my teddy tucked in beside me and my mother's kiss still lingering on my cheek.

The nun came after me like a witch but I did not mind for I knew now that I was going to reach them before she got me. I knew that once I reached my mother and flung myself into her arms the angry witch would stop existing. Once I ran too close to the sea and a wave slopped over my ankle filling my sandal, so that one foot went slop slop slop as I ran the last ten yards to where my family were sitting having tea.

'Come back this minute, Julia Pritchett, or you will be most severely punished,' called the nun, panting, but I was almost there. I did not care a bit.

They had their backs to me. My brother, who was wearing a red sun hat which I did not recognise, was digging a sandcastle with a wooden spade. My mother was sitting back in a deckchair, her head bowed over the book she was reading. My father was standing up, his hand cupped round the bowl of his pipe as he tried to light it in the breeze, his shoulders curved round the flame like a wall.

By now my ribs were so sore I had to cling to them with my hands and my breath was coming out in little noisy grunts. My mother looked up as I approached, glancing from me to the running nun. And with horror creeping up in me I stared into a round stranger's face that was nothing like my mother's at all. The father, who was not my father, and the boy who was not Jem all turned to stare at the approaching nun. Sister's face had gone purple instead of her usual red.

The man and woman hastily went back to what they had been doing, as though embarrassed to be looking at us but the little boy dropped his spade and stared, his mouth open.

Sister reached out and grabbed me by the wrist. She jerked me all the way back across the sand to where all the other children were staring with fascinated interest. She pulled and tugged at me so that several times I was jerked off my feet, but she need not have bothered. I would not have run away. I knew now that I did not have anywhere to run.

I was sent to bed without supper. I had not eaten my lunch that day either but I did not care. I lay there, my stomach rumbling and listened to the sound of the children playing outside in the summer garden. I did not care. I could see the statue of the convent's patron saint from the window. He stood with his arms outstretched in blessing, a smile on his face and a small child under either hand. He was the patron saint of children, Mother Philomena had once told me. I hated him for I was a child and he had taken away everybody that I loved except Emily and even she was not allowed to talk to me.

Then I heard a soft scuffing sound and sat up terrified, thinking that a rat had got under my bed.

Anthony crawled out, his clothes all twisted round, dust in his hair. He clutched hold of something dark and grubby.

'I brought you my pudding,' he mumbled, thrusting the dark handful at me.

For some reason, although the pudding looked disgusting, a great warm wash of tears suddenly rose up in me and before I could stop myself I had put my arms round Anthony in a hug.

'Thank you, darling,' I said. I pulled myself together in an instant though and got my face scowling again. 'Next time you bring me something,' I said sternly. 'Please don't rub it all over the floor first. Wrap it up in a napkin or something.'

'OK, Jewel,' said Anthony meekly.

* * *

A month later Reverend Mother announced that we were all going to go on another trip. I did not listen to what she was saying because I felt certain that, because of my bad behaviour, I would be left out.

'You are all going to Australia,' she said. 'It's a lovely country, full of flowers and sunshine.'

* * *

After that all our lessons had something about Australia in it. We sang songs about Kookaburras and Billabongs, we learnt about kangaroos and wallabies and heard about Aboriginals. Gradually as time went on I realised that I too was to go on this outing. I was not talking to the nuns so could not ask any questions, but we had never stayed away anywhere longer than three days even at Brownie camp, so I thought we would probably be back in a week. I knew I must not be away very long in case Jem came. I felt sure that Jem would be begging and pleading with the aunt and uncle to come and get me.

★ ★ ★

We were all measured up for new clothes for our trip to Australia but the night before we were due to go I woke with a terrible stomach ache.

I can't remember anything much for a couple of days after that. I woke in a hospital and when I tried to sit up I got a dreadful stab of pain in my side.

A nurse came and told me that I had had appendicitis, but that I was better now and in a day or two I would be going home.

'Home?' I shouted, sitting up again and getting another blast of agony.

'Back to the convent,' she said. I saw a look of pity in her eyes.

★ ★ ★

I was taken back in an ambulance. When I got there, there were only two nuns left, Mother Philomena and Sister Patience.

They were packing up the last of the furniture and things.

'Where are all the children?' I asked.

'They have gone to Canada,' said Mother Philomena.

'But I thought we were going to Australia,' I cried.

199

The nuns looked embarrassed. 'There was a bit of a mix up,' said Sister Patience. 'Anyway there are also flowers and sunshine in Canada.'

'What about me?' I asked. 'You'll have to send me to Uncle Harry and Auntie Joan now that the ship has already gone with all the others.' I felt triumphant.

'You are going to Africa, dear,' said Mother Philomena. She looked distressed. 'Apparently you have relatives there.'

* * *

Kitty's baby is a girl. Kitty arrives back, bubbling with joy. 'She's called Mattie because she looks exactly like her Dad.'

Julia surveys the scarlet-faced, bulgy-eyed, new person with its leech-like mouth and almost non-existent nose and is filled with doubt. No man could possibly look like this. She only says, however, 'Is Matthew red haired?' as Rob scrabbles for a look as well.

Kitty giggles. 'Matt'll get a shock, won't he. He'll think I had an affair with the milkman or something. But everything else is his. Mattie has even got his chin.' To Julia the baby does not possess one of those either, but then as Kitty is constantly pointing out to her, she knows nothing about babies.

Rob's tongue comes out, preparing to wipe the minute newcomer in a welcoming lick.

'Fuck off, you bastard,' yells Kitty cheerily, pushing him down. Then to Julia, 'You know what they said in that hospital. That I'd got to give Rob the chop. That he'd be jealous of the baby and try to attack. Can you imagine? The stupid plonkers.'

★   ★   ★

Later that evening Kitty and Julia sit on basket chairs overlooking the waste land, with Mattie asleep on Julia's lap and the huge dog snoring at their feet. There is a smell of cut grass. Swallows are sweeping low. A cow moos softly from the buttercup fields beyond.

Julia says. 'I suppose we'll have to knit her some pink clothes. Everything is blue.'

Kitty says, 'Can't stand pukey pink . . . Wait till you see the kit my gran's made her. Puce and orange, purple and green.'

Julia rests her eyes on the place where her home had once been and to her surprise wonders if she needs it any more. Even if she needs Jem, now that Mattie is here.

She jerks herself out of this foolish thought. The father of the red-haired child will come back then Julia will have to go. She must keep firm to her plan. This land is Jem's as well as hers. She has lost everything twice. She is not going to let it happen again because her heart had been a little bit tickled by a young mother and her red-haired baby.

'It'll probably all fall out and get replaced with something else,' says Kitty leaning across and running her fingers through Mattie's thick curls. It is as though she knows what Julia is thinking.

Julia smiles.

Kitty laughs. 'Look at that. You smiled. I never saw you do that before.'

'Of course I have,' says Julia. 'I often smile.'

'Well I've never seen you smile as though you bloody meant it, then,' Kitty amended. 'There's something I wanted to say to you.'

'What?' asks Julia, raising her eyebrow.

'Ta a load. You've been a mate,' says Kitty gruffly. 'I'd have probably done myself in if it hadn't been for you.'

Julia flushes and looked away. She tries to summon up the vision Kitty had had of a little girl in red coat. She tries to visualise the face of the little boy that must have been there too, as though that would stiffen her resolve.

Kitty adds, 'And when Matt comes he won't half be bloody grateful.'

'I'll get us some supper,' says Julia rising abruptly. She treads on the tail of the sleeping dog who lets out a yelp of outrage.

'Sorry,' she says and hastens on to the kitchen. There she stands over the sink, grasping a tap in either hand and waits for the heat to fade from her face.

★   ★   ★

Shame, she thinks. Emily and now Kitty.

★   ★   ★

A letter from Emily was waiting for me when I got back from the hospital.

'We are going to have to go without you, Jewel, but Mother says you will soon be catching up with us on the next ship. I am going to be adopted by a Canada family in spite of the epilepsy and I will ask them to adopt you too.'

By the time I had asked the aunt and uncle to adopt Emily, it had been too late.

The morning after I was returned to the convent from the hospital Sister Patience packed several dresses and pairs of knickers into the cardboard suitcase that Mrs Rose had given me. 'For your journey to Africa,' she said.

'What will I be doing there, Sister?' I asked.

'Teaching the poor blacks,' she said

smiling. 'You will be representing England. Now that's a big honour for a little girl, isn't it?'

I felt a flush of pride go through me as I took the dresses and began putting them into my case. There seemed an awful lot of them for two days. But then I thought perhaps you have to look especially smart for teaching black people.

'What am I supposed to teach them, Sister?' I asked.

'Being British,' said Sister proudly.

I was packing my red coat in when Sister suddenly reached over and took it from me. 'You won't need that, dear,' she said. 'You are going to the tropics.'

I tried to hold onto the coat, and tell her, 'My Mummy gave it to me. I remember the day she bought it. It's the only thing I've got left that came from her.'

Sister was adamant. 'It's much too small for you already, dearie. And it will be ever so useful to one of the English orphans. You've only got a small suitcase. You won't be able to fit the coat in.' I watched almost hungrily as Sister carried my coat away, carefully folded it, and put it in a cupboard.

'Will I be going to Canada soon after getting back from Africa, Sister?' I asked. I began to worry that by the time I had done the Africa trip the Canada trip might be over and Emily might be back in England again and then I would miss her.

Sister flushed and said vaguely, 'Oh, I don't know about that, dear.'

* * *

The day I left, Mother Philomena came hobbling out and took my hands. 'Goodbye, poor child,' she said. 'I may never see you again.'

'Why? Where are you going, Mother?' I asked, alarmed.

'To Heaven, I hope,' she smiled. 'For I am an old woman. So may God bless your life and make it a happy one.'

I felt surprised. She did not do goodbyes like this when we went to the seaside.

'Now make us proud of you, my dear,' said Sister Patience. 'Make the best use of this wonderful opportunity to make a fresh start in a beautiful new young country.'

* * *

The departure was so confusing that it passed in a daze. I was handed from person to person, travelled in cars and on trains until I did not know where I was, nor hardly who I was. Then I was put onto a colossal ship where I was hurriedly offered up to a strange nun in charge of a group of noisy little boys.

During the first three days on the ship to Africa I felt dazed and fascinated. Nothing like this had ever happened to me before. Nothing had prepared me for a long sea trip. All around, as far as the eye could see, once we were out of sight of Southampton, was dark green wrinkled water with little dabs of white froth here and there.

The other children and the nun in charge, a Sister Nitty, were all strangers to me though they knew each other well. I was different in every way for the others were all boys. Sister Nitty seemed irritated at my being there, talking as though she had had some sort of row about me, as though she had been forced to take me because I had nowhere else to go.

'It's ridiculous, a child like you being sent to Rhodesia,' she said. 'You are not at all what is required.'

Gradually I began to understand that all these other children, these boys, had been sent to Africa by their parents. I understood that they were going to this African country called Rhodesia where they would live in a special house and get a special education. These were boys who had been chosen because of their cleverness. I had got among them because I had had appendicitis at the wrong time.

I had to sleep in the infirmary because there could not be a girl in the boys' cabin. There, amongst people who coughed and wept and groaned all night, I tried to make sense of my situation.

After three days of thrusting on through vast and featureless water, on and on, as though we were going to be surrounded by only sea for ever, the realisation came to me that we were getting further and further away from England and that quite soon we would be so far away that I might not be able to get back to England again.

I kept going to the back of the ship and looking at the trail of foaming white it left and realising that the distance between me and Jem was growing greater every hour. That the chance of Uncle Glossy finding me was getting smaller.

I realised that the grown-ups had tricked me once again, and that this time they had won. For how would a child of seven find her way back, right across the world, across all this enormous water, on her own and without any money or parents or anyone in the whole world to help her?

★ ★ ★

The journey took three weeks, during which I did not manage to give full expression to my outraged fury, for I, as well as most of the other children and Sister Nitty herself, became horribly seasick. I remember day after day of vomiting till my stomach muscles felt as though they were being torn from me. The constant feeling of nausea. The smell of vomit permeated the whole ship.

Sister Nitty tried to urge us on to optimism between bouts of illness. 'You lucky lucky children,' she would gasp. She had become very pale and thin with so much sickness. 'I have always longed for the chance that you are going to be given.'

*　*　*

As the end of our journey approached Sister Nitty got clean clothes out for us. 'So that you will all be looking fresh on arrival,' she said. 'I think there is going to be a welcoming ceremony, so big smiles, everybody.'

She opened my suitcase, counted through the pile of vests and frocks and knickers and said, 'There, that should keep you going.'

'When are we going back?' I asked. 'I can't stay here long. I've got people coming for me in England.'

Sister Nitty frowned, thrust my case of clothes at me, and said snappily, 'Just take those and don't be ridiculous. I have heard many things about you, Julia, and none of them good. Now make yourself look clean and pleasant so that your relatives have a good impression.'

'What is a relative?' I asked.

She frowned impatiently. 'People of your family,' she snapped.

I stared into her doughy face, trying to see truth there, but it was as though she had drawn a curtain over her thoughts. I drew back my breath. My brother was a person of my family. 'Is Jem there too?' I asked.

'Oh, get on with you. Hurry, child. I haven't got all day. Who is Jem?'

'My brother,' I cried wildly.

'Well perhaps he is,' the nun said vaguely. 'Now when you've got that on, turn round and I'll do the buttons.'

I felt trembly with hope and excitement as the nun buttoned me then plaited my hair. 'There, now you look a nice little child for any mummy and daddy,' she said at last.

★   ★   ★

I got overwhelmed by new sights and sounds and smells when we got off the ship at Cape

Town. Somehow we went in taxis through a strange town, sparkling sunshine, clear blue sky, people selling huge and brightly-coloured fruit at the roadside. Several times, on our way to the station, we caught glimpses of a perfect blue sea spilling itself strongly onto yellow beaches.

★ ★ ★

The train journey to Rhodesia took three days. I had a top bunk and once, when the train stopped suddenly, nearly shot out, feet first onto the platform.

★ ★ ★

That was the only moment on the whole trip, I think, that the boys paid any attention to me. They ignored me as they romped and got involved in mock punch-ups and whispered jokes together.

Sister Nitty constantly made it clear that I was an unwanted and unnecessary appendage. All her attention was on these boys, who, it seemed, were destined for such great things.

I did not mind. I wrapped myself in a grateful loneliness, watched fascinated as South Africa flowed past, then day after day of the Kalahari desert.

When the train stopped black people in brilliant-coloured clothes would rush at the windows, and thrust things through for us to buy, carved wood giraffes, their spots done by burning with a poker, clay pots with sparkling mica decorations and huge sweet grapes. Sister Nitty bought a bunch of these for us. I will never forget the sensation of the cool smooth skin against my palate, then the sudden luscious burst of sweetness. I had only eaten grapes once before, that had been years ago.

Then a girl dangled a necklace of green-blue beads in and swung them before my eyes. She must have seen the colossal craving in my face, but I had no money. The girl, however, wore no shoes, and instantly an idea came to me.

Snatching off my sandals I thrust them at the girl and grabbed the necklace.

Sister reached out with a yell and tried to get my shoes back.

The girl, with a cry of delight, went running off along the station clutching my shoes.

'You are a bad, bad girl, Julia Pritchett,' yelled Sister Nitty, as very slowly and keeping my eyes defiantly on her face I pulled my wonderful necklace over my head. 'You wicked child, I've a good mind to take that from you and throw it out of the window.'

Steadily I stared at her and slowly she lowered her eyes. A bright pink colour came into her cheeks. She did not take the necklace away.

★ ★ ★

'We are approaching Salisbury, children,' Sister Nitty said after three days. The boys scrambled about trying to find their shoes under the seats. I had none, so merely sat where I was and tried to rub the train smuts from my face. Then I sat still and stroked my necklace. In a moment I would see my family and then my mother would gently wipe my face properly.

Later I often asked myself if I really expected my parents and Jem to be waiting there at Salisbury station. And knew the answer. Of course I did not. I had been forced to trick myself into thinking this was what was going to happen because all the other alternatives were too unimaginable and frightening.

I thought I was seven. I might have been six, though. Or five. No one had cared much about my age for a long time. I suppose I must have had a birthday and nobody noticed. I was in a completely strange country. I had not been prepared in the very least for Africa. I knew nothing about it at all. I had spent nearly a month on the ship and train with a nun and children who I hardly knew and who paid no attention to me. Something was going to happen to me in Salisbury, and because I could not dare to let my mind speculate on what it might be I invented this certainty that my dead parents would be there.

My later memory, on arriving at Salisbury, was of the boys climbing onto the back of a lorry, while Sister Nitty stood holding my hand and looking this way and that, impatient, tapping her foot, saying, 'For the Lord's sake, where can he be?' She was supposed to be meeting someone. I could see that. Something to do with me. But I did not know what.

Telling the boys to sit still and be good she went with me into the station master's office.

I looked out of the window onto the bustling station, which was so different to any I had seen in England, and behind my back the adult voices talked.

'People called Pritchett,' said the nun.

'No, no one of that name has been here,' the station master said.

'We have to leave. We've a six-hour journey

ahead, apparently and I want to get there before dark.'

'I'm sorry. I can't take the responsibility,' said the station master.

The nun said, 'What are we to do, then?'

The station master said, 'You'll have to take her with you. She can't stay here. It's against the rules . . . '

A man came rushing in. 'I believe you have a child called Pritchett for collection' he said.

'Thank goodness you've come,' said the nun. 'We were just about to leave. You must be the relative.'

The man shook his head. 'Unfortunately it turned out to be a false lead, so the Home has agreed to take charge of her for the moment. We'll keep searching of course. We may still find some of her relatives in the country, though the next problem will be persuading them to accept her.' He whispered something to the nun which I could just hear. 'She's a sullen little thing, isn't she?'

20

The yellow ribbons rattle in the pear tree. A bird is singing there. Julia wonders if it is a thrush. That one's descendant. The warm air is perfumed with cow parsley.

Mattie is a month old. Her hair is scarlet bubbles when the sun shines through it. She has no clothes on, and Kitty is rubbing oil into her skin, sliding her hands sensuously over the soft baby rounds of body, making the baby body curl and chuckle with delight. Mattie has round red cheeks, round black eyes and when she laughs her voice is almost as hoarse and deep as her mother's.

Kitty tickles her and does a pretend nibble on Mattie's fat tummy, making the baby giggle till she hiccups. And when Mattie laughs, Julia and Kitty do too. They can't help it. There is something about Mattie.

★   ★   ★

Then Kitty suddenly falls back on her heels and looks into some terrible distance, an expression of bleak despair on her face. There has been no news of Matthew for weeks and media attention is flagging, although Julia has been doing her best. She has rung radio stations, written to newspapers, even had posters printed and put up round the village, saying 'Free Matthew Wing.' Julia starts to fear he is dead and though she never says it aloud knows Kitty thinks it too. Mattie tugs at her fingers, but Kitty can't find the initiative to start to play again.

Julia turns away. She has known, since the day of the bomb, that nothing is solved by pity.

★ ★ ★

Julia's diary ended on Salisbury station. It ended because all the other things had ended too. Everything she had ever valued or owned was now lost to her, her parents, her home, her brother, her country and even her own name. Over the next few years she was moved from place to place. There were foster homes, a convent orphanage, a few attempts to fit her into some family. Quite quickly the angry silent child was returned to the children's home. They would have sent her back to England if there had been anyone there who would have had her but by now even her name had become utterly lost in being so often wrongly copied. Prichard and Richard,

Pratchatt and Rocket - Julia did not care. Her name was the last thing they could take from her. Let them have it. It had never done her any good. She was the grumpy, unhelpful, ugly red-haired girl who no one wanted. It was a relief to everyone, including Julia, when she became legally old enough to set out on her own. Her birth date had been lost by now as well, so it had had to be done by medical advice and guesswork. She was about fifteen. A tobacco farmer had applied to the home for a companion to his sick wife.

As Julia packed the small amount of clothes they had supplied her with, she overheard one of the children's home staff tell another, 'It won't last any time at all though she can't come back again this time, like before. From now it it's going to be up to her to find herself a living.'

Mr Dikker met her at Salisbury station. He wore a yellow bush shirt, long khaki shorts, and a floppy felt hat. He did not seem to mind Julia's scowl. In fact he did not seem to notice it. She climbed into the lorry cab, and sat down before, for the first time, giving a swift sideways look to see what his face was like. She had expected Mr Dikker to be an old man. Well, a middle-aged man anyway. For otherwise how could he be married, and have a wife who was so ill as well. But this man looked really young. Not much older than Julia, she thought with a shock. He caught her glance and she looked away to stare sternly out of the window.

He started up the lorry then, still keeping his hand on the steering wheel, he pulled a packet of cigarettes out of the breast pocket of his shirt and tried to light it with the same hand. After struggling this way and that for a while, he said, 'Light it for me, would you.'

Determined not to let the man know that she was a novice at cigarette lighting, Julia got the butt into her mouth, lit the match, applied it to the end of the cigarette and breathed in. At once a terrible violent smoke filled her nostrils and throat, scalding and choking her. She yanked the cigarette out of her mouth and yelled aloud at the shock.

The man, making no comment, took it from her with a grunt of thanks.

It looked wet from her spittle as he put it into his mouth but he did not say anything about that. He pulled strongly on it and in a moment the tip went red.

They drove all day in a ball of plum-coloured dust thrown up by the lorry. The roads were strips, two strips of tarmac for the wheels to travel on. Julia had never been so far out in the bush before. In the evening the sky lit up in a blazing magenta and orange sunset, against which birds and the dark silhouettes of bats swooped.

'Beautiful, eh?' said Mr Dikker.

* * *

A man stops Kitty as she is pushing Mattie through the village in her buggy.

'You're the lady who lives in Waste Land Cottage, aren't you?' He is big, ruddy faced, made confident by wealth and thick white hair. He wears a suit which even Kitty recognises is expensive. She nods mutely.

The man leans into the pram and peers at Mattie. 'Lovely baby,' he murmurs. 'Googy googy goo.' Mattie gazes at him sternly, not taken in by this unconvincing display of enthusiasm.

'Are you one of those politicians?' asks Kitty, hastily trying to wipe off the red stain round Mattie's mouth, the residue of a recent lolly. Trying to make Mattie a little more deserving of this top-grade attention. 'Because if so don't waste your frigging time on us. I've got my opinions and this kind of thing isn't going to change them. I only ever vote Green, and you don't look as though you stand for that.'

'Nothing of the sort,' smiles the man. 'Nothing at all. Come in here. Let's have a coffee together. I want to talk to you.' He tilts his head in the direction of the Blenheim Arms. 'My name is Sir Jeremy Burton and it will be to your advantage to listen to what I have to say.'

'Right, I'll listen,' says Kitty after a moment's hesitation. She begins hauling her dog and her pram up the steps, the man going ahead of her.

'Come on, give us a frigging hand then,' she shouts, tangled in an instant, dog lead round ankle, pram tilted sideways risking Mattie slipping out if she goes up another step.

'Ah, sorry, my dear.' He comes back reluctantly. 'I doubt they'll let this lot in,' he says.

'They'd fucking better,' says Kitty sternly. 'What else do you expect me to do with them? And don't 'dear' me. I don't take to it.'

He leans over to take hold of the pram handles and Kitty catches a delicious whiff of aftershave.

As soon as he has got the pram to the top step he hastily thrusts the handles back into Kitty's hands then reluctantly holds the door for Kitty and her entourage to enter.

She stares around her. 'I've never been inside this place before. Bit tacky, isn't it? Bit pseudo. I think it's bloody ridiculous having this kind of poncy hotel in a country village.'

220

Her voice booms through the reception area in which several people are drinking coffee. The receptionist glares. Then shudders.

Rob, sensing hostility, rises onto his toes and glares round the room, hackles bristling. His head reaches higher than Kitty's elbow. Trying to give the impression that he is not to be trifled with he lets out a soft humming growl, offend my woman and I'll have a chunk out of you.

Three ladies in tweed skirts and dark cashmere coats with metal buttons like TV knobs, raise their wavy blue heads in unison and glare even more sternly than the receptionist, as though the sight of Kitty in her tattered and miniscule outfit and her battered pram has turned their coffee bitter.

The porter comes hurrying up and says, 'Sorry, Madam. Dogs not allowed.' Rob leans on his lead and his growl become louder.

'What you going to do about it?' challenges Kitty.

'It's the rule,' says the porter weakly and looks to Sir Jeremy for support.

'I suppose that thing is a bedroom slipper and not a dog,' says Kitty contemptuously, waving her hand in the direction of the three ladies. The Pekinese at their feet is lapping something from a saucer.

Sir Jeremy puts out a restraining hand on

Kitty's arm and tells the porter, 'The lady is with me, George. It's all right.' A piece of money seems to pass from Sir Jeremy's palm to the porter's.

'Oh, sorry, Sir. Sorry,' says the porter, ducking back behind his desk and giving Sir Jeremy an obsequious smile.

'Come, my dear. Let us sit at that table over there so we can have our chat,' says Sir Jeremy. He guides Kitty by her elbow, Kitty pulling the pram in her wake, the dog striding eagerly ahead of her. Rob sniffs expectantly as he progresses over the hushed gold carpets, and the muscles of one hind leg quiver as though he is about to raise it.

'I hope he is house-trained,' says Sir Jeremy as they sink into fat chintz chairs. Kitty's plush airy cushions let out an airy sigh as she settles among them, as though they are tired of being squashed by bottoms. Rob rests his chin on the table and keeps a wary blue eye on Sir Jeremy.

'He has to be bribed not to pee,' Kitty says cheerily. 'Ginger biscuits are his favourite. Although I think it would do this poofta place good to get pissed on.' Kitty's voice has maximum carrying power. The three ladies quiver in unison.

'It must be trying for a young, fun-loving person like yourself to live in a village like this. I'm sure there aren't many people of your own age here. And it must be lonely in that cottage without your husband,' says Sir Jeremy.

Kitty flicks her eyes wide. 'How do you know where I fucking live?' she demands.

'Dear Mrs Wing, I know exactly who you are. Everyone in Britain, perhaps even the world, must know the face of Mrs Wing by now. The voice. And the language.' He says the final sentence without a smile as he lays his hands on the table and gently and precisely touches his fingertips together. His nails are pearly and manicured, his hands soft and rosy, the hands of a man who had never done gardening, thinks Kitty.

The waitress comes. 'Coffee?' says Sir Jeremy.

'I'll have a whisky,' says Kitty to the waitress. 'Neat. Make it a double. And some toasted teacake. With extra butter. Can't bear them dry. Some milk for the baby. And ginger nuts for him.' She indicates the dog. 'And a drink. What's that dog over there drinking?' She gestures to the lapping peke.

'Cream,' said the waitress grimly.

'A pint of cream for Rob, then, too,' says Kitty.

21

Kitty arrives home and tells Julia, huffing with outrage, 'He tried to make me give up the cottage. Said he knew Matt had got a hundred percent mortgage. Said he knew I was having trouble keeping up with the payments. I mean, what's up with these banks and things? Are they allowed to go telling all and fucking sundry about their customers' finances?'

Julia tries not to betray herself with an inward wince.

'Said he'd let me have five thousand, down now, cash, to get out now. I mean the bastard, who does he think he is?'

'Why does he want it?' asks Julia, feeling a chill of anxiety flick her heart.

Kitty shrugs. 'Wants to build on the waste land or something. So I said to him, 'You go to hell and don't you bloody start anything on that waste land either.' And he says to me, cool as anything, 'You'll have to get out sooner or later, so you might as well accept my offer and make something out of it.' Wanker. That's it, Julia, I'm staying bloody here now, even if they try to drag me out. Just

224

because I'm alone he thinks he can come here and pay me to leave home. What'd Matt say if he got back and found the place he loves has been sold to some wanker to build an office block on? Matt is going to buy the rest of the land when he gets back. He longs for it, Julia.' Her breath is coming fast, her eyes are wild at the audacity of it, and filling with tears too as she thinks about Matt.

Julia presses her hands together and tries not to tremble.

She uses the public phone box in the village that afternoon.

'I'll look into it,' her lawyer says. 'I have not been told of any plans to build.'

'A notice has appeared saying that planning permission has been applied for. Find out what's going on,' Julia tells him, and after she puts the receiver down, hangs around the corner shop, waiting for him to ring back.

A young man goes into the box and starts a long conversation, which, judging from the kisses blown down the receiver, is with his girlfriend. After ten minutes Julia taps him on the shoulder.

'Excuse me, I'm waiting to receive a call.'

The young man does a two-fingered sign at her without interrupting his kissing. His call ends at last. Julia suspects he had dragged it out extra long to spite her. He gives her another rude sign as he swaggers away.

It seems like hours before the phone rings. Yes. It seems that a building firm has applied for planning permission to erect flats on the waste land and cottage area.

'The cottage belongs to someone,' cries Julia, her heart pounding. 'How can he apply to build on someone else's land?'

The lawyer said that apparently the land had been registered in the name of a Sir Jeremy Burton. 'Perhaps the people living in the cottage are his tenants and don't own the cottage,' the lawyer suggests. 'But if these papers of yours are all you say they are we may be able to get a temporary injunction.'

Julia returns to the cottage with the hideous vision of her and this apparently wealthy Sir Jeremy Burton locked in legislation, in a financial struggle which she doesn't have the smallest hope of winning. She is almost penniless already.

★   ★   ★

'He's been on the phone, Sir Wanker Burton,' says Kitty. She seemed less indignant. 'He says he's got contacts in Waswar. Might be able to pull strings. Get Matt out. He does huge business with Waswar, he says.'

'You didn't believe him, did you?' cries

Julia. But she looks at Kitty's face and sees that Kitty does.

'His hands were too clean for him to be a proper tricker,' says Kitty.

'Conmen wouldn't have any success at all if they didn't appear honest,' protests Julia, feeling like a maiden aunt. 'Don't do anything till Matthew gets back.'

Kitty glares at her. 'And what if he never does? What if this man is telling the truth and I don't give him a chance and Matt rots in there for the rest of his life because I wouldn't believe this Sir Jerry Wanker? I'll do anything to get Matt out, Julia. Anything. Lick arses if necessary.'

'You really love him, don't you.' Julia feels envy.

Kitty sighs and presses her hands against her heart. 'He is my whole world, Julia. He is the most wonderful bloody thing that ever happened to me in my life. Except for Mattie, of course. Now, every bloody minute of the day he's on my mind so I can't enjoy her like I want. I got Matt jammed in there, inside my head, like when I thought I had that dead baby inside me, rotting. Like a fucking dark shadow. I wanted that brat so much but when I look at her I remember Matt and it makes me cry inside.'

★ ★ ★

Julia thinks, sadly, that if she was held captive there would probably be no one fighting to get her out, no one to cry for her. But then she is cheered by the thought that at least she knows who she is, now. She has possession of her documents and somewhere among them, sooner or later, she may find a clue that leads her to discover people who belong to her. She may find Jem again. Not take the cottage from Kitty. Not yet. Not till Matt is back. But at least find her brother . . .

It had not always been like that. There had been years in Rhodesia when she had hardly thought of her family at all and had had to goad herself into remembering her mother, her father, her home and Jem.

★ ★ ★

When Dick had taken Julia round the farm on that first day he had asked her about her mother. 'Did she have red hair like you?' and she had struggled to answer him, knowing it had been red because she remembered people saying it, but not able to get a picture of it in her mind. Was it short or long, tied up or loose. She could not remember. She could not remember her father, either. She could not even remember Jem.

That first night at Dikkers she had lain,

228

trying to summon up her mother's features, while outside the African night silence was constantly punctured by the sudden cries of wild animals and the strumming of cicadas.

Her mother is gone altogether now. Because her face has never been reprinted on Julia's memory, because every photo of her had been burnt in the fire Julia's mother has become little sentences, occasional episodes, with the mother herself a misty ghost. She remembered her father even less because he had been away in the war so much. She only had him in her mind now as a large protective figure looming over her and protecting her from wasp stings. She could hear his voice, baritone and loving but no face came.

But then, she thought, what was the use of remembering them as they were more than fifty years ago. By now they would be dead anyway, or very very old. Geriatric. Suffering from dementia maybe. The thought almost consoled her. They had been spared that, anyway.

They were spared the kind of suffering endured by Dick's wife, Ann, who, although not old, could only lie in bed, her body helpless.

'A horse reared on top of her,' Dick explained as he drove Julia round Dikkers Farm on her first morning there. 'We had only been married a month. It was the day we got back from our honeymoon. She cries every day, now. The horse had been a wedding present,' he added bleakly.

Julia sighed and looked out of the lorry window. She had not yet met Ann, who had still been asleep when Julia arrived and had still not woken. Apparently she slept a lot because of all the painkillers.

'Tobacco,' said Dick, gesturing to row upon row of bright green, big-leafed plants. Men in khaki shorts and flowered shirts were moving among the rows, hoeing.

When they got back at midday, Dick said, 'Ann will be awake by now, and we'll have to explain things to her. You see, you are not exactly what she was expecting.' He paused then added, 'Bloody trickers.'

Julia felt satisfied because they had tricked Mr Dikker too. He had wanted another kind of person altogether. She learnt later that the head of the home had implied that Julia was middle-aged and accustomed to looking after invalids.

'Wait in the lorry while I talk to her.'

Julia leant back against the hot rexine seat while he went in. The sky was crystal blue, clear, sharp, cloudless and seemed twice as high as the sky of England. She looked across to where mauve mist softened a horizon more distant than any she had ever seen. Some huge birds were striding along it. Mr Dikker's little baccy fields look like children's sandpits in comparison. The bungalow was set in an area of close-cut turf, but behind and beyond and as far as she could see was grass nearly as tall and thick as bamboo canes.

Julia wondered what Mr Dikker would do with her when Mrs Dikker said she did not want her.

Across the compound, through the wire mesh of the veranda, she could see Mr and Mrs Dikker. He was moving around making violent gestures with his arms. She was lying on a long chair. Julia could hear them shouting. They both seemed angry.

Mr Dikker came back after a while, his expression troubled.

'Come and be introduced to Ann,' he said.

She suspected another trick, as she followed him in.

*   *   *

Tricks. She feels guilt flush her, at the realisation that she herself, now, is one of those lying cheating adults. But she is desperate. She has this dreadful need to own her land again, to find her brother, to return to him the place that was his. Surely that is not so wrong of her. She is sorry for Kitty. Of course she is. But Kitty is young, and anyway a town person. Once she was forced into it she would be happier back in London than here on the waste land. That Jeremy Burton was right, it was a lonely life for a girl like Kitty. But she must act fast, get it all sorted out before Sir Jeremy put up his block of offices or flats or whatever.

She had looked through her precious papers a hundred times and now goes through them once again, as though somewhere among them perhaps would be a message from her parents telling her what to do. Or a letter from the fairies showing her how to win Jem's land back in time.

She savours each document as though it is a treasure, a jewel that has been lost for most of her lifetime and now is found again. The joy at finding these papers is tinged with the sorrow that she can communicate her discovery to no one but a lawyer she has only met once and does not like much, her joy tainted with the panic that she might have found them too late.

Sometimes she gets the feeling the lawyer is fobbing her off, is not really doing anything to help her case. He keeps making objections, describing the situation as extremely compli-cated, as needing time to sort out the many tangles, that mustn't on any account be hurried, when as far as Julia can tell it's perfectly straightforward and dreadfully urgent. Someone else has taken something that belonged to her and her brother and if she doesn't get it back soon Jem will lose it forever.

'Unless you get a move on,' she shouts on the phone by the corner shop, 'It will be too late. All the money I have paid to you will be wasted. The land will be built upon and I will have lost it.'

'We can't even say that,' the lawyer tells her ambiguously.

How had that Sir Jeremy found out about Kitty and her financial problems? Julia starts to wonder if Sir Jeremy is her lawyer's friend.

She does not trust the law of Britain that permitted, even aided, a small child to be deported, alone, to a foreign country, to live with unknown strangers. It had connived in depriving her of all the people she knew and was related to, removed her from the chance to inherit her own parents' property and never in all the subsequent years tried to contact her, make any attempt to find out what had happened to her, or offer her any sort of compensation for all it had stolen from her. Such a land, thinks Julia, is capable of any injustice.

Mr Dikker called Julia to the veranda.

'This is Julia,' Mr Dikker said. 'This is Ann.'

Ann was frail and blonde and pretty. She was lying back in a chair but now struggled a little, hopelessly, trying to sit up. She gave up the attempt and falling back, said, 'I am sorry you saw me being angry.'

Julia did not know what to say. No one had apologised to her for anything for a long time. Also she felt she was the one that should be apologising because she was not what Ann had wanted. Ann remained as silent as Julia for a while. Then she said, 'Because I have been ill I have forgotten to think of other people's feelings. I am sorry. We will get in touch with the home and make sure they come for you and find somewhere more suitable for you to live, but in the meantime please be welcome in our house.'

22

Horror echoes through the waste land, Kitty screaming, scares the ducks, sends Rob cringing under the dresser. Drums the river water.

Julia has been setting off down the path, heading to the bus stop to meet the lawyer when Kitty, her face scarlet, tears splashing, Mattie clutched against her, rushes after her. Both are howling together so that Julia can hardly hear the words, 'The bloody bastards have cut his finger off.' Then, 'Where the bloody hell are you going?'

Julia grips her bag, holds her smart hat down against the wind, says 'London.'

Kitty grabs her arm with her free hand. 'How can you go when this has happened. You should stay here and help me. Where the fuck do you go all the time, anyway?'

'I have business interests,' Julia says, trying to wriggle her arm free. 'How ghastly. My God. Poor man. But I have to go.' She could never cope with emotion.

* * *

On the train she opens her newspaper and sees a photo of Mattie, red curls as wide as Kitty's brandy-snaps, black eyes shining, fat red mouth puckered with a kiss. 'Please, please, please, send my Daddy back,' is written underneath.

Julia thrusts the thing away, angry, desperate.

A man is attending a table outside the lawyer's offices, collecting signatures, petitioning the British government to do something positive about getting Matthew Wing set free. Another photo of Mattie, held in Kitty's arms.

Julia signs. He says, 'Have you heard about his finger? Terrible.'

★ ★ ★

The lawyer says, 'I've been in touch with this Sir Jeremy Burton. He is as yet unaware of your claim to the property. It may be that after you have heard me out you will not wish to proceed with your contest. Sir Jeremy is rich, influential and adamant. He fully intends to build on the waste land and the area of the cottage. You are unlikely to win. Mrs Wing will almost certainly be compelled to give up her property.'

'Has he heard about Matthew Wing's finger?' asks Julia.

The lawyer raised his eyebrows. 'That is irrelevant, Miss Pritchett.'

Julia hands him another paper. 'My birth certificate. My surname is Trinkett. Not Pritchett.'

'Amazing,' says the lawyer, not sounding amazed. He fiddles with the paper and waits impatiently for her to continue.

'So first I can prove who I am and then I can prove the land belongs to me,' she says.

'The time factor is the stumbling block,' he says. 'Sixty years is a long time and although you say you were ignorant of the whereabouts of this land till recently and were sent abroad against your will, if it comes to a contest with Sir Jeremy you will have to prove these things in a court of law. You can, as I said earlier, fight, but this will cost a great deal more money than I imagine you have got. And in the end even if you win the land will have been built upon and the cottage pulled down.' He pauses for this to sink in, then adds, 'You have not yet received my first bill.'

Julia listens, knowing he is right. A feeling of chill is growing through her, compounded by the thought in the back of her mind of Kitty's husband being slowly chopped up then killed entirely. Of Kitty's cottage pulled down. Of terrorists' bombs blowing off the limbs of children. Of people who were prepared to go to any length of cruelty for the sake of getting what they wanted. Yes, of course she would never be able to give Jem back his land even if she managed to find him. Of course Kitty would never get back her husband, nor be allowed even to keep her cottage. Pessimism sweeps over Julia in great waves, till she is engulfed in clouds of gloom. As though, like her mother, she is being destroyed by an inarticulate violence that does not even know she's there.

★ ★ ★

When Julia gets home she finds Kitty watching the news and hysterical.

Matt is on the screen, kneeling and wearing an orange jump suit. Behind him stand four hooded men, their faces hidden behind ski masks, only mouths and eyes showing. They hold heavy military weapons. Their posture is triumphant and arrogant, four armed men swanking over the capture of one pathetic shackled victim. Behind the hostage takers is a banner bearing words in Arabic which Kitty later learns are from the Koran and mean 'Praise to Allah. Allah is good. Allah is great.'

'The buggers. The bastards,' Kitty is screaming. 'The fucking bullies.'

Matt has a deep bruised cut across his cheek. His eyes look expressionlessly into the camera. He is speaking. His voice is a little shrill, as though terror is dominating it.

'They are going to kill me if their demands are not met. I am begging the people of Britain to save me . . . ' There is a sound like weeping in his tone.

★ ★ ★

Julia rings the lawyer again. Trying to sound calm she says, 'This Sir Jeremy person says he has important contacts in Waswar.'

'That is correct,' says the lawyer.

'I would like to speak to him.'

The lawyer looks doubtful. 'It's not really the correct procedure.'

'Yes. And I don't expect people trying to wheedle away the homes of women whose husbands are being held threatened with murder is correct procedure either.'

'Please only speak of behalf of Mrs Wing. Do not mention your own claim for the moment.' The lawyer dials a number. After a while he says, 'Sir Jeremy. There is a lady here who would like a word with you . . . ' and hands over the receiver.

A huge and fruity voice booms genially down the line. 'What may I do for you, dear lady?'

Julia launches in without preamble. 'I am a

friend of Kitty Wing. This is not the best time for her to be bamboozled into giving up her home.'

'No one is bamboozling her, my dear.' He laughs softly, rich, unctuous. 'And I really do think that, admirable though your motives are, this is a matter between Mrs Wing and myself. And is nothing to do with you, whatsoever.'

Julia thinks of the yellow waterproof bundles and feels confident. 'May I ask who the land belongs to?' she asked.

The lawyer gives her a reprimanding tap on the arm.

'It is mine, dear lady,' says the man. 'And we need the land upon which Mrs Wing's house stands.' He laughs again. There is no humour in his laughter, only confidence and something close to scorn. 'You are a friend of Mrs Wing's and have her interests at heart, I can see. I am thinking of her too, as well as of my own interests. You must see that that cottage is not the right place for a young, lone woman and a baby. Who knows how long her husband may be incarcerated? It is even likely, given the latest dreadful news, that he will not come out alive. Tragic, but possible.' He lets the words wander sadly, like smoke, through the privileged air.

Julia says, 'But you are going to use your

influence to get him out? I understand you have contacts and influence in Waswar.'

'Ah, Mrs Wing told you that, did she? Yes. I think I may be able to put some pressure on the people who are holding her husband.'

'Shouldn't you do something quickly?' says Julia. 'There doesn't seem to be much time.'

'These things can't be rushed.' He laughs airily. 'But I plan to do my best.' His tone is sonorous and reliable.

'I might be able to persuade her to give up the cottage if you can convince me that these contacts exist,' said Julia.

'You would like to see names? Addresses?' He laughs again, amused, cynical.

'I might be able to negotiate. I have had experience. I have been one of those people in South Africa, during the apartheid years, who was prepared to die, and almost did, for something I believed in. There would have been no price sufficient to pay me off. If I go to Waswar can you arrange for them to meet me? Will you do it?'

'You will go there? To Waswar?' He sounds amazed.

'Why not?' she says. 'If I succeed I will do my best to persuade Mrs Wing to give up the cottage. Is that a bargain? If Matthew Wing is freed because of your introductions?' Julia grips the receiver, leans back and tries to

241

slow her whirling mind. Why is she doing this? Has she gone mad? She made Kitty that promise, but even Kitty could not have expected her to go as far as this. But yet she realises now that this idea has been crawling into her mind for some time. Perhaps it was conceived the moment she put her hands on Kitty's belly and brought the baby back to life. For as Julia had known all her life, every girl needs a father and what she has been deprived of she, herself, might be able to give to Mattie.

★ ★ ★

She leaves the office feeling slightly sick, as though nausea at what she plans is rising into her throat. She stumbles along the road feeling drained and shaken. Cars blow their horns at her as she weaves unsteadily among them. She finds a phone box and rings Kitty.

Kitty's voice is hoarser than ever as though she has been crying ever since Julia left. Julia can hardly understand her at first.

'The fuckers are going to kill Matt if their demands aren't met by midnight. I rang the FO wankers and all the bastards would say was, 'We don't do deals with kidnappers'.'

In the background Julia can hear Mattie

screaming. Kitty bawls, 'The bloody fucking shitty bastards –'

'Now, shut up, Kitty, and put that child down so you can hear what I am about to say,' Julia shouts severely.

There comes a sudden silence as though the sharpness of Julia's tone has briefly silenced both mother and baby.

'I'm going there,' shouts Julia over the roar of the traffic.

'Go on, go away, leave me just when I need someone,' yells Kitty.

Ignoring her, Julia says, 'I make you my sole executor if anything happens to me,' and thinks, how strange and sad that after her long life there was no one except this stranger to take on that responsibility.

★ ★ ★

She might bloody do it, thinks Kitty as she puts down the receiver. Knowing her. Might fucking get Matt out before they top him. She does not like Julia much, but she has learnt to respect her.

She suddenly can't stay at home alone. It is the Danaveda class. She hasn't been for ages and decides to go now. Piling sleeping Mattie into her pram, she takes the dog, putting him on his lead and goes out into the summer night, Rob prancing with delight. Never before has he been taken out at this time. A run in the garden for a wee, maybe, but never a proper walk.

He pulls and dances as Kitty pushes her pram into the village, where people are, where street lights shine, where cars drive by, while Mattie grips the sides of her pram with pink fingers and gazes at the multitude of incomprehensible lights with astonished delight.

* * *

The elderly Indian instructor, in his flowing white robes and prophet-type beard, the very opposite of the idea of a gym teacher, has been joined by a young Western man, tall, darkly tanned, one gold earring. Probably, thinks Kitty, just come back from hitching round India. When she meets him later she finds that this is so.

'Some of you have requested for something with more energy that I am inclined to give you,' says Mr Mitra. 'So I bring you Harry, This is Harry.'

Harry wears a track suit, trainers and a baseball cap turned round the wrong way.

* * *

The class, mostly ladies rather past middle age by now, the young ones having gone onto other more energetic things, clap enthusiastically. Kitty is sorry that most of her friends had abandoned Danaveda, for she would have liked a giggle with them, and to speculate over Harry's married status, is or isn't. Only theory. The girls were all married. All had little kids. But a residue of the hunting girl still remained inside them.

Harry smiles and pushes his hair out of his eyes. His eyes are very blue and linger on Kitty's for a moment. Kitty grins back.

'The silence is there for all of us,' says Mr Mitra. 'And when we find it, all our desires are fulfilled.'

'I'll believe that when I fucking see it,' says Kitty.

'Hush,' urge the blue rinse ladies. They have got used to Kitty, but all the same.

Mr Mitra smiles calmly. 'It's there,' he says confidentially. 'Find that perfect balance and you will be able to make things move, even raise them, with the thoughts alone.' He giggles and makes his joke about the JCB.

Mr Mitra gets the class to take up the series of postures then Harry has them leaping, fending, striking symbolic blows, thrusting invisible swords, shooting non-existent arrows, while Mr Mitra calls out instructions and encouragement. Their trainers thunder and echo round the hall, the soles squeal, the ladies yelp as they nearly slip, there does not seem much room for central silence.

'Good, good, many madams and sir,' says Mr Mitra. 'Now, in the middle of all this movement you must find it. Close the eyes, let it go, feel the power. The day will come when a raging fellow attacks you in the dark and you will deflect him with your mind.'

The blue rinse ladies giggle and shudder.

When the class is over Harry says, 'I am looking for a lady called Julia Pritchett. She was a friend of my dad's. He's been looking for her for years, and saw her on TV. Something to do with the hostage, Matthew Wing.'

'I am Mrs Wing,' says Kitty. 'But Julia's not here any more. She's gone away for the moment. To Waswar.'

The young man stares, trying to take this in.

'She said she was going to rescue my husband, though, fat chance, what can an old woman like her do? And he'll probably be dead by the time she gets there, anyway.'

The young man raises his eyebrows. 'According to my dad she's a fighter. Her dog was attacked by a leopard once and she

246

managed to rescue it.'

'Does your dad know her?'

Harry nods. 'Apparently Julia Pritchett lived with my parents in Zimbabwe for a while when she was young.' He adds, 'Harry Dikker is my name.'

'That great scar on her arm?' Kitty shudders. 'She never told me what did it. A leopard.'

23

Julia, filled with a desperate sense of urgency, hurries through the various formalities required for her trip to Waswar, tries not to imagine how this adventure is going to end, tries not to wish that there will be someone who loves her fighting for her release.

She has forbidden herself to think about Dick but now, in spite of everything he keeps slithering back into her mind. Julia has never cried since she was seven and still can stop herself unless she thinks of Dick. But does it matter now? I can cry, she told herself, and it will make no difference any more.

★   ★   ★

Dick showed her a Rhodesian penny. It had a hole in the middle.

'Can you see the rabbit?' he asked. It was Julia's second day at Dikkers. She peered at the coin from every side but saw no rabbit.

'Can't you see it really?' he said, taking it from her. He looked at it too, then with a burst of laughter said, 'The rabbit must have gone down the hole. That's why you can't see it.' It was the kind of joke her father might have made. So silly. So childish. So . . .

'I've written to the home,' he said. 'But these things take ages, out here in the bush. You may be stuck here for a month.'

Julia felt glad. At least she could stay for a month. She would not think about what would happen to her when the month was over. She would not give it another thought. That would be a worry for the future.

That evening Ann became too hot. Her face was bathed in sweat and her forehead and her nightdress were dark with it and Dick brought a bowl of cool water, and gave her a sponge bath.

'Shall I help you?' Julia suggested when Dick had finished. In the home the bigger girls were often put in charge of washing and caring for the younger ones.

After Julia had helped the crippled girl to dress, pulling shoes onto her useless legs, buttoning up the back of her dress, fetching her brush and comb and lipstick, Julia held up the little tortoiseshell hand mirror that Ann said had been her mother's so that Ann could fill her lips in with glistening scarlet. The lipstick, weakened by the heat, suddenly broke off in a smear of red and, shouting with anger, Ann hurled it across the room where it hit the daga wall with a scarlet splat like blood.

'Why does everything have to always go wrong in this bloody country,' she yelled. 'Other women have a fridge to keep their lipstick in. Not me. They can't get the least thing right. Even when I ask for a middle-aged woman they send me a teen-ager.' She swung round on Julia, furious, her face streaked with lipstick like a clown's.

'I am sorry,' Julia said stiffly. 'But I will become middle-aged in about thirty years, if you keep me till then.'

Ann gazed at Julia for a long moment, her beautiful dark blue eyes smouldering with anger. Then suddenly she burst out laughing. 'Oh, kiddy, kiddy, I adore you,' she cried.

They were going to keep her. Relief flooded through Julia with the rush of an overflowing river.

Julia learnt to give Ann a sponge bath, to pump up the Aladdin pressure lamps and light them, to pick zinnias from the clearing and arrange them in a jar in Ann's bedroom. Dick had two dogs, Rhodesian ridgebacks, that followed him everywhere. He taught her to search their coats for ticks, then dab the swollen blood-suckers with salt till they shrivelled and fell off. And each morning she sat with Ann and they played scrabble, painted watercolours and did crossword puzzles. In the afternoon, while Ann was resting, Julia went round the farm with Dick and learnt about the growing of tobacco. She was happy again. Perhaps she would start writing her diary again, though this time it would be for herself, instead of Jem.

★ ★ ★

'I'm taking you back to Salisbury on Thursday,' Dick told Julia suddenly, four weeks after her arrival. 'They have found us a qualified person at last.'

Julia couldn't believe it. 'Ann agreed I could stay.'

'I think you misunderstood her,' said Dick sadly.

'Where will you put me, anyway?' Julia was shouting now. 'I'm too old for the home, so where will I go?'

'I've talked to the manager of Miekles Hotel. I told them about you, and they are offering you the job of receptionist.'

'I won't do it,' she said.

'Don't be silly,' said Dick. 'The pay is much better than anything I could afford.'

'I won't go,' Julia screamed.

'You have to, ducky,' Ann said softly. 'I need someone more experienced to look after me than you.'

'I can do everything,' Julia cried. 'Didn't I look after you well all this month? Oh, let me stay with you. Let me, let me.'

'It's impossible,' Ann said. 'Don't carry on so. You are exhausting me.'

★ ★ ★

On the morning of the Thursday, before Dick or Ann were awake, Julia slipped out of the bungalow and began to thrust her way through the six-foot-high elephant grass until she reached the vlei, a clearing by the river where, in the evening, all hidden animals would come out to drink.

Now, as the sun began to rise, there was only a lizard, iridiscent, clasped against the rock. It twitched as Julia ran but did not abandon its sunbathing. A huge centipede with the size and colour and gloss of a pre-war sausage poured steadily across the path ahead of her. On the other side of the river the ground rose into a small hill over which blue gum trees had been planted. At the top of this was a kopje, consisting of a round boulder the size of a baby Austin, on which was balanced an enormous one the size of a large bungalow. The top boulder was balanced so delicately that it rocked slightly in strong winds. It took her ages to scramble up to the top. She would stay here all day, she thought. She would not come down till it was too late for Dick to take her back to Salisbury.

She reached the top at last, sweating and gasping, and saw, to her horror, a baboon sitting there. Like the lizard it was taking the sun. He glared at her defiantly and at first Julia cringed back, quailing, under his furious bushy-eyebrowed stare.

It briefly bared its teeth and its hair bristled but when she tried to get out of its reach she could not find a foothold.

Dick had said that baboon's bite is worse than that of a big dog, but all the same, though she was quivering with terror, she forced herself to creep into the shade of a tiny sapling only yards away from the baboon and clutching it for balance, crouch there. She would rush away if it made the smallest movement but would stay here if she possibly could. They would see her from the bungalow if she went down now.

It seemed like hours during which Julia and the baboon sat with only a few yards of rock between them. Gradually the animal's pose became less aggressive and a gentler look seemed to come in his eyes.

Then softly, as though Julia was the wild

animal instead of him, the baboon made a shuffling movement as though inviting her to sit beside him.

By now Julia's legs were aching, her fingers sore from clinging to her branch.

The baboon shuffled his body again, then made a little bobbing gesture in her direction. His meaning was clear. Very softly, so as not to anger him, Julia crawled across from the tree to the hot, lichen-covered rock and sat beside him. For the rest of her life she would be able to recall the strong wild animal smell of him.

★ ★ ★

At intervals throughout the day she caught sight of Dick and his farm labourers apparently looking for her. At one stage some men came to the foot of the kopje and the baboon became nervous. He snarled softly as though he was protecting Julia. Then he reached out a black knuckle, and gently touched her cheek.

'I like you too,' Julia whispered, keeping absolutely still. The baboon's finger rested lightly, half way down her cheek and lingered, cool, smooth and hard. Inside Julia something seemed to open like the petals of a flower, and there rose inside her a tickling feeling as though she was filled with angels that were closing and opening their wings.

* * *

Dick found her there that evening. The sun was setting. She was not hiding any more, but still she sat in the tree on the top of the kopje. The baboon had gone hours ago, but still Julia sat. There did not seem anything else to do.

He looked up at her from the bottom of the kopje and said, 'It's OK. You can come down. You can stay with us. It's OK.' She was hesitant.

He stretched out his arms and said, 'Come on, old girl. Jump. I'll catch you,' and when she still paused, said, 'I promise.'

She got up stiffly at last. Then slowly, on numb legs began to scramble and scrabble down the rock.

'Jump,' Dick urged.

She leapt and landed at last against him, sticks in her hair and scratches on her legs.

He put his arms round her and held her there. She rested her head against his chest till she could hear his heart beating. He smelled of tobacco and sweat. He smelled of Rhodesia.

She felt mad with love.

24

Kitty pours herself a beer, takes the éclairs out of the fridge. She sinks her teeth into cold cream, fills her mouth with cold beer and, moustached with the white froth of both, bolstered with courage, turns on the TV to hear the ten o'clock news.

She misses the headlines, only catches the last words, 'of Matthew Wing.' She can bear no more. She's on a short fuse these days. She hurls the éclair at the screen, where it splats white and chocolate and dims the picture. As though the TV is partly responsible for what has happened to her husband.

'The execution of Matthew Wing,' he must have said.

Rob, not understanding that this is a tragedy not a celebration, rushes at the screen and starts licking. There is nothing he likes more than flung éclair and Kitty is doing a satisfactory lot of this kind of thing lately.

Then through the smear of licked chocolate and cream there appears the face of Julia.

'Miss Julia Pritchett, who is offering herself in place of Mr Wing.'

Kitty gazes, her mouth open with incredulity.

★ ★ ★

When Julia arrives at the hotel in Waswar someone is already waiting to take her to the secret location.

Desperate people cannot afford ethics. She did not expect it. It all might still go wrong. They might take her and still not let Matthew go. But she has Sir Jeremy's assurance that he knows these people, that he does business with them, that he is a person they may well listen to. He had not known, of course, that Julia planned to offer herself in Matthew's place. If he had heard that he would have guffawed contemptuously. Muslim terrorists giving up a man and taking a woman instead. They wouldn't touch it with a barge pole, he would say. These are people that value males. He would have spoken as though he agreed with them, Julia is sure.

She guesses his business with these people. He supplies them with the things without which their struggle would be impossible.

As she slides into the black car she reflects that most likely Sir Jeremy would have been right and they will not accept a female hostage. She would have done her best, though. She would have tried her hardest to fulfill her promise. I am great on trying to fulfill promises, she thinks, as the car crawls along the bomb-holed roads. I promised to look after my brother sixty years ago and I don't even know where he is.

She is blindfolded before being driven. Sounds of explosions echoing through emptiness, no sound of other people or of traffic, always the smell of gunpowder and scorch. She is travelling through what seems to be a dangerous gutted city by a silent driver. She tries to experience what she can of this journey, knowing this is probably her last hour of freedom and so she must savour it.

She wears the clothes she brought for England and they are too hot and heavy here. She remembers coming to Dickers in the wrong clothes too. All those years ago. Saggy frumpy frocks given to her by the children's home, charity clothes. Ann had helped her sew a new frock. 'Have you thought about what you will do with your life,' she had asked, as she turned the sewing machine handle. 'Because you won't want to be here forever.'

'I have to earn enough money to pay my passage back to England,' Julia said.

'Darling, don't you want to stay here, in this lovely new young country? There are opportunities here that you will never find in England. And sunshine.'

Julia explained about Jem. 'I must find

him. I promised my mother. Those were her last words to me, 'Look after your little brother.'

'He has been living with an adoptive family for the past ten years. He must feel that those people are his true parents now. Do you think it's right to go and unsettle him? Why not leave him, Julia?'

She was right. Julia knew it, had known for a long time, really. And also she was worn out with unfulfilled longings. She would never go back to England. She would stay here for ever. It was almost as though, for the first time since her parents died, she had a family again.

Dick taught her how to handle a gun and when he decided she was good enough took her out to shoot deer.

'We have to provide for ourselves as far as possible,' he said as they crept up upon the grazing dikdik.

'The poor creature is looking at us,' Julia whispered, aghast at the idea of snuffing out such a pretty life.

'If you can't face death you should not eat meat,' he said. 'Otherwise it's hypocrisy.'

At about the time of her sixteenth birthday, Julia shot a Kudu, the light rifle reeling thunderously against her shoulder. The deer dropped instantly. Julia cried and felt triumphant at the same time. From the local people she learnt how to make string from a soft and pliable underbark called tambo, how to find a drink inside the wild gourds and prickly pears. She was introduced to the m'hobahoba fruit, brown and rough on the outside, with luscious sweet pulp within.

And because his first crop of tobacco was a success, Dick bought Julia a mare and taught her to ride, holding onto her bit, running round and round the compound, shouting, 'up down, up down,' as Julia bounced desperately around in the saddle, till she got the knack of rising at the trot, and from the verandah Ann began clapping.

★ ★ ★

Sometimes, when there was no work to be done, and neither Ann nor Dick needed her, Julia would take a sandwich and stay out all day, sitting in the vlei, watching the deer come to drink, or wandering over the plains where secretary birds, almost her height, strutted. They had a feather, like a pen behind the ear, sticking out of their heads. Or she would tease the turkey-buzzards, heavy and fat, which only flew if they had to and needed a brief pause from running before their weighty take off, so that if she cantered after them they had to keep on running.

Ann and Dick began to worry about Julia at last, saying that she must start getting out and that just living on the farm with them was not enough.

'Life on the farm was enough for you, Ann,' Julia retorted.

'I was married, that's the point,' said Ann softly.

'You aren't meeting people here,' said Dick. 'You never see anyone except me, Ann and the farm labourers.'

'That's all I want,' Julia assured them.

'It's not enough,' said Dick. 'You must go somewhere where you will meet young men, otherwise how will you ever get married?'

'Do I have to?' Julia asked, appalled. Now that she did not have to look for Jem, she had visualised living here on Dikkers all her life. Growing tobacco crops. She knew all about that now. She could have done it on her own if Dick had not been there.

Dick took Julia to the tobacco auction. They walked among the square, hessian-wrapped bales that were arranged in rows. The sun shone in through dusty glass, stabbing the great corrugated iron shed with long drifting motes. Fifty, perhaps sixty people in the misty hall, yet there was a silence here broken only by the crooning nasal voice of the autioneer, a rhythmic singsong unintelligible to outsiders – 'And a one and a one and a twotwotwo and a two and a half and a half and a half –' Fifty or so sellers all craning urgently, hearts in mouths, willing the bidding to rise. Sellers from abroad signalling with a raised thumb, a nod of the head, a tap of the shoe.

Afterwards Dick took her to the bioscope, where they sat side by side in the dark and when a frightening bit came she reached out and took his hand. She held it for a long time and felt sad when at last he gently released his fingers. The feel of him had sent fireworks of wonder up her arm.

★　★　★

Now, hammering over the rutted roads of Waswar, a black bandage over her face from which sweat trickles, going to a dark place from which she might never emerge, she thinks, I have those years to look back on. The happy years that Dick and Ann gave me. Until the desire became uncontrollable. Unendurable.

★　★　★

The phone rings. Kitty rushes for it, her feet tangling in the wires, tumbling over Rob.

'Hell, bloody, blast and fuck,' shouts Kitty as she scrambles among the sofa cushions for the fallen receiver.

It is the man from the Foreign Office. His voice is muffled with sofa.

'Shout louder,' she yells. 'I can't hardly fucking hear you.'

The man from the Foreign office tells Kitty that Matthew has been released.

'I don't fucking believe you,' she says.

'It is true. He is already free and on a plane home. We will send a car for you to meet him at Heathrow.'

25

Matthew is wearing a back-to-front baseball cap, like Harry of the Danaveda class, as he comes down the steps of the aeroplane. This is the first thing Kitty notices. Notices particularily because such a hat is so much not his style.

Because of the clamour of the crowds shouting welcome and the vast mob of media waggling fur-clad mikes, shouting questions, Kitty can hardly get to him.

But at last he is somehow eased through the crowd and is standing in front of her and Mattie in her buggy.

'You're back then?' she says sillily, as though he's back from a weekend's pheasant shoot. Her cheeks feel hot as though she is blushing.

'Kitty, my queen,' he says. His voice sounds hollow, and slightly artificial. Cameras flash and pop as Matthew reaches out and embraces her. She tries to not look at the hand with half a little finger missing.

His body feels shockingly thin. He smells musty as though touched with the damp of the grave.

Then he stares incredulously at Mattie. 'Who is that?' he asks.

'Your daughter,' she says, flushing with the glory of it. 'Mattie.'

'Mattie?' He bends down and examines the baby. Mattie stares back at him with round and fascinated eyes, grins, puts out her fat hands to grab Matt's amazing yellow beard.

When he straightens Kitty sees that his eyes are the same grey, cool and sensible, but troubled things seemed to have happened to the face all round it. There are lines in his forehead, a sagging of his chin, dark rings under his eyes.

He says, 'It's been three days without sleep.' He speaks as though he is making an excuse for some lack on his part.

Kitty says, 'What do you think?' She smiles upon Mattie. Mattie giggles happily and waves her hands at her newly restored father.

In the car Kitty reaches out and takes his hand, squeezing his cold fingers between her warm ones. His hand in hers. Her fingers encounter the raw stump and forcing herself she tries to stroke it, but he jerks his hand out of her grasp and she feels a quiver passing through him as though some ghastly memory has been awakened.

'Everything's going to be fucking OK from now on, darling, darling, darling,' she whispers and strokes his cheek with her released hand. She speaks like a mother reassuring a child after a nightmare. 'I'll bake you a cake when we get home.'

He puts his hand up to hers, takes hold of it again, presses her fingers cautiously and says with a laugh so dry that it sounds as though it is hurting his throat, 'Your cakes. Oh, your cakes.'

She does not know what he means.

At home Rob comes to the door raging at the sound of Matthew's voice. 'He doesn't know you. He'll get used to you,' says Kitty, making excuses.

Matthew flinches. 'What in God's name is that?'

'It's Rob. The puppy.'

'It was a spaniel.' Matthew goes inside, skirting the snarling dog, his foot ready to kick at the sign of attack.

★ ★ ★

Kitty feels flustered that evening, trying to insert Matthew into her routine and wishing Julia was there to take over some of the chores, perhaps bathe Mattie while she, Kitty, concentrated on Matt. She tries not to allow herself to dwell on Julia, fearing that this would lead, now Matthew was free, to feelings of guilt and worry. Imagining Julia, instead of Matthew, chained to a radiator and bundled into the boots of cars.

As she tries to feed Mattie with one hand, and make Matt some tea with the other she wants to ask what they had done to him but his closed-down face forbids inquiry.

★   ★   ★

Straight after supper Matthew goes to bed and falls asleep instantly, although it was only seven-thirty. She studies her reclaimed husband, trying to see into his heart, to read his soul.

His breathing is uneasy, he turns and stirs and murmurs, though before he had been a heavy sleeper, flinging himself across the bed like a child. Thundering. Before he had been taken hostage he would thunder across the bed and heave heavy limbs over her body in surges of unconscious loving. Now he holds himself small as though he will be punished for taking up too much space.

His temples were tinged with grey before, but now his hair is grey all over. Pity fills her in a warmth of rising tears, fills her mouth with a longing to make him glad and young again, fills her heart with a determination to wipe away the scars that mark his heart.

From this day on, thinks Kitty, she will do all the things that are necessary to repair the damage done to the darling of her soul, the beloved of her life.

Cautiously, so as not to frighten, she reaches out a finger and tries to caress away the frown that furrows his forehead. His eyes open instantly, he jerks upright and stares into Kitty's face with a look of wild alarm, as though for a moment he does not recognise her but thinks she is the enemy. She can hear his breathing speeding suddenly and thinks she can even feel the hammering of his heart.

If Julia had been here she might have stroked Matt's soul with her healing fingers and made him well again, like she had restored life to the baby. The thought of Julia makes Kitty feel like crying, but she does not dare in case she makes a sound and Matt is troubled.

Once Julia comes into Kitty's mind she cannot get her out again. For hours Kitty lies, wondering if they are doing the same things to Julia that they had done to Matt. Worrying that the day will come when Julia, too, will wake full of panic because someone touches her forehead.

★ ★ ★

'Do you want to tell me what the bastards did to you?' Kitty asks next morning.

'No.' He kisses her, says, 'Forget it. I want to.' His mouth tastes sour as though he has been eating lemons. His fingers, where he holds her, bite into her skin.

'You're hurting me,' she tells him, laughing a bit but trying to pull away. But he holds her tighter and says, 'Have you stopped loving me? Often I thought you must have stopped loving me.'

Mattie begins to bawl from the other room.

'I've got to see to the brat,' she says.

'Tell me. Answer me,' he demands, still holding her.

'I love you to bloody bits, Matt,' she says, still pulling at her arms.

'Why didn't anyone try to free me?' he asks.

'Every person in the country did,' Kitty cries. 'Me and Julia worked our butts off.'

The baby screams louder. She is spluttering as though she is going to choke.

'Let go of me, Matt. I have to go to her.' She wrenches herself away from him and races to the bedroom. Mattie's face is purple.

★　★　★

When she brings Mattie back, Rob is cowering in a corner, glaring at Matthew.

269

'Where did you get him?' asks Matthew.

'I told you,' says Kitty, starting to feel desperate. 'He's that same puppy.'

★ ★ ★

Julia, in Waswar, sits in a dark room, alone, without news. She does not know that Matthew has been set free. She does not know what is going to happen to her.

'Why have you given your life up like this for someone who you say is no relation and you do not even know?'

Julia shrugs. 'I have no husband. No children.'

★ ★ ★

She forgot Jem, for a while, when she was sixteen because the whole of her mind, her body, and her soul, were filled with Dick. She had become like the waters of the Victoria Falls, helpless in her thunderous drop, rainbowed in the deliciousness of love and in the depth of her mind lay a fuzzy image in which Ann and Julia would share Dick from now on. If Dick's fingers inadvertently brushed hers a wild fire would spring up in her. She would feel her face go scarlet, her breath rapid.

'Jewel, you must decide what to do with

270

your life.' Dick said. They were in the hottest of the tobacco barns. The heat and redness that sprang into Julia's cheeks came not only from the sudden flare-up of the furnace.

'I would like to be a tobacco farmer.'

Dick said, 'Well, you'll need a husband. We'd better find a way for you to meet some young men.'

'I don't want to get married,' said Julia.

Dick laughed. 'Until I met Ann I did not have the least intention of getting married either. And once I'd met her I could think of doing nothing else.'

'You were dreadfully young,' Julia said.

'Eighteen. Can you imagine.' He laughed. 'I was working as a trainee farmer and fell in love with my manager's daughter. That simple.'

'That simple,' Julia said, stifling her pang of envy.

26

Matthew is getting better. The dull pasty look is fading from his skin, his eyes are starting to shine again, his step is getting its bounce back.

He begins to go round the village greeting people as though he has only been away on a foreign holiday.

He drops in at the pub while Kitty cooks supper. He is greeted as though he is a pop star or a newly returned hero.

'Come on, young man. Get a pint inside you. I bet you never got any of this stuff where you've come from.'

'No,' agrees Matthew, taking the foaming spilling mug. 'Cheers, mate.'

Their eyes look and pretend not to, at the stump where his finger had been.

'Will you be helping to free the woman who has offered herself in your place?' someone asks him.

Matthew shrugs. 'I don't know anything about her,' he says. 'Is there really such a person? Perhaps she's an invention of the media.'

'She was living with Kitty while you were kept hostage. She put a lot of effort into getting you freed.' But they do not press the point too hard for they disapprove of Julia, suspecting her relationship with Kitty. They don't voice their doubts, though, not wanting the newly freed hero to feel distress.

★ ★ ★

When he gets home he has drunk too much beer and Kitty has already gone to bed. He shakes her awake. 'What about this woman, then?' he demands. 'Who is she? Why did she give herself over for me?'

Kitty sits up, rubbing her eyes. 'She was bloody decent to me, Matt. And to you.'

★ ★ ★

During the day Matt takes his gun and walks over the fields. Not wandering lusciously, reclaiming lost summer English days, but striding wildly like someone let out of a cage, like someone hunting for an enemy.

'Take the dog, why don't you. Start training him, Matt,' Kitty suggests, but Matthew ignores her, shutting the door on the dog's face as he goes out.

He returns, exhausted instead of exhilarated, carrying rabbits that look mangled, as though he has used them for target practice.

He brings pheasants with their heads blown away. Kitty has a struggle to remove the multitude of pellets, finds it hard to cook such broken game.

He takes to shutting himself into the sitting room for long hours, telling her he is busy writing his memoirs and that he must not be disturbed. If Mattie cries or the dog barks he bursts out suddenly, looking angry, telling her to shut them up.

They have not made love since Matt came back. He lies still and after a while, as though her touch irritates him, withdraws from her.

'What's bloody gone wrong, Matt? Don't you love me any more?' She knows she will not be able to bear it if he says no.

'Of course I love you,' he says.

'Shall we make love tonight, then? Shall we make this into our wedding night?'

He nods and drawing her to him, kisses her gently.

That evening she rinses her mouth with freshener and wipes her body with eau de cologne. She rejoices as, like a bud unfolding, the old Matt returns. She can feel his love as though it is something tangible, tingling from his hands, as he caresses her. Then suddenly he pushes her away. It comes out of the blue and she is so filled with shock for a moment that she cannot take in what has happened.

'Have I done something wrong?' Kitty whispers.

He makes a slight sound, like a groan.

'Couldn't you try to explain, so that I can try to understand?' she says.

'That baby,' he mutters. His teeth seem clenched.

Kitty thinks back, wondering if Mattie had been crying, and in her delight she has not noticed.

'That child of yours,' he grunts.

'But yours, darling, too,' she cries. A chill possesses her.

'You bitch,' Matthew whispers.

The terrible word hangs on the beautiful night like evil.

'And the dog,' he says. 'Who gave you that dog?'

'You, Matt,' she whispers, though she knows it is hopeless.

★ ★ ★

Julia sits in the dark and remembers the past, for without companion, books or pen and paper that's all she's got now. She gives herself titles. Joy for instance. Then goes back through her life trying to recall moments when she experienced such a thing. Fear. Hope. Fun. She compels her mind to

275

concentrate on her self-imposed exercise of memory, one of the many techniques she had invented during her imprisonment in South Africa, to avoid sinking into despair and fear. She always keeps love for last, like the jam sauce on a boring pudding. Love. Something happened to her in that first year at Dikkers, that made her able to write her diary again. Now she has to remember what she has written but because she has read it so often, that is not hard.

★　★　★

For my nineteenth birthday, Ann and Dick gave me a gelding called Dan. 'I'm in love, Dan,' I whispered to the horse as we set off along the dust track. I had not meant to tell anyone, but I could not stop my secret bursting out. Dan pricked back his ears at the sound of my voice. 'I'm in love,' I told Dan, over and over again as we galloped across the grasslands.

A bird was calling. It sounded as though it was saying, 'Go away, go away.' I closed my ears to it.

Dan would be foamed like a seashore, panting in snorts, his nostrils wide and scarlet when I got back to the bungalow again. Steam would be rising from him, dimming the flies that buzzed around his ears. When I leapt off and handed his sweat-slippery reins over to the cow man, who acted as groom as well he would reprimand me. 'You ride too hard, n'kosikasi,' and I would scowl at him as I strode inside. Love had pruned away my manners. I would rush indoors, steaming too, the horse's hot sweat mixed with my own. Steaming inside me as well as out. My face crusted with the dust of the veldt. My breeches dense with sweat and horse hair. My heart shaking with an urgency to see Dick again as though a month had passed without an encounter instead of only hours.

Ann must never know how my heart was betraying her.

★ ★ ★

Sometimes Dick would ask, 'You are looking thoughtful, darling. What's on your mind, Jewel?' and I would shake my head, amazed he did not know.

★ ★ ★

A strange smell began to permeate the bungalow. From Ann's room I heard the sound of chanting.

'What's happening?' I asked.

'She's got a witch doctor with her. He's doing something with smoke.'

Through the daga wall we could hear the sound of the witch doctor chanting and the beating of his drum. The smoke that filled the bungalow kept changing its smell.

★ ★ ★

Later, after the witch doctor had gone, Dick said, 'Let's go and see if it worked.'

I followed him, but, for some reason, felt reluctant. As though I had a premonition that this was going to change everything.

Ann's legs were glistening with the oils the man had rubbed into them, her face was shining with hope.

'I really do think he's done some good. I think I can feel a tiny tingling in my toes,' she smiled.

I tried to smile back but my lips were stiff.

27

My days became burning waiting, yearning for the moment when, on the moonlit verandah, and Ann had gone to sleep, I would be again alone with Dick.

Because there was no hospital, nor even a chemist that the Dikker farm workers could easily go to, Dick had always tried to treat his workers himself. At first I went round with him, and helped, but gradually I learnt more and more about how to treat the minor common illnesses of the farm till this became my responsibility. I borrowed medical books from the farmers' club library and each time we went to Salisbury, I bought a stock of medicine.

Each day, when I went round the farm, giving out medicine, putting drops into people's eyes to cure opthalmia and rubbing iodine onto wounds, I would wish there was a medicine that would ease the ache of love inside me. I would put my hands on others' illnesses, often curing them, and wish that there were hands that could cure me of my inside pain which was greater than any piccaninny's stomach ache. An ache that was not eased by my hands that could heal almost anything else, dog's paws, women's labour pains, men's broken bones. My breaking heart was absolutely incurable.

Sometimes during the day there would be some job we did together, Dick and me. Mending a fence, coping with a violent cow, doling out the labourers' pay. Together we would dip the cattle. As Dick herded our cows into the ever narrowing fenced way to the dip I would be on the side, ready with a hooked stick, waiting to pull up the head of any animal that seemed about to swallow the poisoned water. Standing next to him as though I was his wife. Sometimes our bodies would touch. When our eyes met I would frantically try to read something more than affection and understanding in his.

But it was only in the evenings when I truly owned him. Then, with cicadas strumming from the garden, bats slashing the moonlight with their swooping shadows, wail of hyena, sudden distant roar of a lion, I would lie back in the wicker chair and listen to his voice, hardly hearing the things he said. Just revelling in the soft, deep, slow rhythm of his words.

'Don't you agree, Jewel?'

'What?'

'That we should plant gums in the lower

land, or make another cattle grid at the north gate. I wonder if we could get a little hospital started for our workers. The children are not getting any education. Have you ever thought of becoming a teacher, Jewel? Perhaps you could get a teacher's degree, then come back here and start a school for our children.'

This last one alerted me. This was the one that jerked me out of my feelings of anxiety. Suddenly there seemed to be a future for me, here at Dikkers. My heart began to pound with hope. I told him that I had always wanted to teach, which was not true at all. The idea had never crossed my mind before.

* * *

Dick provided me with a little schoolroom to teach the labourers' children.

In my spare time I still worked with Dick on the farm. Being near him calmed my craving somewhat. I could bear anything as long as I did not have to be away from him. He did not have to touch me, kiss me, hug me. He never held me. Perhaps even he realised that contact was dangerous.

* * *

The witch doctor's potions were working. Steadily Ann improved until at last she no longer lay, supine, on the sofa, but as long as Dick or I held her arm, she could walk a little way along with us. Then further. Then we hardly had to hold her at all.

And then she was walking on her own.

★   ★   ★

After that Ann came with Dick and me when we went on outings. Taking off in the jeep to see a pride of lions, exploring caves with ancient paintings, trips to the town where we went, the three of us to the bioscope, the races, to watch polo. To Miekles for dinner after. To the Honeyani Hotel for a weekend.

'What's the matter, Jewel? Why do you look so miserable? Cheer up, ducky. Life's marvellous.' Ann was bubbling with the happiness of being better.

Dick would reach across the table, take her hand, then mine. Look from one to the other of us. 'My lovely girls. Smile, darling Jewel. Look how wonderful everything is. Ann is better. We are, well, not quite rich but well enough off. We are together. Smile, my love.'

★   ★   ★

The three of us went on holiday to the Leopard's Rock Hotel in the Vumba. A hotel perched among mountains, steep drops, wild views, lakes, distance.

'Do try to enjoy yourself, ducky.' Ann was getting irritated with me.

There, balanced on a purple fall of mountain mist, Dick put his arms round me and held me. 'What is the matter? Can't you tell us, Jewel? We love you and we want you to be happy.'

I was silent. How could I possibly tell him? I stayed very still in his embrace, so as to keep his arms around me for as long as possible.

Back home I began to be overwhelmed with bouts of silent fury, to stalk the bungalow, my face scowled into a rictus of anger, slamming doors, shouting when they spoke to me. Throwing things, books, cushions, even once a vase of flowers, wildly across the room.

Dick stopped asking, 'What's the matter, Jewel?'

And no longer could my rages be eased by Anne's caress. She was the reason for them. She only tried once to draw me in her arms and comfort me. My rejection was so violent that she never tried again.

They let me be when the angers came. I shut myself into my own room and shouted, threw, punched the walls, beat my head against the bed. Wept. Longed for things that could never happen.

★ ★ ★

The three of us were walking through our orange grove, Ann's eyes sparkling with happiness. Dick's arm linked in hers. Me coming along behind, my face sulky.

Ann reached up and picked an orange. Turning, she handed it to me.

'There, Jewel, for you,' she said. 'See. I can pick my own oranges now. I don't need help any more.' She looked like a child, clear eyes, rosy cheeks, fine blonde hair fluffing in the perfumed breeze.

★ ★ ★

She had lain, helpless, unable to move her legs for three years and because of the oils, smoke, and incantation of an African witch doctor, Ann, who had been written off as hopeless by Western medicine, was cured.

★ ★ ★

There were flowers as well as fruit on the orange trees. That's how they grow. If ever I smell the perfume of orange flowers now and the stinging smell of orange skin warmed by the sun, a sadness darkens me. The sun was shining, sharp and clear as Ann's laughing eyes, at the very moment that the light in my life was dimming.

* * *

I took the warm fruit from her hand without looking at her. The smell of orange flowers was everywhere. That is how I remember the moment. The sad moment. The wonderful moment. Saturated in orange flower-perfumed breeze.

'I am having a baby, Jewel.' That is when she said it.

'Ann is pregnant.' Dick's face was alight with the marvellousness of it.

* * *

I remember following them home slowly, knowing it was over. Wishing in an evil little corner of my soul that Ann had not been cured.

* * *

I got a job in Cape Town.

Spent lonely evenings trying not to think about Dick. Failing. Going through every single thing I could remember about him. Conjuring up in my mind his very presence. Ticking off, detail by detail, the way his ear had a little crinkle in it, the way his hair was fairer near his face. The way the tan had never penetrated the radiating laughter lines round his eyes. The way his voice was rich, and dark, and deep.

I would re-invent my life, pretend Dick and I had made love together, floating Ann away for a while and being Dick's wife instead. Floating away the baby that had destroyed everything.

Dick was a blister in my heart, killing me, yet inescapable. He appeared suddenly, without warning, at my flat in Cape Town.

'I will pour you a drink,' I said. My hands were shaking as I unscrewed the gin. 'How are you? How is everything. How is Dikkers?' I could not bear to ask him anything about the baby. About Ann.

After we had both sat down and he had taken the drink from my hands, he said, 'Why do you never come home these days?' I could not speak. I could not look at him.

Then suddenly he asked, 'Are you in love with me, Jewel?' He spoke calmly, throwing out the sentence as though he was making a comment on the baccy crop. 'I have been thinking about it.'

It came so suddenly that I felt as though I had been biffed. Winded. It took me a moment or two to get my breath back, during which he waited in silence.

'Yes,' I said at last. The word came out like a little burst of breathing. 'Yes. Yes. Oh, yes.'

'I see,' He said. He was thoughtful for a while, then rising he came over to me. Took hold of my hands and gently drew me into his arms. There he held me tightly to his body, so that I could feel the hammering of his heart inside his chest. He pressed me to himself as though he could feel the pain inside me and was using his own body to heal me. As though his own healthy warmth could warm the icy cold that lodged inside me.

Outside, through the open window there was an orange moon, huge and hot, streaming light on us.

He did not kiss me. There was no passion in his hug, only love. I felt ravaged with desire, my whole being screaming for more. I was desperate with thirst. A thirst that only Dick could quench, but not like this. Not with the embrace of a friend.

Something seemed to burst inside me. Tears came gushing out. The firm substance of myself began frothing over, like a shaken bottle of lemon pop. I was shivering. I had hungered too long. I had controlled too much. The pent-up passion that I had kept so frantically locked inside me spilled out and went galloping wildly like a wild horse, freed.

'Make love to me,' I said. Grabbing him around his neck I wept, implored. Pressing my wet face into his, clutching at his body as though I was drowning and he might save me, I sobbed, 'I beg you, Dick, make love to me.'

He stroked my hair, he kissed me softly on my forehead, on my cheeks, he murmured loving things, there there darling. It will be all right, you will see.

I felt like a sleeping person who is thirsty and dreams of drinking water.

'Puppy love,' Dick whispered, 'A crush. You'll get over it. You'll meet some nice young man.'

I pushed him away hard. 'Go. Get out,' I said. 'Go away. Never come back. I hate you.'

He backed out, shocked, dismayed.

'Go, go, go,' I yelled.

★   ★   ★

I rang a month later and told him I had a boyfriend.

Dick's happy relieved laugh came down the phone, rang in my ears like misery. 'I am so glad. I was worried about you.'

* ★ ★

I would have to fight hard to stop my voice shaking when I described my fantasy lover after that. I had to be careful not to make him sound like Dick.

My invented lover took on a reality. I talked about him, quoting him, 'Piet says the only thing that can execute your soul is hypocrisy.'

'He sounds like a frightfully worthy fellow,' Dick said, laughing. 'When are we going to meet him?'

I hated Piet. I would have killed him if he'd been real.

'Piet and I are going to Canada. We are going to get married.'

I was lying when I said it, but against my will, years later my lie became a truth.

I was imprisoned twice because of my activities with the ANC. After I was released the second time, I went on working for the cause from various hiding places, but the police were catching up with me and not only did I begin to be a danger to the people who were helping me but I knew that if I was caught this time, I would be executed. In the end I was forced to flee South Africa. Once again everything I loved was taken from me, even my beloved country.

*   *   *

I never saw Ann's baby, though I heard he was a boy and remembered that they had called him Harry.

*   *   *

At least, thinks Julia, I have made it all right for Kitty in a way that it will never be for me. She will be Matthew's wife and the mother of his children because of me. After Julia knows that Matthew is free she feels that whatever happens next will seem more bearable.

On Julia's second day, someone is thrust into the room. Julia, as ordered, is wearing her blindfold and only knows this newcomer is a girl because she is weeping.

Her name is Laila, she whispers later that day. They are not permitted to speak aloud, but must talk in whispers. Julia bears an aching bruise on the side of her shoulder, marking the moment she forgot this. They share a sleeping mat on the floor and because they only have a single blanket, cotton, during the cold part of that night Julia holds the shivering girl close to her own body.

'My father is a government minister,' she says. 'So they have demanded an enormous ransom for me.'

Julia and Laila are imprisoned together for fourteen weeks. They invent whispered futures, punting together on the Thames, skiing together on the Alps, singing in a choir. Neither has ever punted, skiied, or sung. They invent husbands and children, they invent jokes, tell each other stories, sing songs. They invent recipes, design meals, compete for the most delicious dishes as they eat the sour, raw bread and occasional banana. Sometimes one or another becomes ill and seems about to die and then it is as though the world is ending. In those chained months in the Waswar dark Laila and Julia are each other's worlds.

Laila is an artist and describes to Julia the details of her paintings, women in action, dancing, fighting, running, self portraits of herself painting pictures.

Sometimes they hear the screams and pleadings coming through the walls and then they look into each other's eyes and silently pray that at least each other will be spared.

'One day, if my father does not find the money soon, they will come for me,' Laila tells Julia. 'One day they will take me out and rape me. Then they will kill me.' She tries to smile when she tells Julia this, but Julia feels Laila's body shaking. 'Not you, because you are a foreigner. They will not rape you.'

Laila's father had so far not managed to get

together the money demanded by the kidnappers. Perhaps he never would. There had been other girls before, whose fathers or husbands had failed to find the money. They had all been raped, tortured, then put to death.

Julia puts her arms round Laila, holds her tightly and knows there cannot be a god, not Christian, not Muslim, not any other kind, for if there was he would not allow a person like Laila, young and beautiful, clever and brave, to be locked up in the dark and facing a possible horrible death.

28

It is three months since Matthew has been set free and Julia imprisoned.

★ ★ ★

Matthew kisses Kitty, after he hits her.

He has never struck her before, and although the blow was light and did not hurt, the shock has pained her.

'Why did you do it?' she keeps asking.

'It's nothing,' says Matthew. 'Stop going on about it. Why don't you do something about getting this place in order instead of moaning. The baby. That dog. The house looking so messy. Chaos everywhere.'

His voice ends on a querulous note that makes Kitty suddenly sorry for him. 'I'll get the dump perked up, love, I promise. I'll keep the brat quiet.'

He smiles, bright again. 'I'll work on that vegetable garden today. It'll be nice to have home-grown vegetables.'

'Do. Julia worked so hard on it.'

Matthew presses his lips together, his sudden relaxed mood clouded.

Kitty's heart misses a beat. 'What the fuck did I say?'

'I just wish you would stop talking about this Julia person all the time.'

Kitty puts her arms round him and this time instead of wincing away he stays in her embrace. 'I won't ever mention her again, you jealous old bastard,' she says cuddling him. 'But can't you tell me why?'

'She's interfering in our lives,' he says vaguely.

Kitty feels she understands. 'It's only us from now on.' She visualises her and Matthew sitting on the lawn, the baby playing on a rug on the grass. She remembers how often she has been like this with Julia and has wished it was Matthew instead. Now it is.

★   ★   ★

Matthew hoes, digs, rakes wildly, as though by working with every last fibre of his strength he can drive away the memory of the past. Kitty longs to ask him to come in and rest but she says nothing, only watches and feels anxious. He brings out his gun and shoots the pigeons that are eating the cabbages.

Rob keeps trying to follow Matt, creeping along after him, not a devoted gun dog but a suspicious watchdog keeping an eye on the enemy.

'Can't you keep the bloody creature inside?' demands Matt. 'The pigeons take off the moment they catch sight of him.'

Rob comes into the kitchen yelping and limping. He is spattered with shot, blood daubs several parts of his yellow bristly fur. He hops on three legs, the fourth held up, bleeding. A part of his ear has been shot away.

'That'll teach the bastard,' Matt shouts from the vegetable garden and lets go another burst of shot into the sky at a handful of flustered pigeons trying to settle in the waste land trees.

★   ★   ★

That night Matthew makes love to Kitty for the first time since his release.

Mattie sleeps in her cradle as Kitty and Matthew re-explore each other's bodies. Tomorrow, she thinks, he might even start loving the baby and liking the dog.

Next day, as though the lovemaking has changed everything, Matt is on the phone, getting back in touch with his clients.

He grins joyfully, the old Matthew back, as he puts the phone down. 'They all remember me. They have all been waiting for me to start work again. You would be amazed at how nice they were about me being set free.'

'I should hope so,' she laughs.

★ ★ ★

The phone rings while Kitty is bathing Mattie.

'I'll answer it,' Matthew said. He was back again to his old energetic self. 'It's probably a client.' He runs downstairs eagerly.

Kitty massages soap into Mattie's head, soothes her fingers into the baby's tender skin and feels that happiness is starting properly at last.

Matthew's footsteps, as he comes back up, are slow and heavy. Kitty's heart contracts a little again, and some of the happiness ebbs.

He stands in the bathroom doorway. She is holding the baby, fresh smelling and delicious from her bath wrapped in a soft white towel.

Matthew's face is dark and angry. 'It is her,' he says.

'Who?' asks Kitty, pressing her child against her body and starting to shiver.

He reaches out and strikes Kitty across her face, cracking it with the side of his hand, the kind of blow that strong men use to break bricks.

It breaks Kitty's eyebrow in a rush of blood. Staggering, keeping her grip on Mattie, Kitty tries to move out of his way, frightened that the next blow might land on the baby's soft skull. Clutching Mattie she stares at Matt, shaken with the shock, while the blood runs trickling down her face.

'Don't look at me like that,' he says. 'It's nothing. Only a little cut.' Taking the end of the baby's towel he dabs at the bleeding, while Kitty tries not to shriek with pain, while she tries to understand what has happened.

'There, get that child into bed,' he says. 'And I'll make you a cup of tea.'

Holding Mattie tight against her body she watches him go. Her heart is pounding hard against her ribs. Somehow she seems to need a huge amount of effort to get Mattie into her cot, as though the baby has become heavy as lead in a moment.

He comes back after a while, carrying a daintily arranged tray. He is smiling, calm, looks cheery, as though Kitty's brow is not swelling and gouting blood from the blow he has just delivered.

'My God, Matt, that was some fucking blow,' says Kitty as she shakily starts to drink. Her head still rings with the thunder of it.

'Snap out of it, Kitty,' he commands. 'For God's sake woman, a little clip on the head and such a fuss. I suffered a hundred times worse than that when they . . . in my . . . I suppose I did hit a bit harder than I meant to. I just don't know how strong I am, these days.' He pauses thoughtfully, then goes on, 'All the time I was there I practised. I needed to keep up my courage. And my strength,' he says. 'I worked out all day long in a cell two foot by three. I chipped bricks from the wall with my bare fists.'

Kitty sips her tea. 'It's fucking weird that you worked so hard to learn how to hit the person who loves you most.' She pauses, but needs to know. Takes the risk. Asks, 'Was it Julia? Is she free?'

His fist clenches again and she is afraid he's about to hit her once more. But he only shrugs, scowls, says, 'Seems like it. Though was she ever imprisoned?'

'She's free? She's out?' Kitty tries not to let Matt see her happiness.

'She wants to come and see us tomorrow.'

'Fabulous,' cries Kitty. 'What time? I'll make some of those squashy buns. I used to stick two together with chocolate cream and call them bums. It made her laugh.'

Matthew shudders fastidiously, then examines Kitty's face. 'I've made a bit of a mess of you. You can't let her see you like that.'

'Oh, I'll tell her that I bumped into the

cupboard door,' Kitty says cheerily. Suddenly everything is getting all right again. 'I was always leaving them open and she kept banging into them and blaming me.'

'I don't want you to see her.' He speaks flatly.

'She's my mate,' Kitty protests. Then, seeing the dark shadow start to fall across his face, says quickly, 'All right, my presh.' After all Matthew was more important to her than any friend.

★　★　★

She feels regretful, all the same, next day, as she pushes Mattie in her buggy, Rob on his lead, across the fields. Julia must be wondering, she thinks, why Kitty isn't there to celebrate. Must think Kitty's absence churlish and unfriendly. Wonders what excuse Matt will think up for her not being there when Julia comes.

She feels terribly tired and the injury on her eye is throbbing as she shoves the pram over the bouncy grass.

She stays out as long as possible but in the end can bear it no longer and sets off back for home. As she comes into the back door she knows she is too early, for she can hear Julia's voice from the sitting room.

Rob pricks his ears in excitement at the sound. He has a passion for Julia. Kitty clasps her hand round his muzzle to stop him barking and pulls off Mattie's outdoor things with her free hand.

Julia is leaving, Kitty can hear her saying, 'Goodbye.'

She runs upstairs with Mattie and as she watches Julia go, Matthew comes in.

Kitty turns to him, laughing. 'I hope you told her you were bloody grateful for what she did for you.' Then her laughter fades as the dark shadow begins to creep over his expression.

He strides across the room.

She manages to get the baby down onto the bed and to safety before he reaches her, before the blow strikes, crashing into her breast, knocking the breath out of her, sending her flying across the room.

'I told you to keep out of the bloody way till she was gone,' he roars.

She struggles desperately to her feet, shaking all over. A new hot pain is searing through her body.

That night he wakes at midnight, suddenly, jerking up, grabs Kitty, pulls her thighs apart and begins sex, in silence. It feels like rape and Kitty, with a sudden anger, a surge of humiliation, tries to thrust him away, but holding her by her thigh, he hits her. He starts to hammer into the parts of her that are hurt already, he presses his fingers into her throat till she feels like choking. On and on, beating at her naked body, pulverising her. He will kill her if he goes on like this. She tries not to make a sound but a scream bursts out all the same. It wakes the baby.

Matthew gets to the cot first and grabs Mattie up. His movements are slow and calculated. He is not acting in red hot rage now.

'You bugger, don't you fucking dare.' Kitty rushes to intervene her body between her child and him.

He is too fast and strong for her. He swings the baby through the air. Mattie, gripped by his hands, is silenced instantly with shock and breathlessness. Kitty can hear her take in air gulps chokily, panicky.

He is going to crack Mattie against the wall. Thwack her, head-first, into the bricks.

Kitty leaps, snatches, catches his fists. Mattie lets out a great, inward, gulping shriek.

From below, on his cushion under the kitchen dresser, Rob guesses and howls in his desperation.

Mattie's face is growing blue.

Matt fells Kitty, sending her reeling across

the room, then swings the baby at the wall.

In a single wild movement Kitty manages to throw herself onto the bed and grab the child just a moment before her tiny body hits the bricks.

The silence that follows is short, shocked, panting.

Matt turns away as though suddenly disassociated from the situation. As though he has grown bored.

'She's your own fucking kid, Matt. Why are you bloody trying to kill your own kid?'

'I know she is not mine because she has got red hair and also because you were not pregnant when I left. When I find out who the father is I shall kill him.'

29

When Julia understands that it is only she who is to be released, she tries to force her way back into the cell room that she and Laila had shared all these weeks.

'Keep me and let her go,' she begs. But the silent female guard, holding Julia's roped arms against her back so she cannot turn and see her captor's face, has tied the hated blindfold tightly round Julia's eyes and shoves her out onto the road and into some kind of vehicle.

Inside the car Julia shouts to her unseen captors, 'She is young and my life is finished,' and, 'Sir Jeremy, who is my close relation, will pay you all over again to set me free,' until someone strikes her mouth, making her lips swell and words impossible. As the car drives away, Julia thinks she can hear Laila crying.

★ ★ ★

They dump her, still tied and blindfolded, after about an hour of driving and after she has been untied by a passing motorist and taken to the nearest British Consul, she phones Sir Jeremy Burton.

'He is away on business.'

'When will he be back?'

'End of the week, maybe. Though you can never tell with him.'

With sinking heart Julia puts down the receiver. She cannot bear to think of Laila alone in the dark for another week, or maybe more. The only other hope is Kitty's husband, Matthew, who would be sure to help, for after all it was she, Julia who had secured his freedom. By now he had become famous and a hero. Julia has no doubt that he will help Laila, and will surely agree to campaign on her behalf. She would go to Waste Land Cottage and tell Kitty how the land was really hers but that someone called Sir Jeremy Burton was claiming it, at the same time she would get Kitty's husband to do something about Laila. Perhaps some kind of bargain would be possible. Julia would protect Kitty and Matthew from Sir Jeremy in exchange for Matthew saving Laila.

⋆   ⋆   ⋆

The moment she gets back to England, she sends a message saying she is coming. All the way to Waste Land Cottage, as the bus trundles through the countryside, she keeps saying to herself, over and over, 'It's all right, Laila. I am going to get help for you. You won't be there much longer.' As the bus approaches the village, Julia becomes filled with excitement at the thought of seeing Mattie again. It is several months since she had seen the little girl, and she might even be talking by now. Perhaps she was old enough to say 'Aunty Julia.'

The cottage door is open and Julia's first surprise is that no Rob comes rushing out to greet her. She goes inside, calling out but no one answers. The house seems empty though there are chaotic signs of Kitty and Mattie everywhere, thrown toys, dirty crockery, half-eaten food, shed clothes. After calling again and still getting no answer she goes through and into the garden where she finds a man prowling among the vegetables with a shotgun. Matthew. Julia knows him at once though he looks older than the TV pictures Julia had seen of him when he was held hostage. There is something weak about his mouth, a child's mouth, petulant. He twists his lips now, in a little grimace that looked like part distaste, part shyness. Round his chin and mouth the skin is paler than the rest of his face as though he had recently removed a beard. There are dark stains under the loose skin of his eyes as though he suffers from insomnia.

There is no sign of Kitty or Mattie.

Julia had expected Kitty to be waiting for her, thrilled to see her back, grateful for all Julia had done to secure the release of her husband and feels amazed and also shocked when Matthew tells her that Kitty had gone out with the baby and might not be home for a long time.

'I'm getting some weeding done,' Matthew says. 'Kitty's let the place turn into a jungle.'

Perhaps he does not know that Julia has taken his place as a hostage. That she offered herself to save him. That must be why he is not mentioning it, is not thanking her. Or maybe he does not want to be reminded of his terrible experiences in Waswar. She only says, 'The vegetables look well tended.' The cabbages were plump and bluish-bloomed. Radishes burst up like scarlet bosoms. Leeks were neatly clasped in paper. 'I planted them, you know' she adds.

'Really?' She thinks she hears contempt in his tone.

He leads her into the kitchen. 'Things are a bit upside down at the moment.'

The kitchen is a mess, dirty dishes stacked, the cooker greasy.

Sitting down at the kitchen table Julia asks,

trying to keep her feelings out of her tone, 'Where are Kitty and the baby then? With her granny?'

Matthew does not answer her question and only says, 'There is something you want to discuss?' He seems hostile, as though he feels resentful, rather than grateful.

She has been going to beg him to help Laila. But now, instead, stabbed by anger at his rude ingratitude and filled with a desire for revenge, she says angrily, 'I own the land your cottage is built on.' It had not been meant to come out like that. As soon as she has spoken she regrets the words.

He laughs. 'Come on,' he says. He thinks she is joking. She feels red rage flood her cheeks as she opens her bag and pulling out papers, shows him the title deeds that had been buried in her mother's box.

'Proof enough for you,' she asks savagely.

He studies them carefully then looking up, raises his eyebrows. 'What do you want me to do about it?'

Julia says, 'I have a brother.'

'So this is partly his, then.' Matthew makes an expansive gesture round his home, then laughs as though at a joke.

'It is all his. I want it for him. I have been searching for him for years, but all the time have been using the wrong surname. Now I know what we were really called, so it should not be very long before I track him down.'

'You want us to leave?' asks Matthew.

Julia shrugs. 'It seems that a Sir Jeremy Burton has registered it in his name and plans to build on it. As it belongs to my brother and me, I may be able to prevent that.' Julia is feeling increasingly annoyed. The man's attitude was not what she had expected. 'But I need your support.'

'Why should we support you if you are going to turn us out?' Matthew asks.

She wants to say, 'You owe me a favour, surely?' She wants to tell him about Laila, but the hard look in his eyes deters her. She fears that, after all, anything he did might make things worse for the girl. Instead she says, 'Would you want to stay after Sir Jeremy Burton's flats are there? If I own it there will be no building and there may be some way for you to stay on.' This idea has only just come to her. She, living on the waste land too, watching Mattie grow up.

There comes the sound of the back door opening. Julia thinks she hears the squeak of pram wheels, the muffled voice of Rob trying to bark.

'Sounds as though Kitty's back,' she says.

Matthew shakes his head. 'I told you. She's away.'

There comes another muffled bark and then the sound of a baby burbling. Julia looks at Matthew questioningly.

Nodding his head in the direction of the scullery, he says, 'I left the radio on.'

He rises, in a sudden hurry for her to leave. 'I shall be in touch with my lawyer,' he says. 'I fear you will not get very far with that.' He gestures towards the ancient crumpled title deeds. 'I would suggest it would need a good deal more proof than that.'

Julia had thought that this conversation would never take place. She had thought the Waswaris would keep her for a long time, years may be. Perhaps she would have died in Waswar. She had thought that decisions for her future had been taken out of her hands.

* * *

She is just leaving when she remembers the present she had brought for Mattie.

'What is it?' asks Matt, his tone suspicious as he takes the parcel.

'A red coat.' She had had to search the shops for ages before she found one that she thought must be similar to her own that the nuns took from her before she left for Africa all those years ago.

309

All that day Kitty tries to keep out of Matthew's way. She pushes the baby in her buggy round and round the village, with Rob on his lead and tries to pluck up courage to go home. When she passes the village hall she sees that it is the evening of the Danaveda class. She feels cold and tired. She has not been back since Matt came home, but now, on an impulse, she goes in.

Two blue rinsed ladies from Blenheim Terrace are in the hall. They beam large-toothed smiles on Kitty.

'That's a nasty bruise you've got on your eye,' says one. 'Has your husband been beating you?' She and her friend laugh heartily at the joke. Lovely Matthew Wing, national hero, beating his wife.

'Yes,' says Kitty.

The pair laugh louder.

Today Harry Dikker is the only teacher. Mr Mitra is unwell, apparently.

★ ★ ★

Leaving the sleeping Mattie in her buggy and tying Rob to a bench, Kitty joins the class. Avoiding movements that hurt her ribs, she tries to follow the postures as best she can.

310

She is feeling safe for the first time for ages, feeling Mattie is safe too.

Harry Dikker is showing them the total self defence posture when there comes a sudden crashing of the door.

The class turns to look. Rob rises stiffly and the hair on his shoulders begins to bristle.

Matthew stands in the doorway.

'Ah, there you are, Kitty,' he says. His voice is calm. Rob tenses up and shows his teeth. Mattie wakes with a jerk and lets out a little scream.

'I'm so sorry for interrupting,' Matthew says to Harry Dikker. ' I've been looking for them everywhere. I was getting worried.' And to Kitty, 'Come along, my queen.' He strides across the room and seizes the buggy handles. 'Come on, Kitty, love. You are holding these good people up.'

He seems the very picture of fatherly and husbandly concern.

Untying Rob's lead and chivvying the reluctant dog along, Kitty catches up with Matthew as they reach the swing doors.

★　★　★

Out of the light of the street Kitty, knowing what is coming tries to duck away, but she cannot avoid him without abandoning Mattie.

'You lied to me. You told me your teacher was an old Indian man. Now I know who you have been fucking while I was held hostage, dirty bitch.' He strikes Kitty in her throat. Still clutching the pram handles she staggers, sees sparks, can hardly breathe, but dares not make a sound. She fights back the choking, holds in the coughing, in case anyone hears. She must let him hit her if she is to protect Mattie.

★ ★ ★

At the first light of dawn, while Matt is still asleep, Kitty creeps out of bed.

Taking up Mattie she tiptoes into the kitchen. She does not dare wait to change either of them out of their night clothes, only pulling coats over the top of them. The red coat that Julia gave Mattie fits the baby perfectly.

Rob rises stiffly from his cushion. He has become a nervous dog by now. She silently signals to him. As though he understands the urgency of the situation he follows her without a sound.

★ ★ ★

Gran opens the door on Kitty's third ring. 'I was just making a yam stew for lunch,' she says. 'There's plenty. There's cooked mutton for the dog as well.'

Kitty is not hungry, but they have had no breakfast and the food has the taste of home and safety.

On the floor at Kitty's feet Rob gobbles up the bowl of mutton Gran has given him.

'You didn't get nits, then?' says Kitty's gran.

'No.' Kitty shakes her head.

Kitty's gran runs her fingers through Mattie's mop of bright hair and without looking up says, 'A man tried to beat me once and I strangled the bastard.'

'I bumped into the cupboard door,' says Kitty.

Gran holds up her enormous hand. It is heavy with rings, great knobbled stones, fractured and glittering. Rings are her passion.

'Of course you are not the woman that I was. You've got too much namby pamby white blood in you.'

★   ★   ★

Kitty is planning to phone the Citizen's Advice Bureau and ask them how to find a woman's refuge when there comes a footstep on the concrete stair.

Rob shrinks and snarls.

'I thought I would find you here, Kitty.' Matthew is here. Smiling, coming towards Kitty, arms outstretched. 'I was worried,' he says.

'Yes, you take her home, and look after her better,' says Gran. 'I don't like to see her in such a way. She's bruises all over.'

'I don't either,' smiles Matthew. 'Just going off without a word, after you had that nasty fall. I've made an appointment with a psychiatrist. He's going to see you tomorrow.' To Gran he says, 'She's had bad nerves since the baby. Coming on top of me being imprisoned. It's got to her. She's been doing funny things.'

★   ★   ★

Kitty, lost already, clinging to Rob's lead, pulling her buggy, struggles down the stairs like someone drowning.

30

Julia rings Sir Jeremy's office every day, but he is still not back, and they still cannot say when he will come. She can't put Laila, alone there now, out of her mind.

While she is waiting she tries, once more, to see Mattie. The chubby baby with the scarlet cheeks and the cloud of red hair. Julia's baby. Mattie, the first person of her own since she had lost Jem. Swallowing her pride, she rings Waste Land Cottage again, but there is no answer. Perhaps they are at Gran's. She has the number from the day she and Kitty spent in London together.

Gran answers just as Julia is preparing to put down the phone, gasping and groaning as she says, 'What do you want?' She sounds like someone who has run up three flights of stairs to answer the call, not taken four paces across a tiny room.

'It's me. Julia. Kitty's friend,' she says.

'Did you ever see an elephant sitting on a marble?' chortles Gran. 'If you can get it to sit, you can pull it along by a little bit of string. I told Kitty.' Her voice is so loud that Julia's ear-drums ache. 'Of course persuading the elephant to sit on the marble is the difficult part.'

'Is she with you now?' Julia asks.

'She and that dog ate all the stew. But don't you worry. I'll be quite buggering happy making do on biscuits.'

'What time did they leave?' asks Julia, feeling increasingly deflated.

'When that husband came to fetch her I told him, you look after her better in the future,' roars Gran.

'What was wrong with her?'

'She said she bumped into a cupboard door. Looked more like bumped by an elephant to me. Big eye. Sore bruising. No fucking nits though. I didn't have to bloody shave her.'

★ ★ ★

Matthew is going at eighty and has one finger on the steering wheel.

'You drive like that we'll have a fucking crash,' says Kitty.

Perhaps a car crash in which she and Matthew are killed will be the best. In fact, she thinks, if it wasn't for Mattie and Rob, she would have been tempted to snatch the steering wheel and let the car plunge into the barrier.

But she knows, for them, she must try to stay alive.

'Let's start again. Start all over again,' he says.

'Definitely we will start all over again.'

'This other man's child. You can get your grandmother to take her. Bring her up. Or perhaps you could get her adopted. Find some good family. There are always people wanting to adopt healthy white children. And they will not know, you know, about her background, her great-grandparents.'

'All right, Matt,' says Kitty, bowing her head submissively.

'And the dog, Kitty. He must go. When he is gone everything will be all right. I will be able to forgive you then. You do understand, don't you?'

Kitty nods. 'I understand perfectly.'

'We will be like newly married people.' He speaks dreamily. 'I have been very sad about it all. Your betrayal of me. But soon it will be behind us and we will be able to pretend it never happened.' He is silent for a while then says, 'You should be grateful to me, Kitty. For isn't this your night for your Danaveda class? Tuesday? You would have missed it if I had not come to fetch you.'

For some reason Matt's words make Kitty shiver.

When they reach home a man is on the waste land, hacking brambles.

'What the hell are you doing?' Matthew shouts, leaping from the car.

'They're putting flats up, mate. No one told you?' says the man.

'No one's putting any bloody flats up in this place,' says Matthew with an icy fury.

The man shrugs. 'I'm only doing what I've been told.'

'Bugger off,' yells Matthew.

The man shrugs again as though confronting a loony and goes on hacking at the elders.

Matthew launches himself upon the man, knocking him over and sending him flying, face first, into the nettles.

The man emerges raging and brandishes his sickle. 'I'll have the police on you, mate. You just wait,' he says and goes shambling off, shaking grasses out of his hair.

★ ★ ★

Something about her conversation with Kitty's gran starts worrying Julia. Then she thinks back to the conversation on the phone with Kitty. That too does not seem right. Alarm begins to grow in her. Kitty, who is not scared of anything except ghosts, had sounded afraid. That is what Julia realises.

She decides to try ringing Waste Land Cottage again. Kitty and Matthew should have reached home by now.

Kitty answers. 'Julia. Where are you? Can you come . . . ' Then the phone seems to be seized from her and Matthew's voice takes over.

'We need a bit of peace. To be left in peace. That is what we ask.' He is panting as though he has been running. The receiver is slammed down before Julia can say anything.

★ ★ ★

The previous year a doctor has given Kitty sleeping pills and now Kitty crushes some into Mattie's milk then waits till the child has fallen into a deep drugged sleep. At last she gets up softly and goes out locking the bedroom door behind her, the baby safe for the moment though she must think of some more permanent way of protecting Mattie.

'I'm taking the dog to Tim's this evening,' says Matthew when she gets downstairs.

'The vet's? What for? Rob's not sick.'

'He's going to put the creature to sleep. I described how the dog behaves and Tim agrees that such a dog is sure to be dangerous with children.'

Keep calm, keep calm, Kitty tells herself. Her heart is beating fast. She knows better than to argue by now, though.

'The bugger's ever so scared of the vet,' she says. 'He went like a fucking wild thing when I took him for his boosters. The vet couldn't hardly hold him down.'

Keep calm, keep calm. To Matthew she adds, 'You won't get Rob into the building, probably, the way he hates you.'

Matthew glares at Rob. Rob snarls back. Matthew says, his voice grim, 'I'll get him in. Don't worry.'

'You'll have to drag him every fucking inch, him growling, those old cows in Blenheim Terrace telling each other how fucking useless you are with dogs.' She pauses, then says carefully, 'Couldn't we do it here?'

He frowns and looks at her suspiciously. 'It costs more for a vet to visit.'

'Matt, you get the stuff and the needles and things and we'll stick it in. You gave him injections when he was a puppy so you know how. And Tim's your friend. He'll let you do it.'

'I gave injections to a pedigree spaniel puppy that you got rid of.' Matthew's fury was starting to mount again. 'I'm going to

320

take this bloody mongrel and have it done away with.' He grasps Rob's collar. The dog squirms out with a yelp of anger mixed with fear, scuttles across the room and cringes under the dresser.

'Get him out,' Matthew commands Kitty.

Kitty makes a feeble effort to pull Rob out, that is only half play-acting. The pain in her arms and chest are, in fact, making it almost impossible for her to use any strength. Matthew stands behind her shouting, 'Go on. You aren't even trying.'

She stands up after a while. 'Let it be done here,' she begs. 'Me holding him. I'll get the clothes line round him then you can pull him out. It'll be easier like that, I swear.'

Matthew looks from her to the dog, then back to Kitty. He shrugs. 'OK,' he says at last. He is, Kitty thinks, more persuaded by the prospect of the shame of having to drag the unwilling dog through the village. 'I'll go and ask Tim.'

Matthew leaves hurriedly, as though he can hardly wait for the thing to be over and the dog out of their lives.

★   ★   ★

Matthew is back in half an hour. 'We'll have to put sticky tape round his mouth. I don't want him biting me.'

'I'll do it,' says Kitty. She winds Sellotape round the dog's muzzle while he stares into her eyes with an expression of bewildered horror.

'Do you think we should tie his legs too?' says Matthew.

'Not necessary. The clothes line will hold him tight,' says Kitty.

She gets her arms round Rob, holds him, whispers into his ear, 'There, my love, there my soldier. Don't be afraid. It won't hurt.'

Matthew fills the syringe and taking hold of Rob's thigh prepares to plunge it in.

Rob shrinks, snarls and somehow gets loose.

'For God's sake, Kitty,' Matthew yells. 'You've let the bastard go. I said we should have tied his legs.' He and Kitty chase Rob round and round the kitchen, Rob making muffled growls through the Sellotape and skidding this way and that among the kitchen chairs and table legs.

Matthew makes a grab, gets the dog by the leg and manages to pull him down. 'Now hold him properly this time while I give the injection,' says Matt.

'He's too strong for me,' says Kitty. 'You hold him and I'll do it.'

'You've never given anything an injection in

your life,' says Matthew.

'I have,' says Kitty. 'I squirt cream into the éclairs with a thing like a bloody great hypodermic syringe. It's only a matter of sticking the needle in.' Kitty, who has never been the least bit of good with a needle. Kitty who could not even darn her own clothes.

Matthew shrugs. 'If you really think you can do it, let's give it a go. You have to bang it really hard, though. Skin is much tougher than it looks.'

Handing the hypodermic to Kitty he gets his arms round Rob's struggling body, hauls the heavy animal to the floor and throws himself on top of it. 'Right. Now. I've got him. Quick. He's as strong as an ox.'

With a great stab, as though thrusting a dagger, Kitty plunges the needle into Matthew's arm and presses the plunger.

31

For ages after her visit to Waste Land Cottage, the idea keeps coming back to Julia that there is something wrong. Matthew's behaviour was so odd, and she felt sure, in spite of what he said, that Kitty and the baby had come into the scullery. In the end the worry is so insistent that she decides just to turn up without warning. And maybe this time she would manage to see the baby. She did so long to see Mattie again who must, she thinks, be walking by now. Maybe she will be wearing the red coat when Julia arrives.

As she approaches the cottage the birds are singing and a small breeze is ruffling the trees and the limpid water of the river. Now she is here she wishes she had not come. By now Matthew will have told Kitty that Julia is claiming the property, will realise that Julia's friendship had never been true. That from the start she had planned to take her and Matt's house away. All the same she walks on along the road, towards the waste land.

Julia has to remind herself to ring the bell instead of merely walking in. Julia does not live here any more. She has to remember that.

This is Matthew's house now. After she has rung the front door bell, as she stands waiting, Rob rushes out and hurls a wild welcome at her.

There come footsteps and after a while the front door opens. Kitty stands there. There is a vast black bruise over her eye. Her body is crooked as though she is in pain, and her face is very pale as though she has had a shock. She stands, gazing at Julia, saying nothing, not asking her in.

Somewhere in the house Matthew must be listening, probably is about to call out, 'Who is it?' or even to order Kitty to send the visitor away.

'Still leaving the cupboard doors open, I see,' smiles Julia, looking at the eye. Kitty puts her hand up to the injury but her face stays grave.

'You weren't here when I came the other day.'

'Everything's all right,' says Kitty as though Julia has asked a question. 'I had the hell of a fucking problem, but it's all sorted out now.' She seems very calm. Almost cheerful, though, paradoxically, her eyes are red as though she has been crying. 'Come in.'

'It's a bad time. I can see,' says Julia.

'Come in,' repeats Kitty. This time her tone is urgent.

Rob laps Julia with barks and kisses as she comes into the hall.

'What's happened to his muzzle?' asks Julia. 'It's stuck over with something.'

'Sellotape,' says Kitty. She does not explain.

'I'd love to see Mattie,' says Julia. 'Is she asleep? Is that possible?'

'Wait here,' says Kitty. 'I'll go and see. I've locked the door, but she's safe now so I'll just go and get the key. Wait here,' she says again. She turns to go, lets out a groan and puts her hand against her side.

'Is there something wrong?'

Kitty shakes her head. 'Open fucking cupboard doors all over the place,' she says.

Julia follows her to the kitchen but at the door Kitty pushes her back, says sharply, urgently, 'No, don't come in. I'll get the key. You stay here.' She speaks with the desperation of someone hiding something. Comes out a moment later carry a key, and firmly shutting the kitchen door so Julia can't see in.

Julia understands. Matthew is in there. He does not like Julia. Kitty is protecting him from her. She shrugs and waits in the hall till Kitty comes down again.

Kitty returns. 'She's still asleep.' She takes Julia's arm and pulls her into the drawing room.

'Why did you lock Mattie in?' asks Julia, worried.

'To keep her safe,' says Kitty.

'From what?'

'From cupboard doors,' Kitty says.

'Is she walking yet?'

'Not Mattie any more. I call her Tilda now.'

'Tilda? Too muddly having a Matt and a Mattie, I suppose.'

'She loves the coat you gave her,' says Kitty. 'She wears it all the time, even when she's in bed.'

'When will she wake up?'

'She won't wake up for hours. I gave her sleeping pills.'

Julia looks bewildered. 'Sleeping pills? Why?'

'To keep her quiet,' says Kitty.

'Kitty, that can't be the right thing to do.' Suddenly all Julia's apprehensions wake again.

'I had to. But it's all right now,' laughs Kitty. Or is she crying? Julia sees a wave of shining tears suddenly well up in Kitty's eyes and the sound that seemed like laughter suddenly sounds like sobs.

Kitty goes into the kitchen and makes tea, and when she returns, Julia sees that her hands are trembling. They sit in silence.

Julia tries to think of something to say. 'It's

Tuesday. Don't you go to the Danaveda class this evening? Or have you stopped doing it?' she asks at last.

'I still go when I can but the teacher is a handsome young man these days, instead of old Mr Mitra. He's called Harry. He'll be going past the cottage soon on his way to the class. He used to drop in, have a cup of tea with us and we'd go to the hall together, but he stopped coming in because . . . ' Her voice tailed away and Julia saw the tears filling her eyes again. 'But things are all right again and I can invite him in this evening. If you wait till he comes I'll introduce him to you.'

'Is Matthew away then?'

Kitty stares at her for a long moment, then slowly nods her head.

'Well, perhaps it's a good moment to discuss something else while he's not here. I suppose Matthew told you that I have a claim to this piece of land.'

Kitty stares at her, as though trying to remember.

'He hasn't told you?' Julia feels surprised. 'I was hunting for the box my mother buried here with the title deeds to the land in it. That's what I was looking for.'

Kitty still says nothing, but goes on staring blankly.

'I am sorry, Kitty,' Julia says. 'I did not

want to deceive you. It just came out like that.'

'Oh, it doesn't matter.' Kitty waves her apology away, suddenly brisk, businesslike. 'I won't stay here anyway. I shall go back to London soon.'

'Does that mean you forgive me?'

'I don't understand all that.' Kitty makes a grimace. 'Anyone can have this fucking place. I'm done with it.'

'What about Matthew? I thought he loved it.'

'I've killed Matthew.' Kitty pauses, teapot poised, as tears start running down her cheeks, her spilling eyes fixed on Julia's face, waiting for a reaction.

Julia tries a smile, attempting to see the joke, but Kitty stares back at her, serious. 'You don't believe me, do you?'

Julia's mouth starts to dry with foreboding.

Kitty says, 'Come and see if you don't believe me.' She leads the way along the passage, Rob dancing in her wake. She flings the kitchen door open wide and says, 'There.' She points, gasps, lets out a little scream.

'What?' demands Julia. 'For goodness sake, Kitty.'

★　★　★

Julia looks out of the kitchen window and sees Matthew. He is standing among the trees at the foot of the waste land. He holds his shotgun. He leans against a tree, and looks groggy, as though he has been drinking.

Kitty is staring at Matthew, her face ashen.

★ ★ ★

Julia, shaking her head at her own silliness in coming all this way for nothing, leaves at last. Kitty, still staring to where Matthew stands, gun in hand, seems abstracted, hardly hears her.

She walks to the bus stop feeling annoyed. When she gets there, stands waiting. Then sees someone who makes her gasp, audibly, with shock. She thinks she sees Dick Dikker walking along the road towards the waste land. For a moment she is certain it is Dick, tall, long legged, thick light brown hair, an easy way of moving his arms.

But a moment later she knows it cannot be, for this man is far too young. She gives one last look, as the bus arrives, at the young man who is so like Dick. Even after she gets onto the bus she finds her heart is still beating extra fast at the extraordinary likeness.

★ ★ ★

Matt is a good shot, Kitty is telling herself, as fear creeps through her. Harry will be in range when he comes out from behind the trees and passes the foot of the waste land.

* * *

Julia travels back to London feeling regretful because she has gone through all this worry, made the journey for nothing and has not even seen Mattie. Giving the child sleeping pills! Only a little idiot like Kitty would dream of doing such a thing. And just to keep the baby quiet.

She looks back once, as the bus turns the last bend, and sees a JCB approaching the waste land. Sir Jeremy Burton going into action already. Julia becomes filled with a sense of desperate urgency. She must meet this Sir Jeremy and as well as getting help for Laila from him, stop his building activities before they go any further. She curses her lawyer, who clearly has not told Sir Jeremy of her, Julia's claim to the land.

* * *

Kitty, from the kitchen window of the cottage, sees the JCB approaching too. And hears it. The roar of its engine has already drowned out the sounds of bird song from the waste land, the hum of traffic from the motorway.

Kitty considers dialling 999 but what's the use? By the time anyone comes to help it will be too late. And even if they do manage to come in time, she does not think they will believe her when she tells the police that her hero husband is waiting with a shotgun to kill Harry Dikker. And that afterwards he will kill her and Mattie-Tilda.

Harry is fifty yards away now. Only one more group of tree shields him from Matt's gun.

The JCB has come onto the waste land.

Matt is concealed in the weed and rubbish-ridden centre, the place where no one plays, where people never go, the place from out of which disaster comes. The place they had said was haunted.

Kitty opens the back door softly and steps out onto the waste land.

He turns. Sees her. Stares, his jaw tight. Keeps his gun trained on Harry. He will turn it on Kitty later. He has plenty of time, and now the roar of the JCB will hide the sound of gunshot.

Kitty shuts her eyes and carefully following Mr Mitra's instructions, makes her mind blank and powerful. Offers herself to infinity and the Absolute until the universe fills her and she is everything and everyone. I am a strand of forever with a mind that can move matter.

The JCB has reached the spot where, a year ago, Kitty heard the explosion and saw the red-haired child screaming, 'Mummy, Mummy.'

Matthew is waiting for a particular moment, only half a minute away now, to pull his trigger.

There is another explosion.

The front of the JCB rears up like a spirited horse.

The driver hurls himself from his cab as the whole front of the machine curls up into a crumple of burst-apart metal.

Matthew's body flies up into the air and seems to separate there. The shotgun twirls round in the air, popping out little explosions of its own.

Tilda comes out of the cottage screaming, her scarlet curls bouncing, the coat Julia gave her billowing out like a crimson flag.

Still shrieking, 'Mummy, Mummy, Mummy,' she runs towards the smoke and flame that has just engulfed her father.

$$\star \quad \star \quad \star$$

'Bloody hell,' yells the JCB driver. 'So it was true, what all the people said. That there was a second bomb lying in there, ever since the war.'

32

The lawyer sends Julia a message. It is waiting for her. He has found the people who adopted Jem. 'We should have Jem's address within the week.'

Julia feels light-hearted as she sets off to meet Sir Jeremy Burton, who is back at last and staying in the Langham Hilton.

She enters the hotel and recognises Sir Jeremy across the foyer. Kitty has described him already, large, white haired, florid faced, wearing all the attributes of success.

He rises, frowns as she approaches and gestures her into the seat beside him. 'You, my dear lady, have caused me lot of trouble. Why the Devil did you have to go and offer yourself in exchange for Mr Wing? It has cost me a fortune, getting you out.'

'That was very nice of you,' says Julia grimly.

'Have no illusions. I did not do so out of any altruistic motives. In fact as far as I am concerned you deserved everything coming to you. But if there had been a hooha about your kidnap and a connection had been made with me, my whole business would have come under scrutiny. I risked being caused great embarrassment. I trusted you and for obvious reasons I cannot approach these people myself. I knew of your activities in South Africa, understood you were accustomed to dealing with terrorists, that you had secured the release of other hostages, but I never for one moment imagined you would be so foolish as to put yourself into these people's custody.'

'I tried talking to them,' says Julia. 'But they would not give an inch. I had no option, in the end, but to agree to go with them and hope that they let Matthew Wing go.'

His frown deepens. 'Well, it's water under the bridge now and all's well that ends well.'

'All has not quite ended,' she says. 'There is a young girl still held hostage in Waswar. Her father cannot raise the ransom. I have come to ask you, since you already are in contact with these people, to pay it and get her freed.' When Julia explains who Laila is, Sir Jeremy Burton lets out a burst of scornful laughter. 'My dear lady, the kidnap of this Waswarian businessman's child is no threat to me.'

'Out of compassion?' pleads Julia.

He shakes his head and shrugs. 'If I start that sort of thing, paying ransoms for anyone captured by the terrorists, I will be made bankrupt in a month.'

'Not anyone. Just one girl.'

'Out of the question,' says Sir Jeremy Burton. 'No harm whatsoever can come to my company because of the capture of this Waswar girl, so you can forget it. Now, let us forget the past and concentrate on the future. A happy future. Mr Wing is out and we can all live in peace and I can take possession of my little piece of land.'

'You are my only hope, her only hope,' says Julia and wonders if she can still bargain. 'There's a problem, still, about the waste land.'

Sir Jeremy stares at her. 'I am in a hurry to start building,' he says. 'My contractors are already clearing the land. I hope we are not going to have any more trouble from either you or Mr and Mrs Wing. Remember that you promised to persuade her to give it up without fuss.'

Julia frowns, trying to decide how to approach her subject.

'You look doubtful, my dear Miss Prinkett.'

'Trinkett,' said Julia.

'As though you do not trust me. I can assure you I am not the kind of man to take advantage of a family at a time of stress.' He laughs a laugh that is deep and warm, at the very outrageousness of the idea. 'I shall most certainly compensate them for the inconvenience of their move as well as repay them their deposit on the mortgage. Let me reassure you that I am not a con-man.' He laughs again at the absurdity of the idea. 'Look, here are photos of my family.'

He pulls his wallet out and places, one by one, the photos before Julia. 'My wife and children.' Large confident looking people, with big teeth and optimistic expressions.

'This is my eldest, Ashley. He's something big in the city, earning two thou a week. Here is Robert. He's working for his PhD. Science, biology. Then there's Julie, our only girl. She's still at university. Lovely, isn't she? She's the star of her Daddy's life. And this is Henry. He's the youngest and is still at Eton. And my wife, well she's the best wife and the most perfect mother any man ever had. And she's a marvellous cook, to boot.' He lingers his thumb over the picture of the lady, fortyish, frightfully well dressed, wearing jewels that looked like the real thing.

'Her father was Lord Albertine. She will inherit a castle and five hundred Scottish acres,' he says. 'We have a holiday home in the Algarve. We go skiing in Chamonix every winter, and we spend our summers in the Bahamas. And this is our home. A beautiful thirteenth-century farm house, now completely modernised in the most tasteful way imaginable and bliss-fully comfortable to live in.'

The vast house, bent and darkly beamed with age, stands in a garden the size of a park. A large lake gleaming in the background, a smart looking rowing boat tethered to the bank and beyond clumps of huge and ancient oaks under which spotted deer shelter.

'I hope you now see me as completely bona fide,' says Sir Jeremy.

'Why do you want this scruffy bit of land if you are so well off?' asks Julia.

'Because I am a businessman, my dear. Because, although some of my money is inherited, I have made most of my own wealth by seizing business opportunities when they arise. And I see, in this dull little village, a business opportunity.'

'How did you acquire the waste land in front of Kitty's house?' asks Julia.

'Really, dear, I think this is no business of yours.' Sir Jeremy smiles as if Julia is a cute but cheeky child.

'I would be grateful if you would tell me, for I think it is my business,' Julia says.

'I've no idea what you mean,' says Sir Jeremy. He frowns. 'And moreover I cannot imagine why you should need to know, but so that you may be perfectly certain that I am above board I will tell you. I inherited it. It was left to me by my parents.'

Julia represses a gasp. 'Your parents?' she says.

'Yes, dear.' Sir Jeremy leans toward. 'You look as though you have seen a ghost. I spent my first four years on that piece of land, so as you may imagine I feel rather sentimental about it. My parents' house was blown up by a bomb during the war and they were killed. I was subsequently adopted by a Mr and Mrs Burton and have had a long legal battle to regain my property. In fact I have only recently succeeded.' The waiter arrives with the tray. 'Yes, put the drinks there.'

In a voice that came out as a croak Julia asks, 'Did you inherit the whole property? Were there no brothers or sisters to share it with?'

'You seem amazingly curious about my private life,' smiles Sir Jeremy. He laughs. 'But I have agreed to tell you all, haven't I? So, no. I have no siblings. I am an only child. The whole parcel of land belongs to me alone. I am sole inheritor, sole executor. That should have made things simple, but it was in fact immensely complicated. Luckily, though, I was able to afford an excellent lawyer. I had to struggle hard to claim the property that was legally mine and now it indisputably is I intend to make good use of it.' He pauses.

Looks Julia up and down. 'Surely you can see that, Miss . . . Trinkett.'

'You can call me Jewel,' says Julia faintly.

For a moment something seems to flicker in his face, like an ember about to take light. Then it dies out again. 'Jewel, charming,' he said.

Julia leans back in the chair, lets a mist of dizziness pass over her then says, her voice weak as though she has been hit in the throat, 'I found the fairy train.'

He stares at her uncomprehendingly. 'The what?'

When she rises and starts to pull her coat back on he says, 'Your drink. You haven't touched it.'

Slowly, through the fog of shock, Julia gathers up her gloves and bag.

As she goes out through the swing doors she turns once. He is staring after her. She cannot read his expression.

★　★　★

Had Sir Jeremy lied when he called himself the sole inheritor? Or had he forgotten? The memory is a strange thing. It is good at blotting out. It does not allow the mind to endure too much pain.

She has followed a trail for more than half

a century and feels as though she has found the Holy Grail and it is made of plastic.

The sole executor.

The soul executer.

Her soul has been executed and her existence made worthless.

Suddenly the whole shabby structure that has been her life has fallen apart. Julia's life, her aspirations, her hopes, her desire to do the right thing, have been shown up to be void and useless.

★　★　★

Julia goes back to the waste land once, not to see Kitty. She does not even let Kitty know she is there. To return the fairy train. She throws it over the wall from the road, hears it fall into the vegetable garden, as near to the place where she had dug it up as she can get it. She does not go up to the cottage. She does not even try to look over the wall, try to catch a glimpse of Mattie. That is all over. She knows it now.

She puts a note through Kitty's door telling her that she is going back to Waswar and that it will probably be for ever. It may not work this time. Without any money to offer them they probably won't let Laila go. But at least, even if they do not free Laila, Julia will be there with her, in the dark. There is nothing here for her, nothing for her anywhere. At least there is someone in Waswar who needs her.

It seems like days later. Julia is waiting at Heathrow. The Waswar plane is two hours late. A man comes walking towards her.

Reminding Julia of someone.

Making her heart leap up for a moment.

But of course, it could not be him. Dick was far away, in Zimbabwe.

★   ★   ★

She turns away and blots Dick from her mind. She has spent forty years forcing herself not to look for Dick. She knows how to do it now. She has total self control as far as Dick and love are concerned.

When she looks round the man is coming closer and looks more like Dick than ever. Like Dick must look now, not like that young man, that younger version, she had seen walking along the road the last time she visited Kitty. She must be hallucinating out of shock, she thinks.

He is very near now, tanned as ever, his blue eyes sparkling with laughter, his hand outstretched as though, as soon as he reaches her, he will fold her in his embrace.

Julia has run away from Dick for so long that now she has to force herself to stay there, to stand and watch him approach her.

He comes and stands before her. His arms are still outstretched but he does not touch her.

'Jewel,' he said. There was no question in his tone. Only certainty. Only a great warm reservoir of love. 'My son, Harry, said you would be here.'

'Your son?' she gasps, then adds, breathless. 'I am just leaving.'

'What about your husband? Is he here too. Piet?'

Her face flushes scarlet as she says, 'There was no Piet, Dick. I invented him. But I can't wait. I must rush. I'm catching a plane.'

'You really hate me so much then?' he asks softly.

Julia looks out to where planes stand. To an English sky, not really grey, not yet yellow. A sky she had often tried to remember when she was a child in Rhodesia. A sky she had thought she longed for. She does not look at Dick because she knows what he looks like. Has always known. His face is etched in her heart. His eyes are the colour of Rhodesian skies. He does not fit here, she thinks.

'You do hate me, don't you,' he says softly. 'You never forgave me.'

343

This is too difficult, she thinks. Too complicated. I am not up to it. She tries to teasel out the various aspects of their relationship. Employer. Lover. Friend. And then, forlorn, the husband of Ann.

'We could just start again from here,' he says.

She feels a sudden surge of anger as though he is mocking her. 'There is no here.' Her tone is fierce.

He reaches out and tries to take her hand.

'I can't stay,' she says. 'You know that. I have to go. Don't try to tempt me, because it makes it hurt the more.'

Dick Dikker laughs. 'You never change, Jewel. One would have thought the years would have mellowed you, but you are as sharp and ferocious as ever.'

'You are married to Ann,' says Julia.

'She died, Julia,' says Dick softly.

Julia gasps and presses her hands against her mouth. This changes everything. She says, 'Oh,' and feels a dreadful sorrow because she has not been able to say, 'goodbye' and 'thank you'.

'I did not know,' she says and thinks, it is too late now. I should have told her I loved her years ago, but it is too late now.

'She knew you loved her, Jewel,' says Dick as though she has spoken the words aloud.

'She knew that was why you left us.' He takes Julia's hand. 'I have been looking for you for a long time.'

Julia's mind is seized and swirled with hope, thoughts bumping and splashing like clothes going round in a washing machine.

'I live in South Africa now. I have a farm near Johannesburg. Not baccy any more but dairy cows. Jerseys. Beautiful, golden hair, mascaraed eyes. And the orange groves. And grapes. Come back to Africa with me.' He is watching her all the time with his eyes that are still as blue as the sky of Africa.

Stinging dry skies, thinks Julia, so bright they make your eyes wince. Spring, laden with the smell of orange blossom. Summers roaring with the rage of bougainvillea, zinnias, canna lilies. The wild calls of jungle birds, echoing hollowly among the kopjes. Animals punctuating the nights with cries like shouts of pain. No tenderness. Nothing cute or small. Skies so huge you could get lost just looking up in them. Nights made of dark blue satin, ruched, soft, tingling with cicadas and nightjars, glittering with sharp stars, per-fumed with jacaranda.

Julia has longed for years for that vast African land, longed for the uncomplicated blues and reds and blacks of sky and soil and men. She is tired of dipping her fingers

345

cautiously into these little British matters that always seemed to end with loss and disappointment.

★ ★ ★

She remembers the white wicker chairs on the meshed verandah, she and Dick sitting there at sundown, looking out onto the brass-bright grass, watching it turn crimson in the sunset. Dikdik, kudu, duiker, springbok, glowing with sunset purples and poppies as they emerge from among the thorn trees and the acacias, on their way to the water hole.

'We will ride together again. I will get you another horse like Dan. We will ride across the veldt all day and drink gin and lime on the stoep in the evening.'

She feels warmth steal across her heart. Feels lightness begin to fill her, realises this is the sensation of happiness and that she had not at first recognised it because she had not experienced it for so many years. 'I love you, Dick,' she says.

He says, 'Marry me, Jewel.'

33

Julia is going to be happy, like other people. She is going to step into sunshine and love at last. Julia Dikker is coming home to Africa.

Julia thinks, I will take a red coat even though it is too hot for Africa. She does not have to touch him. Every cell in her body knows he is there, near her, will be by her for ever.

Then she remembers Laila. Turning to Dick a face gone suddenly gaunt she says, 'I cannot come with you Dick.'

'Why? Why?' He seizes her wrists and looks pleadingly into her eyes.

She tells him about Laila. Laila, who had shared the room with her during the months of their captivity. Laila who had been bundled along with Julia into the boots of cars, who had shared with Julia the shackles, cold and hunger. Laila who was twenty-three years old and did not deserve to die. Laila whose presence had helped Julia to endure the unendurable.

★ ★ ★

'I beg you darling Jewel,' cries Dick, holding Julia by her hands as though, unless she is forcibly pinned, she will fly away on the spot. 'Be sensible. You are owed a life as well. It's your turn for happiness.'

'I have to go,' she says. Her throat has gone dry as though some of her is already dying. 'I have to go.' The words grind out and hurt like grit against her heart.

He lets go of her hands and looks away. 'Write to me.' He seems suddenly old.

'If I can,' she says.

After that they become silent, not knowing what to say any more. Bowed with the sadness of it. Dry with the absence of hope.

She does not look back, later, as she goes through into passports.

She does not look back. That would be fatal. Her hands are shaking and a veil of tears is blinding her as she tries to pull her papers out.

Then she hears Dick shout.

The man examining the passport looks up. Dick can be seen beyond the barrier, waving wildly. 'Jewel, Jewel, come here a minute.'

'I'll see what he wants,' she tells the passport officer and taking her passport back, pushes her way back, against the incoming queue.

Julia and Dick face each other across the barrier.

'How much was it?' asks Dick.

'How much was what?' People are jogging her as she stands in the way. 'I must go, Dick, or I'll miss the plane.'

'The ransom. For Laila.'

'Oh, Dick, don't imagine that if it had been possible I would not have got it,' sighs Julia and names a figure that is enormous.

He looks aghast for a moment. Then says, 'Come out, Jewel. Let's discuss it.'

'There's nothing to discuss, Dick,' says Julia, gathering up her bag again, turning to go. 'I have to hurry.'

'I will get the money,' says Dick.

'Oh, how? And why?' Julia laughs as though he is joking.

'I am not poor, Jewel and I can get that much together even though it means selling everything I've got.'

'Don't be ridiculous,' she bursts out. 'You are going to sell everything you value to free an unknown girl in a foreign country?'

'I am going to sell nearly everything I value to get something I value most of all,' says Dick softly and taking her hands pulls her gently back through the incoming crowd. 'We will be broke,' he says as he kisses her. 'We will be old too. But we will be happy.'

We do hope that you have enjoyed reading this large print book.

Did you know that all of our titles are available for purchase?

We publish a wide range of high quality large print books including:
Romances, Mysteries, Classics
General Fiction
Non Fiction and Westerns

Special interest titles available in large print are:
The Little Oxford Dictionary
Music Book
Song Book
Hymn Book
Service Book

Also available from us courtesy of Oxford University Press:
Young Readers' Dictionary
(large print edition)
Young Readers' Thesaurus
(large print edition)

For further information or a free brochure, please contact us at:
Ulverscroft Large Print Books Ltd.,
The Green, Bradgate Road, Anstey,
Leicester, LE7 7FU, England.
Tel: (00 44) 0116 236 4325
Fax: (00 44) 0116 234 0205

SALT & HONEY

Candi Miller

In a southern Africa violently split during Apartheid, Koba is taken away from her Kalahari desert-tribe after witnessing her parents being murdered by a party of white hunters. She slowly learns to adapt and survive in a dangerous but beautiful environment. However, she is plagued by the knowledge that unless she leaves those who have grown to love her, she faces exile from her own people. The only answer may be to risk all through the brutal laws that condemn her.

THE ATTACK

Yasmina Khadra

Dr. Amin Jaafari, an Israeli Arab, is a respected surgeon at a hospital in Tel Aviv. On the night of a bombing in a local restaurant, he works tirelessly to help patients brought to the emergency room. But he is horrified when his wife's body is found among the dead, her injuries typical of those of a suicide bomber. As evidence mounts that his wife, Sihem, was responsible for the bombing, Dr. Jaafari is torn between memories of their years together and the realisation that the woman he loved had a life far removed from their comfortable, assimilated existence together.